PEACHES

PEACHES

A SADDLEBROOK FALLS ROMANCE

MICHAELA JEAN TAYLOR

PEACHES

Copy Editor: Britt Tayler

Proofreader: Brooke Crites at Proofreading by Brooke

Cover Designer: Cindy Ras

Internal Formatting: Michaela Jean Taylor

For the kind of love that shatters through the dark. It lives in all of us—we just have to be brave enough to let it shine.

AUTHOR'S NOTE

This book contains scenes with discussions of mature subject matter including cancer, death, grief, alcoholism, depression, anxiety, sexual kinks, gambling and an on-page gun fight and is intended for mature audiences.

CHAPTER ONE

RHETT

Cigarette smoke curls around from the back patio to where I stand, digging my driver's license out of my wallet. Spurs only opened a few months ago, but by the looks of the line forming behind me, it's doing well. The fact there's even a bouncer scanning IDs at all is telling—most bars around here don't give two shits about who comes in, so long as they have money to burn. It's probably the most "hip" thing to come to this part of Texas since . . . well, ever.

A grumble climbs my throat when I step through the door and see how packed it is—so much for trying to take the edge off. I've got half a mind to get back on my bike and ride the fuck out of here, but I promised Colt I'd meet him tonight. I haven't seen him in months.

Dozens of people crowd the bar, shouting their drink orders over the blaring music. Chris Stapleton's "White Horse" pounds through the speakers so hard I can feel it pulse against my chest. At least it's not that hokey shit they've been playing on country radio lately.

I spot Colt at a high-top against the wall, his face shadowed beneath a wide-brimmed cowboy hat that looks new, eyes glued to a group of girls jumping around on the dusted dance floor. Their skin is a kaleidoscope of color from the dozens of neon lights hung on the far wall, like some sort of poor man's art show, and Colt's hooked in. A few have danced their skirts up their thighs and almost disappeared them altogether—his type to a tee.

"Don't be a perv," I mutter as I slide onto the leather stool opposite Colt.

His eyes bounce from the girls to me, his grin widening, and he reaches over the table for a one-armed hug. "Bennett," he says warmly. "Always a party-pooper. Good to see you, man."

I shake out of the embrace and straighten my jacket. "The fuck is this place?"

He gestures around with both tattooed hands as if presenting a gift. "Every country boy's dream," he declares. "Cheap beer and hot girls."

I huff out an unamused laugh. "God, you're dense."

"Says the fella who walked out of the bar I last saw him in with not one but *two* hot girls on his arm." He flips his pointer and middle fingers up for effect, then finishes off the dramatics with an eyebrow raise.

The memory of the two barrel racers we met at the Foxborough rodeo earlier this year sparks to life, and I force a shrug. "Nothing special." It was the truth: nothing happened with either of them. A long afternoon in the heat led to cooling off with some ice-cold beers at a nearby saloon. We'd all had way too much to drink, and when we got to the parking lot, one of them started crying about missing home in Cheyenne. Her friend took that as a cue to shuffle them both into a cab. All that to say, drunk girls' emotions could turn on a dime, and I tried not to make a habit of sleeping around, despite what Colt—and everyone else, really— seemed to think. I don't care enough about it to correct him. "How you been?" I ask instead.

He leans back against the wall, bright eyes bouncing around the bar. Always on the hunt. I swear, the world could be ending, and this fucker would still be looking for the right girl to end it with. "Good, man. Got a cattle run to get through next week . . . Moving the herd out to the neighbor's pasture down south."

"Need help?" I don't have a lot of experience with cattle, but Colt knows I'm good on a horse.

"Nah." He shakes his head. "Dad called in the cavalry—my uncles and cousins are coming in from San Antonio on Tuesday."

"All right." I nod. Colt's dad has been running cattle for nearly forty years. He met my dad when they were both in their twenties. Back then the local bar scene was even smaller than it is today and stories of bar fights crossed county lines, turning them into the stuff of legends. Amos and Dad did a stint in jail together after taking on a biker club in Dallas. When they got out, they started an illegal gambling ring that Colt and his brothers still keep alive almost thirty years later.

I got in deep with it a few years back, and when Kasey found out, he cold-cocked me in the hay barn. That punch had felt like a train barreling into my face, and I remember spending the rest of those frosty pre-dawn hours seriously wondering how the fuck life had landed me there.

Needless to say, he'd threatened to tell the rest of the family if I didn't quit. It took a while to pay Colt back what I owed, but I got it done with a few months' worth of bar tips. I don't think Kasey ever found out that Brooks was a part of it too, but that's not my business.

Actually, I'm not certain Brooks ever really stopped.

"How's the family?" Colt asks, and immediately my stomach tightens.

"Been better," I say honestly. "Melody's sick."

Colt turns to face me. "Shit, how bad?"

"Not good. Doc says it's cancer—Brooks is really torn up."

"Fuck."

"Yeah." I nod. Life at home has been chaotic these last couple of months. Melody's cancer is complicated enough that it took a long time for anyone to realize what it was, so they got a late start on fighting it.

With Brooks so focused on her and the boys, Kasey and I are practically running things at both the ranch and Wild Coyote. Wells has stepped up a lot too, but he's only home so much. Rodeo's been keeping him busy as hell, and no one has the heart to ask him to slow down—not after all the shit he's been through in the past year, losing his best friend and love for football in one fell swoop.

"I'm sorry," Colt replies with a level of sincerity that's rare coming from him. "Anything I can do to help?"

"We're managing. But I appreciate it."

He nods. "You know I'm there in a heartbeat, brother. If you ever need anything, just say the word."

My chest constricts further, and I'm not sure how to respond. Thankfully, a waitress in a tight black tank top sidles up to the table. "What can I get you boys to drink?" she asks around a piece of gum.

"Men," Colt corrects, flashing her a smile.

I cringe inwardly and point my chin at the bottle of beer he's holding. "I'll take one of those, please."

"And two shots of your best whiskey," Colt cuts in.

The waitress grins. "You got it."

"That whiskey's going on *your* tab," I mutter to Colt as I prop my boots on the stool's footrest.

He chuckles and takes a swig from his bottle.

Honestly, the anticipation of the burn from some whiskey nearly has my hands shaking. I told myself I wouldn't have any of the hard stuff tonight—I still have to get my ass home later. But with everything going on, sometimes it's the only thing that loosens the tension. My family's a fucking mess right now, and I don't know how to make it better.

Isn't that always the damn case though?

I shove the thought away as the waitress returns, balancing a bottle of Bud and two shots of whiskey on her black tray's glossy surface. She places the bottle and a shot in front of me before dropping the second shot for Colt. "Y'all need anything else? We got wings on special tonight."

"No thanks, honey," Colt says with a voice like velvet. "But feel free to join us when your shift's over, yeah?"

She lets out a surprised giggle, twirling a strand of hair around her index finger. I suddenly realize how young she looks—can't be much older than nineteen or twenty. "Tell me how I *already* know you're bad news," she purrs.

Colt makes a show of looking wounded. "Let me prove to you I'm not," he volleys. And then he turns to me. "Rhett, please tell this sweet young lady how nice I can be."

I bring my bottle up to my lips. "He *can* be nice," I confirm, taking a sip and swallowing. "But he won't be with you."

Colt scoffs. The waitress laughs, her smile bright, and I wipe my mouth to hide my own. "You boys be good now, ya hear?" She sashays away, the empty tray tucked beneath her arm.

"Dude," Colt whines beside me. "What the fuck?"

"That girl is way too young and . . . *nice* . . . for you to be fucking with. Leave her alone."

He relents, throwing a hand up. "All right, all right." He lifts his shot and waits for me to do the same before saying, "Cowboy up, Bennett."

I relish the way the liquor heats my tongue and throat, welcoming the fire as it slides all the way down to my chest. Immediately, the pressure on my shoulders lifts.

I already want another one.

"We got a card game coming up. After we move the cattle. Ellis has been working on it for weeks—a lot of money on the table."

Colt watches me intently, no doubt trying to see if it's enough to bait me. I chuckle dryly. "You know I don't fuck with that shit anymore."

He grins. "Rhett, when I say there's going to be a lot of money on the table, I mean a *lot* of fucking money. Our biggest night yet."

Can't help it—my curiosity is piqued. "How much?"

"Maybe half a mil."

"Jesus," I choke out. "How the hell do you have that kind of bread lined up?"

He shrugs, turning his focus back to the girls dancing out on the floor. "Ellis made some new friends in Cheyenne."

"Ellis is going to get you all killed," I bite out, keeping my voice low. Colt's brother, the eldest of the Rustler brood, has been organizing these illegal card games since his father handed over the books a decade ago. "For fuck's sake, Colt—you guys are taking this shit too far."

I watch as Colt bristles. "Yeah, why do you think I'm asking for you to be there?" His eyes move back to me, burning with focus. "We need more people we can trust at the table. Figure it's only right to have a Bennett there. For old times' sake."

Brooks must not be attending lately then. I shake my head in disbelief . . . but I can't deny the old tug of recklessness. Kasey would put me in the ground himself if he knew I was even considering this. Our family gets enough heat as it is.

But little does he know I've gotten away with a lot more over the years. No one ever found out about my years-long stint pedaling pills so I could pay off some of Dad's debt to society. I'm not sure anyone even knew he'd accrued a debt to begin with.

He made sure *I* knew though.

I blow out a frustrated breath and take a long pull from the Bud bottle.

"Oh shit," Colt says, his focus now somewhere near the front door. "Dark hair, silver dress—just walked in." I turn lazily to find the girl he's talking about. "Dibs," he's quick to say, and I can't help but smile.

She's . . . fine. Definitely attractive, but not quite my type. "All yours."

I glance at the girl behind her though, and my attention snares. Thick auburn hair frames her round face, only reaching the top edge of her bare collarbone. Her cheeks are flushed like she might be cold—or excited, maybe. She's wearing a black dress with little bows on the straps, and I'm already imagining what it would be like to pull them loose. "Damn," I whisper as my eyes trail down her body to her long, gorgeous legs.

Something about her feels familiar, but I'm not sure why. *Fuck*, I think. *Have I met her somewhere?* One of the disadvantages of my deep-seated love affair with whiskey is I don't always remember nights when I'm looking to unravel parts of myself. Sometimes I unravel so far I leave important pieces behind—like my memory. It's one of the many reasons I'm trying to hold back these days, from both booze *and* girls.

Colt and I both watch in a mutual transfixed silence as the girls navigate their way to the bar. I'm halfway off my stool, ready to buy them both a drink and invite them over, when the silver-clad one slides her hand up the back of some dude in a backward hat who sits belly-up to the bar's counter.

"Dammit," Colt mutters.

Another guy sitting next to the first one turns to look at the girl in the black dress, the one who has somehow stolen the breath from my lungs, and reaches out to hug her.

Yeah, I think. *Dammit.*

CHAPTER TWO

OLIVIA

"What's your favorite position?"

Trent's face, although objectively beautiful, is hazy with the buzz he already had when we showed up. Ivan snickers from the other side of the booth we just moved to, hiding his mouth behind both hands as he looks down at his lap.

"What?" I ask, though I heard him loud and clear. My gaze slides across to Charlotte, and I see hesitation in her pinched brows that I'm sure matches my own.

"What's your favorite position?" Trent repeats, and Charlotte sighs. The apology in her eyes shines beneath the stained-glass chandelier hanging from the ceiling, one of several odd details I've spotted since we got here.

It's my first time at Spurs, a brand-new bar in Williamson County. Despite its name and the country music blaring, there isn't much else that makes it feel like a country bar. It actually still looks a lot like the restaurant it was before.

Italian, if I had to guess.

I give Char a soft smile—there's no reason for *her* to be sorry. Sure, she may have dragged me out here for this awkward (and blind, on my part) double date, but she's not the one asking rude questions before we've even ordered our food.

I turn back to Trent, finding him eyeing me with curiosity. The heat from his body so close to mine in this shared booth puts me on edge—only twelve minutes in and I already know I never want to see him again. "Who let you out of your cage tonight?" I quip.

The insult doesn't land as intended. Instead, Trent belts out a high-pitched laugh, nodding his approval. "Sassy." He scratches at his beard and looks down at his phone as he fires off a quick text to a contact I can't help but notice is saved as *Houston Big Tits*. "I like it."

I roll my eyes.

I suppose there are *worse* situations to be in. I could be stranded in the rain with a flat tire and no one around for miles to help me. Or I could contract a violent flu that wipes me out for days. Still . . . when I agreed to drive the half hour to get here, I didn't anticipate having to deal with such an asshole.

"I'm going to get some drinks," Ivan says. "Do you guys want anything?" He looks nervous, and I don't blame him. He and Charlotte only started dating a few weeks ago, and she trusted him to bring a friend tonight that I might like. Unfortunately, I think the one he chose is going to lose him a *lot* of points.

I look back to my best friend and see the question in her eyes. *Do you want to stay?* they seem to ask. She met Ivan last month at a Noah Kahan concert in Dallas. Despite not being able to find anyone to go with her (I couldn't get away from the café that weekend), she'd decided to go it alone and ended up standing near Ivan and his group of friends in the amphitheater's crowded lawn section. At some point, Ivan realized the girl beside him was there by herself, so he ushered her into his huddle of people.

Charlotte said it was fate, and she'd been giddy the next day when she recounted the way he couldn't keep his eyes off her when he thought she wasn't looking. How, in the few quiet seconds between "Dial Drunk" and "Your Needs, My Needs," she'd brazenly fisted the front of his shirt and kissed him.

I give her a discreet nod—I'm not going to let some stupid guy in a *Demon Slayer* T-shirt get in the way of my chance to get to know her new man better. She likes him—like, *really* likes him, I can tell—and if anyone deserves the heart-swooping roller coaster drop of a new fling, it's Charlotte.

It's just clearly not my turn to have that sort of thing. Not yet, anyway.

Trent nudges my knee with his under the table, and I have to fight back a grimace at the contact. "Let's get these ladies some shots. What do you like, babe? Tequila?"

I swallow a sigh, shaking my head politely. "No thanks. I'm driving tonight."

Ivan eyes me warily. His regret is evident, which makes me wonder if it's possible that Trent isn't normally like this. Maybe he's having a bad day, letting loose a little *too* much. Maybe he's normally a stand-up guy who wouldn't treat a girl he just met so . . . offensively. I find it hard to believe, but still . . . it's possible? I give Ivan a small smile that I hope conveys my assured forgiveness and add, "I'll take a ginger ale, please."

He nods, turning to Charlotte who asks for her standard vodka cranberry and treats him with a quick kiss on the cheek before he scoots out of the booth. "So." Charlotte angles toward Trent, propping her chin in the palm of her hand. *I know that look*, I think. She's about to get a few licks in. "You don't get out much, do you?"

Trent's mouth opens and closes a couple of times before he settles on, "What do you mean?"

"Asking a girl what position she likes literally minutes into meeting her? What kind of animal are you, Trent?"

His brow furrows. "I . . . don't understand."

Charlotte grins. "I imagine you wouldn't, honestly. But here's the thing"—she leans in real close—"Olivia is my best friend.

She's actually one of the best people I know. But she's *way* too tolerant of asshole behavior. *I*, however, am not. I think it's clear you're not going to get anywhere near Liv after this, so let's make a deal, yeah?"

She waits patiently for Trent to respond. To his credit, he gives her a wide-eyed nod.

"Cut the shit. In fact, maybe just don't speak for the rest of the night. I have a feeling we won't be here long anyway." She pushes her hair behind her shoulder. "Can you do that for me, Trent? Can you be quiet?"

I watch as Trent registers he's being bested, the divot down the center of his forehead splitting his face in two with an effect that I might find comical if not for the anxiety this entire confrontation is giving me. As someone who's worked in hospitality since the ripe age of twelve—when I was finally strong enough to hold a tray full of plates and drinks—my go-to response to conflict has always been de-escalation.

"What the fuck?" he says, just as Ivan returns with a handful of drinks. "Why are you such a bitch?"

"Hey!" Ivan snaps. "Don't call her a bitch. What the fuck is wrong with you, Trent?" He sets the drinks down in a disorganized jumble that sends liquid spilling over onto the table, but he remains standing at the end of the booth, towering over us all. There's an icy heat in his eyes I would never have guessed he could conjure, and my anxiety spikes as I realize I'm trapped between him and the target of his hostility.

Damn. He must really like Charlotte.

Maybe I could just slip down to the floor and crawl out around Ivan's legs . . .

I'm just about to try my luck when the screeching sound of metal dragging on hardwood precedes a shuffle from somewhere to my left. No one else seems to notice, but something pulls me to lean back so I can get a better view of the bar behind Ivan—and that's when I see him.

Rhett Bennett.

My stomach lurches at the sight of him. He's standing next to a high-top table, and he's looking right at us. Another man in a tan cowboy hat sits at his side, staring up at Rhett with surprise splashed across his dark features.

My gaze jumps back to Rhett, and I find him watching me with so much blatant interest that it causes the hairs on the back of my neck to rise with a shiver. Rhett Bennett, a man of mystery with a reputation in Saddlebrook Falls for trouble, is looking at me like a coyote who just found a plump rabbit.

I nearly shiver again at the implication of what it would mean to be his rabbit.

But he also looks . . . angry.

"I'm sorry, man," Trent says next to me, pulling my focus back to the booth. "But she's acting really rude, calling me an animal and shit."

"That's because you fucking are, asshole!" Ivan's voice is laced with frustration. "You've been a jackass from the moment we got here. You knew this night was important to me. What's gotten into you?"

I catch Charlotte's eyes across the table, widening my own to convey that we need to talk. "I think I'm going to go to the bathroom," I sputter out.

She tilts her head as she tries to translate my face. "I'll . . . go with you!"

Trent huffs and reaches for his drink, distracting himself with his phone. As if ignoring Ivan's glare might somehow get him out of trouble. "What is it with chicks and the bathroom?"

Ivan sighs, moving out of the way so I can stand. "Honestly, dude? Hundred bucks says they're going to talk shit about you."

Charlotte smacks his arm as she slides out the other side of the booth. "Ivan!"

"What! You know it's true."

"I'll give you that. Also, thanks for defending me." She leans in and plants a smacking kiss on his cheek, then turns back to me. "Let's go."

I follow her through the crowded bar and down a dark corridor with a RESTROOMS sign hanging above it. There's a line for the bathroom, but I don't even care at this point. I slump against the wall, letting it cool my skin.

"I'm so sorry about Trent," she's quick to say. "I had no idea Ivan would be friends with someone like that. Everyone he was with at the concert was *way* cooler."

I shrug. "Not a big deal, and not your fault. I'm a big girl," I tell her, brushing it off. "But, um . . . did you see who's here?"

"No, who?"

"Rhett Bennett."

Charlotte's eyes grow wide. "No way."

I nod. "Yeah. Sitting at a high-top across the dance floor. And he was looking right at us."

"Hm," she considers. "I mean, he probably recognizes us— I'm sure you've served him coffee after a bender or two." She grins when I tsk at her—his reputation is no secret, but everyone knows it's customary to feign ignorance, not speak of it aloud. "Maybe we should go talk to him."

"Are you crazy?"

"Why not?"

"*Because*. You know that family is dangerous. *Especially* Rhett. Didn't he beat Scotty Pearce to a pulp for asking him for a cigarette?" Rhett and Scotty were a few years older than us and had graduated by the time we got to high school, but there were tons of stories about all of the Bennett brothers. The youngest, Wells, was in our grade—but he hardly talked to anyone. The whole family keeps to themselves . . . except for when they're causing trouble, I guess.

Charlotte rolls her eyes. "I heard Scotty was talking shit about their dad and deserved it."

I blink at her. "Who could you have possibly heard that from?"

"Micah's girlfriend's older sister was in their grade and at that party—she saw it happen. She said the rumors about Rhett punching him over a cigarette weren't true, and that Scotty was practically egging him on and looking to start shit." Micah is Charlotte's older brother, and he's been dating Eileen, his girlfriend, since they were in middle school. I forgot Eileen had an older sister. "You know how things get twisted over time," Charlotte continues. "I also heard the gazebo fire might not have been him."

"Wow, really?" Of all the stories about the Bennetts, that fire is one of almost legend at this point. Apparently Rhett, who was drunk and angry about a girl standing him up, set the wooden gazebo in the town square on fire. The whole thing collapsed before they could douse the flames, and it took months to replace it. For a long time, you could still see the charred remains of the surrounding grass, but it's since grown back.

"Yeah," Charlotte says, taking a deep breath. But then, before she can dump every detail she has on standby about this, something flashes on her face—a look of pure shock.

"Evenin'," a deep voice rumbles from behind me. The sound expands in my gut as I grow rigid, the wall behind me now my personal support beam.

Charlotte's eyes flit back and forth cartoonishly from mine to a spot just over my shoulder, and it doesn't take a clairvoyant to know who's behind me. Squeezing my eyes shut, I internally count backward from five before pivoting around and opening them again.

Rhett Bennett is standing less than two feet away from me, gaze moving across my face as if he's looking for something. A black hat with a simple band sits low across his brow, dark curls begging to be freed barely held in along his temples. His gray eyes —or maybe they're a pale blue—spark even in the low light of the hallway. They're near thunderous, and the corners of his mouth are tipped down into an obvious frown. I can't help but feel like I've done something wrong.

"Um . . . hi," I stammer. "We were just talking about you!" I say way too loudly. I regret the words before they've left my mouth.

His frown deepens, and my stomach sinks with it. "I'm sure," he says, so low it's a wonder I can even hear him. He's got that familiar hotheaded anger on full display, and I've never been more uncomfortable in my life to be on the receiving end of it.

A group of girls burst out of the bathroom like fireworks, laughing at something I'm sure is far less stressful than the awkwardness I'm stuck in, but his eyes don't leave mine. "It looked like those guys might've been bothering you."

It's not a question, and my mind blanks as I attempt to draw out a response from . . . *somewhere*. Surely there's a single neuron still firing. Thankfully, Charlotte must sense my frozen state. "Oh, that's just my boyfriend and a friend of his," she says, stepping up beside me with a confidence she wears like a suit of armor.

Rhett's gaze moves to her, and the relief I feel is nearly tangible. "Your boyfriend was shouting."

Charlotte waves a hand like it's nothing. "Yeah, his friend called me a bitch. Honestly, his friend sucks. Liv and I just met him tonight . . . but I doubt we'll see him again." She laughs, and I can hear how forced it is.

Rhett's focus moves back to me, and . . . *yep*, I feel the damning effects of it all over again. "You good?"

Something sparks to life inside of my chest, like the click of a gas burner. I don't understand his question. "Am I good?" I parrot. But he doesn't say anything, just keeps looking at me with that stoic frown. I flip the question around in my mind before finally finding my voice again. "Um, yeah. Yeah, I'm good."

He nods once, the dip of his chin infinitesimal, before stepping around us. Charlotte and I turn in sync to watch him disappear into the men's bathroom.

"What the *heck* was that?" Charlotte whispers beside me.

I can't tear my eyes away from the closed door, knowing Rhett's in there. "I have no idea."

Charlotte turns to look at me. "I think he likes you."

I almost choke on my own saliva. "I'm sorry," I sputter, finally looking at her. "That's . . . that's impossible. We don't even know each other."

Her brow raises. "Why else is he so concerned about you?"

I scoff. "He's not concerned about *me*. He's . . . he's probably just looking for a reason to punch someone."

She tilts her head, considering. "Hm."

"Also," I rush out, attempting to change the subject as we move forward in line. "Don't think I missed you calling Ivan your boyfriend."

She rolls her eyes. "Please don't tell him I said that. It just felt easier to explain."

"Mhm." My smile is saccharine. "Whatever you say."

CHAPTER THREE

RHETT

I pull a worn box down from the top rack of the storage closet and send a cloud of dust flying across the small space, immediately sending me into a sneezing fit that, quite frankly, pisses me off. I've been irritable all day, and I know going out last night is part of it, but it's also the bone-deep exhaustion of life lately, of feeling like I'm always waiting for something else to go wrong.

Maybe going out to Williamson County last night wasn't the smartest move, but I needed to blow off a little steam. It's not even that I drank enough to be hungover—I cut myself off before Colt could drag me into his mess—but I didn't get home until well past midnight and was up again not four hours later when James started crying from the room down the hall.

Melody's been in and out of the hospital over the last four months. When the doc found the cancer, everything in my family's world changed on a dime. Melody was immediately sent to a bigger hospital in Houston where they started her on rounds of aggressive chemo and radiation. Brooks spent most nights there to be with her, and the rest of us took turns watching the boys and filling in for him on the ranch and here at the bar. It's been a lot.

Initially, I figured the impact of her diagnosis would be like anything else that had struck the Bennett family: quick and disastrous. And while I was right about the disaster it caused, I was dead wrong about it being quick. For four months my family has been in an ongoing cycle of hell, trying our damndest to support Brooks while Melody fights for her life.

Carrying the box back out to the public bar space, I set it on the seat of the nearest stool and look around to inventory all the holiday decor that needs to come down. I hate that it was even put up—such a waste of time. Our family didn't have much good to celebrate this year, and people don't exactly come to Wild Coyote looking for a dose of holiday spirit.

Nah, this is a place people come to hide from the rest of the world. In addition to the ranch itself, Wild Coyote has been a decades-long fixture for town corruption and lawlessness. This is where people come to lose themselves to the bottom of a bottle, to sit in the dark with their misery and pretend like everything outside these four walls doesn't exist. It's no secret most of the Saddlebrook Falls townsfolk give it a wide berth, but we still have dedicated regulars who help keep the lights on.

My great-grandfather opened this place during the Great Depression, when breaking wild horses wasn't bringing in enough money to keep the ranch afloat. He figured people had plenty of reasons to drink, and he was right. The bar kept him and my great-grandmother from having to sell off pieces of the ranch—a move that's undoubtedly categorized as the biggest failure any Bennett could bring upon their family.

That land has been in my family's name since before Texas became a state, and my great-grandfather Earl wasn't about to lose it because of a stock market crash and bank failures that had nothing to do with our family name. He figured out a way to push through—same as we've been doing my whole life.

"Hey." A voice sounds from near the front door, and I drop the piece of red tinsel I just plucked out from an old wall sconce. I turn to find Kasey standing with two cases of beer stacked in his hands and another on the ground at his feet. "Could use some help here."

I shove past the box and reach him in a few strides. "Sorry," I mumble. "Didn't hear you come in."

He cocks his head. "You okay?"

"Yeah, just . . . busy mind, I guess."

Kasey deposits the cases of beer onto the bar top. "Wells said you got in late last night."

I roll my eyes, setting the third box down beside the others. Leave it to my little brother to rat me out. "Yeah, well, it was my first time out in almost a month. I needed to get out of that house. It ain't a crime."

Kasey spends nearly every night in his own cabin on the ranch. Sawyer was home for a month during the holidays, but he had to head back to school about a week ago. Wells has been spending more nights at the big house than his own cabin lately—he and his girl, Layla, have been pulling night duties with the boys while Kasey and I run the bar. He bartends too when we need him to, but Layla is so good with the kids and, despite all the heartache, I think he likes playing house with her.

Everyone knows I'm better suited here than at home, trying to wrangle three little boys without hurting their feelings over my complete lack of patience. Kasey is good with them like Wells is, but he's been managing all Bennett-related business operations since Brooks has been away—something no one would trust me with. Honestly, no one trusts me to help with anything outside of breaking horses and pouring drinks, and I can't say I blame 'em.

"You have your own cabin, you know," he says, pulling me back to the present.

I don't have the heart to tell him that the cabin our parents handed down to me is depressing as hell. It's the one Dad used to live in, before he and Mom took over the big house when Grandpa got too old and tired to run things. I was only a kid back then—before Wells was even born and Sawyer was still running around in diapers—but I remember how hectic life was for us in that little two-bedroom space. It was before Dad's accident but well after his heavy drinking had taken root, and that cabin was much too small for Mom to hide it from us.

"Yeah, well," I respond, "figured Wells might need help with the kids."

Kasey's eyes narrow. "At one in the morning?"

I shrug. "James woke up not long after, looking for a snack."

Kasey sighs, his eyes softening. "He's been hungrier than a hog lately. Must be going through a growth spurt."

Thinking about those boys growing up without their mama around to see them twists a knot in my stomach, and I busy myself with pulling down the Christmas lights that are stapled around the door frame. I'm still annoyed we have this shit up at all, but Kasey wanted to decorate, like he does every year. Says it helps lighten the mood in this place.

I hear the clinking of glass as Kasey fills the fridge below the bar with the bottles he's just brought in. "Gonna be another busy night," he calls out from where he's hunched over.

No shit, I think. It's Saturday, our busiest night of the week. Fridays are a close second, though I'm sure Wells was still able to get out of here by nine last night to get back to Layla and the boys. I'm on closing duty tonight, but Kasey will still probably be here until around eleven. "How'd things go last night?"

"Eh." He knocks a shoulder up before reaching for more beers. "Not too bad. Old man Gerry closed the place down with me—most everyone else was out before midnight."

Gerry was the oldest person in Saddlebrook Falls. He knew my grandfather well and is one of the only people who ever defended him to the rest of town. Things between the Bennetts and everyone else didn't grow sour until Grandpa grew into a feral teenager and caused trouble everywhere he went. He had a wild hare up his ass and tore through this town like a tornado on wheels, chasing girls and starting fights with anyone who looked at him sideways. He calmed down in his old age, but the damage to our family name had been done.

Our dad certainly didn't help things. As the oldest of three boys, Dad should have been a good example for his younger brothers, just like Brooks and Kasey were for us. But Dad was wilder than Grandpa ever was, and we've all been dealing with the repercussions of his actions for as long as I can remember.

"How is that old man?" I ask.

Kasey smiles. "Still kickin', that's for sure."

I grin before I pull out my pocketknife to pry the staples from the wooden frame.

FOUR HOURS LATER, THERE'S A STEADY STREAM OF people flowing through the door. At max capacity, the cramped bar holds about forty patrons, which isn't a whole lot compared to most other bars. But the way these people suck down liquor keeps Kasey and I busier than two beavers in a hurricane, and I've already lost what little scraps of patience I had today.

"Rhett," Sunny Cooke calls from the corner of the bar, his sweat-stained collar stuck to the side of his sun-weathered neck. "Beer me!"

I hold up the four bottles of Coors Light I've got between my hands. "Little busy here, Sunny," I bite back.

"Yeah, yeah," Sunny mutters, turning back to his brother Boone, whose eyes are already glazed over.

Sunny and Boone aren't technically from Saddlebrook Falls—they live in a run-down shack out past county lines, selling fresh eggs from their chickens and whatever else they can find worth a quarter or two. I can't imagine they're able to make much money that way, but they still somehow end up here a couple times a month and spend enough of it to get piss-drunk. We usually have to drag them out the door because they don't stop drinking 'til we force them to, and by the looks of things, Boone is halfway there.

I bring the bottles I'm holding to a high-top out on the floor and drop them on the table's surface between eager hands, scooping up the empties before I head back for the bar. The jangle of the bell above the door sounds and, on instinct, I turn to look at a young couple walking in.

My gaze immediately locks in on the girl, on her smokey green eyes surrounded by long lashes and strawberry blonde hair curled to frame her pretty face, the strands much lighter than they'd looked in the dark last night. I stop dead in my tracks.

Olivia.

Those beautiful eyes grow wide as saucers when she sees me, like she didn't expect to find me here. Not sure how, since this is my family's bar . . . but I've also never seen *her* in here before, so her surprise could be genuine.

I watch her throat bob before she looks up at the guy she came in here with, an uneasy smile spreading across her face. I, too, turn my attention to the lanky kid next to her and frown. *Jesus*. Didn't take her long to find a new one. The guy grins at her, wrapping a long arm around her shoulders and leading her farther inside.

I move behind the bar where I have a better angle to study him. He's an angular-looking city boy with slicked-back hair and a shirt so starched it's practically wearing him. Looking back at Olivia, I find her flushed as she takes off her denim jacket. Blood flows to the surface of her soft cheeks in a way that both excites and irritates me. Something about the way she can't stop glancing in this direction, like she can sense my impatience about this whole thing, has me standing a little straighter. The smell of her perfume from last night—sweet and ripe like a basket full of peaches—floods through my memory, and I have to force my attention onto a stack of cocktail napkins.

Thankfully, Kasey notices when they sit down and works his

way over there. We've all been in this godforsaken town our whole lives, so I know Kasey and Olivia know each other, but neither of them rushes to mention it. "Evenin'," Kasey greets them warmly. "Can I get you folks something to drink?"

"Two White Russians," City Boy replies, and I almost snort. Figures he'd order something with fucking milk. I'm pretty sure the open gallon in the fridge has been in there for almost a month, but I don't stop Kasey as he turns to work on making their drinks.

I need to distract myself before my tongue starts flying, so I bend to grab two bottles of Miller Lite from the fridge and walk them over to Sunny and Boone. "'Bout time," Sunny mumbles bitterly as I set them down.

I plant both hands on the bar top and lean down to look him right in the eye. "You know something, Sunny? I'm getting real tired of you two comin' in here and actin' like the world revolves around your sorry asses. You don't like the service? Find somewhere else that'll deal with your shit."

Boone starts laughing, a wheezy, obnoxious sound, and slaps his brother on the shoulder. "Aw, Sunny, lighten up. These boys treat us good."

I grin. "Yeah, see. Listen to Boone."

Sunny clicks his tongue. "Listenin' to Boone never leads us anywhere fucking good."

Boone stops laughing, eyes squinting as he tries to look serious. "Well, fuck you, Sunny."

"Hey," I warn. "Don't get yourselves all twisted now. You start fighting with each other in my bar and I'll be the one to finish it, you hear?"

"That a threat, Rhett?" Sunny looks at me like this would be a fair fight.

"That's a promise," I confirm before stepping away, inhaling a deep breath through my nose to stem the tingle in my fingers. I shake out my hands and beeline it for Kasey. "Those two idiots are on their last drink."

He looks in Sunny and Boone's direction. "Already?"

I nod. "Yep."

"All right. I'll give them the good news when they're done with that round." He pats my shoulder and gives me a once-over. "You cool?"

"Yeah. Just . . . annoyed."

"Okay. Well, take it easy and let me handle them. I'm gonna grab some more bourbon from the back—you okay for a minute?"

"Yeah," I say through a sigh. "I'm good."

Kasey nods and heads for the back office, and I see City Slicker is headed for the hallway too, likely for the bathroom.

I take the opportunity to plant myself right in front of Olivia.

She straightens, her manicured fingers reaching for the square napkin that rests on the bar between us. "You're here," she says, the words slipping through full lips I can't resist watching.

My own mouth curves into a wide smirk. "You thinkin' about me, peaches?"

The napkin crumples in her hand and her cheeks flush crimson. It's a beautiful display of what I can only assume is her discomfort, which leaves me feeling a bit at odds with my ability to have that effect on her. "I didn't know you worked here," she says in a hushed whisper.

"It's my family's bar," I say back. She winces, like somehow that's worse than me just working here. The lingering silence is taut. "You really didn't know I'd be here?" I ask.

She shakes her head, straightening in the tall barstool. "No. If I'd known . . ." A flare of determination settles over her, a confidence that makes my chest spark. "I knew your family owned the bar, but I guess I didn't realize you'd actually be working in it. I didn't know where else in town to meet Tony without anyone noticing."

"Tony?" I parrot, looking toward the dark hallway he disappeared down. "Who the fuck is Tony?"

"My date," she says coolly.

I scoff, shaking my head as I stand back to my full height. I don't have time for this shit.

"What's so funny?" she asks, defensive.

I take in the ferocity in her eyes, the tight press of her plump lips. God, she's one hell of a looker. Too bad she wastes it all on guys like *Tony* and the greasy douchebag from last night. "Nothing, sweetheart." I knock my knuckles against the bar's surface. "Have a good night with your date."

She looks like she wants to fire back, but Tony comes walking around the corner and stops her from saying another word.

CHAPTER FOUR

OLIVIA

My annoyance spikes as Rhett walks away and Tony sits down. I feel him slide a cold hand down my spine as he settles next to me and resist the instinct to shake him off. *You wanted this date*, I remind myself—though I'm already having a hard time remembering why.

"You know," Tony says with an arched brow as he looks at me. "You're prettier than your profile picture. I almost didn't swipe." He smirks and picks up his drink—can't say anyone's ordered me a White Russian before—then proceeds to suck down its contents through the small black straw. It suddenly feels like last night all over again—except this time, I don't have my best friend to act as a buffer.

When I let Charlotte download the dating app to my phone last weekend, I wasn't sure I was actually going to do anything with it. She's always been much bolder and braver when it comes to interacting with men, but she's also lived through her share of dating-related horror stories that, quite frankly, should have been more than enough to keep me away from online dating.

But spending night after night alone in my quiet house has been increasingly depressing. Not even keeping myself busy with work at the diner has staved off this suffocating . . . *boredom*. I've spent the majority of my life in this cramped and dusty town, surrounded by people who care more about spying on their neighbors for a juicy piece of gossip than making lasting and heartfelt connections with each other.

That's not to say I've never dated. But nothing ever lasted more than a few weeks . . . and I certainly didn't find any of *those* men online. It's not even to say I haven't dabbled in gossip. It's just . . . I want more. For my life, for myself. And I just don't care if Jenny hired the latest teen mom at her salon or Ed from the post office is delaying his retirement.

"Oh," I mumble into my own drink, unsure how to respond to what I'm *choosing* to believe was a well-intentioned compliment. "Really?" I take a long sip and almost spit out the foul concoction. Something tastes . . . rotten.

"Yeah." Tony laughs, seemingly unaware as he takes another swig. "I mean, don't get me wrong—you're easy on the eyes in that picture. It's not like anything was a turn-off, you know? But I consider myself to be pretty picky, and I guess I just wasn't sure if it'd be worth it."

I squint at him. "If what would be worth it?"

He shrugs. "You know"—he waves a hand around as if to indicate anything and everything it took to get here on these stools together—"this date."

I can only stare at him in disbelief.

"But it is," he insists, perhaps recognizing the massive offense in what he's saying. "Like I said, you're a *real* looker. Very pretty." He smiles. "I don't even care that you're just a waitress."

Anger pinches deep in my belly, a sharp and uncomfortable pressure. "I'm not—"

"Get out," a deep voice gruffs.

I turn to find Rhett standing on the other side of the bar, his scowl trained on Tony. His dark cowboy hat is sunk low over his head, and it makes him look even more menacing than I already know him to be.

Tony shifts to give me a look like *Who the fuck is this guy?* before addressing Rhett. "What?"

Rhett points a thick finger at the door. "Get the fuck out of my bar."

Tony's face crumples into a frown. "I don't understand."

I begin to rise from my own stool, utterly mortified, but I know better than to cross a Bennett.

"Oh no," Rhett says, turning his attention my way. His pale gray eyes bore into mine and I feel the weight of his focus press into me. "Sit down."

"All right, man," Tony interjects. "You talk to her like that and we're going to have some real problems."

Rhett smiles. "Oh yeah?" My stomach coils with dread— Tony isn't from around here and has no idea who he's talking to. Rhett Bennett is the *last* person he should be fucking with.

This is what I get for trying to have some fun. Charlotte is going to lose her mind when I call her later.

Tony throws him a hard look. "Yeah. You know what? Where's your manager? I'd like to talk to someone about your behavior."

Rhett smirks, a dark and dangerous thing. "Tell you what, City Slicker . . . instead of focusing on my bad behavior, why don't you take a minute to reflect on your own?"

An older man who shares Rhett's nose and jawline—his brother, Kasey—rounds the corner from the back with two bottles of liquor in hand. He pauses when he notices Rhett's stance. "Something wrong, Rhett?" he asks cautiously.

"Yeah," Tony answers instead, his voice an octave higher. "This guy is trying to tell us to leave for no good reason—"

Rhett shoves a finger right in the middle of Tony's chest, and Tony's eyes bulge out of their sockets. "No, asshole. I'm telling *you* to leave because you're a sack of shit and I don't want you stinkin' up my bar."

"Rhett," Kasey warns.

"She stays," Rhett continues, eyes flicking my way for a beat before bouncing back. "Date's over. Get out."

Tony turns to look at me, brows pinched in a furious show of indignation. "What the hell kind of place is this, Olivia? Shitty bar in a shitty fucking town . . ."

Now I'm the one throwing a daggered expression. "This is my home, asshole," I retort, surprised at my bravery in such a contentious moment. But I've put up with enough shit in the last couple of nights—enough to last me months—and it's about time I stood up for myself. "You know what? I wish you *hadn't* swiped. Hell, I wish I hadn't swiped. This whole thing was a mistake."

Tony's ears glow bright red. "Wow." He shakes his head as he stands, doing his best to save face. There are other men around the bar watching the scene unfold, most of them I recognize as the husbands of some of Saddlebrook Falls's most notorious gossip mongers, and I realize how easy it would be for all of this to get back to my mother. She'd have a field day if she knew I was meeting strangers from the internet.

Tony stands and shoves his drink toward Rhett, causing some of the white liquid to spill onto the bar top. "This tastes like shit, by the way," he says before striding out the front door.

I turn back to look at Rhett and find him already watching me. Kasey stands a foot away from him, looking back and forth between us. "Want to tell me what that was about?" he asks his brother.

"Nope," Rhett answers, keeping his eyes fastened on me from beneath the brim of his dark hat. The black felt contrasts the gray storms in his eyes, painting them almost onyx in the low bar light.

Kasey sighs. "Right." He walks away, mumbling something incoherent under his breath.

Rhett crosses his arms over his chest. "You have a kink for this shit or something?"

I balk, my shoulders rising to my ears. "What?"

"You were with a douchebag last night, which I'd hoped was just a fluke," he says, uncrossing his arms to lean over the bar. He brings his face within a foot of mine, his glare sharp and biting. "But now I've got you parading another one around—in *my* bar, no less. I don't have time for this shit, peaches."

Peaches. What the heck?

"I'm not parading anyone around," I argue. I'm just . . . *dating!*"

He has the audacity to smile, though the way his face twists reflects zero humor. "Right," he says, shaking his head. He backs away from me again, leaving room for me to gulp down a deep breath.

I watch him examine a stack of dirty drinking glasses, tossing their remaining contents into a wide trash can before moving them to the sink behind the bar.

"He was right, by the way," I mumble. Rhett looks at me, brows dipped in question. I drag my glass back and forth through its puddle of condensation. "This is terrible."

"Yeah." He nods. "Milk's 'bout two weeks past old."

I grimace, looking down at the liquid I thought was supposed to be curdled, and cough to mask my gag.

"I don't know why you're wasting time with guys like that," he grumbles, abandoning the dirty glasses to reach for a bottle of whiskey from the well below.

"Guys like what?" I demand irritably.

He looks me square in the eye, a clear challenge. "You know exactly what I mean." He pours the whiskey into two water-spotted shot glasses before pushing one toward me.

I stare at it hesitantly. "No, I don't. And I didn't order a shot."

"It'll kill whatever bacteria's in your mouth from that milk."

I frown. "You shouldn't have served rotten milk to begin with, asshole."

"Fine." Rhett shrugs, reaching to pull the shot back toward himself. He sighs before lifting the glass to his lips and tipping the whiskey into his mouth. I watch as his jaw works around a heavy swallow, still in disbelief that this is what the night's come to. He sets it down on the bar's counter with a loud thud and immediately picks up the second one, downing that too.

"I don't think you can do that," I say.

"Do what?" he snaps, that buzzing frustration on full display.

"Drink on the job."

"Says who?" He makes a show of looking around, like Sheriff Joe or some suit from the Texas liquor board might suddenly appear out of thin air.

I roll my eyes. "I'm just saying . . . it's a little unbecoming to watch the bartender down shots faster than his customers. Seems a little messy, don't you think?"

"Peaches, everything about my life is messy, haven't you heard?"

That name again. "Look . . . I should go." I pull the straps of my purse up onto my shoulder. "I'm sorry about Tony—"

"Wait," Rhett interrupts. He reaches to lift his hat off his head before settling it back down, then crosses his arms over his chest again. He seems . . . anxious. Like all that frustrated energy rolling through him has no place to go. "Stay."

I'm pinned with that heavy focus again, like he's trying to make sense of me, and I'm not sure what to make of it. "Stay?" I ask.

"Please." He sighs, scratching at his jaw with the knuckle of his middle finger. "Just . . . stay . . . 'til I'm off. And I'll take you home after."

I glance back at the door behind me, knowing it would only take me a half hour to walk home from here. Maybe less. Rhett's not going to be off for at least another few hours; if the steady buzzing of conversation and riotous laughter is any indication, it's a busy night at Wild Coyote. Plus, I *just* watched him down two shots of whiskey, so even if he is done with work soon, I don't think getting in a car with him is a smart move.

Every logical consideration in my brain tells me it's time to bail on this whole weird night and find reprieve in the comfort of my little backwoods bungalow.

But when I pause to study Rhett, I find a sincerity in his eyes. Something protective and concerned and . . . tired, I think. It's the same look he gave me in the hallway at Spurs last night, the one that hooked under my skin and left a mark I don't know how to describe—exactly what's happening now. So, against all reason, I lean into the instinct to stay and see this—whatever "this" is—through.

My purse slides off my shoulder, hooking in the crook of my elbow. I hold eye contact with him as I settle back onto the stool. "Fine," I say quietly.

If he's relieved by my choice to stay, he doesn't show it. All I get from him is a quick dip of his chin before he walks away, busying himself with making a drink. To my surprise, he drops it in front of me when he's done, rumbling out, "A real drink," before he plucks the White Russian off the bar with two fingers and disappears into the collection of tables behind me.

I take a tentative sip of the new drink—a strong Jack and Coke—and cough to clear the burn in my throat. But warmth spreads down my chest with it, and I decide I like the feeling.

Turns out, I don't have to wait too long. I spend some time reading a book through an app on my phone, and it feels like only a few minutes have passed before Rhett's standing in front of me again, a stoic look on his face. "Ready?" he asks. He's wearing a brown fleece-lined work jacket zipped up to his chest, hand stuffed in the front pockets.

"Already?" I say.

"It's been almost two hours."

I glance at the analog clock hanging on the wall above the beer taps, confident I'll find 8:30 flashing back at me, at the latest. But sure enough, it's almost ten. "Oh," I say, realizing just how lost in my book I'd gotten as I tuck my phone back into my purse. "Yeah, I'm ready." I wrap my own jacket—my favorite: distressed denim with sewn-on pearls and rhinestones—around my shoulders and stand to follow him out the front door.

The air outside is cold and sharp as it slices right through all my layers, burrowing into a bone-deep chill, and I wrap the front of my jacket tighter around my middle to seal in as much warmth as I can while trailing behind Rhett into the parking lot. Rhett, who doesn't appear affected in the slightest by the freeze of winter. I distract myself by trying to match a vehicle to the man, assuming he's probably driving some fashion of a truck.

Unlike most of the businesses in Saddlebrook Falls that sit together in town square, Wild Coyote is an isolated establishment tucked behind a few layers of tall trees and wild brush. You wouldn't know it's there by simply passing it on the main road— even at night, there are no exterior lights that shine like beacons to attract new customers. The bar itself doesn't have any windows for indoor light to spill out of, so it's only by moonlight that we're able to see anything out here.

But when Rhett stops walking, there's no mistaking what he's standing next to.

"No way," I protest, looking at the two-wheeled deathtrap parked at the end of the row. Silver metal bars jut up toward the sky, only dimly illuminated by the stars.

Rhett unties a strap to free a dark helmet from the seat and holds it out to me. "Put this on."

A nervous laugh bubbles out of me. "Sorry, I don't think you heard me. There's no *way* I'm getting on this thing." I've seen Rhett on a motorcycle before, rumbling through town, mean-mugging everyone who so much as looks at him. But for some reason, I figured he'd have a second vehicle—something practical for everyday use that isn't so . . . risky.

"I heard you," he clarifies. "I'm just hoping if I ignore your spiral, we'll get to the part where you cowboy up and get on the bike quicker."

"That's a little bold, don't you think? To just assume I'd be okay with getting on . . . *that*." I hike my purse up my shoulder. "You know, you've been making assumptions about me all night."

Rhett's head tilts with an amusement that feels dangerous as his gray eyes assess me, cocksure and oozing confidence. "Oh yeah? What sort of assumptions have I been making?"

"That I'm on some sort of *loser* kick, trying to find douchey guys to date me. That I purposefully decided *your* bar would be a good place for it, as if I'm trying to, I don't know, mess with you or something?" My eyes jump back to the motorcycle. "Or that I would ever get on a dangerous hunk of metal destined to spread my blood and guts across a highway."

A little dramatic perhaps, but I'm making a point here.

Still, Rhett smiles. And I want to stomp my foot and scream.

"Olivia," his deep voice rumbles. "One, you *are* on a loser kick. Exhibits A *and* B are the assholes I've seen you with in the last twenty-four hours. Two, I find it pretty fucking coincidental that after seeing you last night two towns away, you ended up right in front of me again tonight. But you said you didn't realize I might be there despite it being my family's bar, and I believe you. And three"—he tosses the helmet at me in a low-speed underhand move that still has me shrieking as I easily catch it—"I would never let anything happen to you on this bike." He says it like it's a simple fact.

I look down at the helmet and then back up at him. "I watched you take shots."

At this, the cockiness slips. Like I might have touched on the one thing that could actually poke a hole through his plans.

"Yeah," he agrees. "I probably shouldn't have done that. But it was a couple hours ago, and I promise I don't feel anything. I've had plenty of water since . . . I'm pretty sure any trace of that whiskey would be gone by now. But . . ." He pauses, shifting on his feet. "If you want to go back to the bar and watch me down a cup of coffee before we leave, I'll do it."

His words unspool in me a steadying calm. For as much as he grumbles and glares, he wants my trust. I'm not sure what to make of it. I mean, he's a *Bennett* for goodness' sake.

This is exactly what you wanted, a small voice unhelpfully chirps inside of me.

I try to shove it down, but it's no use, because it's right. Getting on the back of a dangerous man's bike is pretty much in line with the kind of fear-inducing rush of adventure I've been craving for longer than I care to admit. It's what prompted me to let Charlotte download dating apps on my phone in the first place.

The truth is, I've reached a level of boredom with my life that rivals studying for the SATs or listening to the same song on repeat for years on end. If my life were a reality show, it would only exist on C-SPAN, and that's *not* to knock on the episodes of *American Writers* I get hooked on late at night when I can't sleep.

To be fair, my mother vehemently raised me to believe that risk is an unnecessary undertaking, especially as it relates to romance. And while growing up I mostly felt thankful that she'd set me straight and helped me avoid so much of the embarrassing drama my peers fell victim to as they navigated love and, inevitably, loss, I can't help but now feel I may have missed out.

Sure, I have everything I need for a decent life—I signed a lease on my first home last year after Gus Romano's sister passed away and he put her vacant property up for rent (by which I mean he posted a sign in the window of Mustang's Pizza to advertise to everyone who walked in) and am paying for it all on my own with money I saved working at the café. The café my mother owns and will someday hand over to me.

It's not like she's scared me away from men altogether. She just wants me to steer clear of the ones who stand as a threat between me and my carefully guarded heart so that I don't end up desperate to fill a hole the size of Saturn in a perilously broken one when one of those men inevitably shatters it. It's me who's never been sure how to tell the dangerous ones from the good ones, so I've avoided men altogether in hopes that someday I'd figure out the difference—just in time for my own Prince Charming to walk into my life and sweep me off my feet.

But I haven't figured out anything other than I won't ever know if I don't try, which is what led me to making plans with both Trent and Tony this weekend. Admittedly, both dates were catastrophic failures. But I'd be remiss if I didn't see the opportunity right in front of me, shaped like a hostile cowboy with a clear fetish for danger.

It's enough for me to find my bravery, to grip the sides of the helmet and pull it over my head, the pressure of it squeezing uncomfortably against my ears. "No, it's okay," I finally say.

Even through the dark-tinted visor in this unlit parking lot, I catch the surprise in Rhett's features. After a beat, he steps toward me, reaching to gently fasten the helmet's straps below my chin. His fingers are careful as they make adjustments to tighten it against my skin without choking me, just until the helmet fits snugly. He gives it a light shake for good measure, and when my whole body moves in response, a new smile plays on his lips.

"Thank you," I say, though I have no idea if he can hear me through all the plastic and fiberglass.

He inhales a breath and lets it out in a whoosh before turning back to the bike, pulling a pair of gloves from one of the bags that hangs from the side. When he pushes the key into the slot and turns the ignition, the bike comes to life with a thunderous roar that racks my whole body.

He turns to look at me as he pulls off his cowboy hat, tucking it carefully beneath a bungee strap on top of the back wheel well. "You ready?" I force myself to nod, though I'm second-guessing this thing with every moment that passes. He swings a strong leg over the seat and sinks down, knocking the kickstand up with the heel of his boot. "All right," he calls back to me over the noise of the engine. "Get on."

I must hesitate for too long because he turns to look at me. His dark curls are wild from being trapped in his hat all day, a lock seemingly glued to his forehead, and I realize he doesn't have a helmet for himself. That he's given me the one *he* wears. "Olivia," he presses again, "get on the bike."

The command is soft and somehow knowing, but his assured-ness in our safety is a balm over the rattling anxiousness I feel expanding inside of me. It's what finally pushes me over the line in the sand, pressing my hands down on the backs of his shoulders for balance as I mimic his move and swing my leg over the seat of the bike.

I settle behind him, my head heavy beneath the weight of the helmet, and slide my hands down his back, fearful that if I lose any ounce of contact with his body, I might spontaneously tip right over and onto the ground. I band my arms around his middle, and before I know it, he takes off with a jolt.

CHAPTER FIVE

RHETT

I get all the way to the main road before realizing I never asked Olivia where she lives.

Guilt washes over me for convincing her to get on my bike in the first place—she was obviously scared of it. Plus, I have an iron-clad *no girl* rule for the bike that I've upheld for nearly four years. Just like everything else in life, I've had to learn the hard way that I have no business being responsible for anyone else. I mean, no one's ever gotten hurt from getting on the back of it, but that doesn't mean I haven't been reckless. More reckless than I care to admit, especially to someone as good and sweet as Olivia.

Shame clenches tight. Serves me right for getting involved in any of this in the first place.

It's not that I have a *thing* for her—I know damn well to stay out of Saddlebrook Falls when I'm looking for the company of a lady. This town is full of people who have made a mockery of my family over and over and over again—it would be blasphemous against everything I stand for to start crushing on some girl who exists right in the heart of it all. Everyone knows her mother's café is practically a hub for the gossip-obsessed old birds who'd sooner snicker and laugh about an old man when he's down than try to help. It's a wonder they don't burn on the spot when they walk into their cherished church every Sunday morning.

I can't stand to think too much about the hypocrisy of it all. As if these people haven't experienced their own shit.

Olivia's always been nice enough, but I could never trust someone like her. I don't know what came over me tonight . . . I guess hearing the words *almost didn't swipe* and *just a waitress* coming out of her loser date's mouth sent a violent wave of fury through me so overwhelming, I didn't realize what I was doing until it was already done. And while kicking that guy out of the bar was well worth it—and helped to siphon out some of the hostility that's been brewing in me for months—seeing the shock and hurt on her face was jolting enough to make me wonder if I'd done the right thing.

She waited for you, I silently counter. That has to count for something, right?

As pissed as she is at me for ruining her night, she still stayed.

It spins something loose inside of me, something long wound tight, and I'm not sure what to make of it.

"Hey," I shout over the rumble of the bike, hoping she can hear me. "Where am I taking you?"

I feel her shift behind me, her arms squeezing tighter around my waist as she leans her head forward over my shoulder. "What?!" she shouts back.

I turn my face toward hers as far as I can while still keeping my eyes on the road. "Where am I taking you?" I try again.

"It's good, thanks!" Her chin swipes across the shoulder of my jacket as she pulls her face back.

A low laugh spills out of my mouth as I slow the bike down. There's a turnout up ahead where I can pull over and get her address. Carefully navigating the bike over crumbling asphalt onto the loose rock of the wide shoulder, we come to a stop and I brace the weight of us on both legs. Before I can even turn the engine off, Olivia is climbing off the back of the bike.

"Careful!" I shout, suddenly terrified she's going to burn her leg on the engine. She's wearing jeans, thank god, but still—the last thing I need is her getting hurt, especially after I promised her she wouldn't.

"*Wow*," she exclaims as she stomps over gravel, shaking her arms out around either side of her, completely oblivious to my warning. "That was incredible!" She looks at me with eyes full of wonder, and even through the bulk of my helmet, her beauty nearly knocks me right off the bike.

"What was?" I ask, moving my focus back to the bike as I turn the key and shove the attraction away.

She waves a hand around. "*That*. You. The ride."

I'm almost ashamed at the sheer pride roaring to life inside my chest at her words. "You liked it?"

"*Liked it*?" she repeats, tipping her head back like she's about to howl at the moon. "I loved it! Can we go again?"

I try like hell to hold back a laugh, relieved that this harebrained scheme of mine isn't going as badly as I thought it might. "Of course we're going again," I confirm, nudging the kickstand back down. "You think I'm going to make you walk from here?"

She shrugs like she's only just realizing we're pulled over in the middle of some country back road along the edge of town. "Why *did* we stop?" she finally asks, squinting at me.

"I don't know where you live."

Recognition sparks in her eyes. "Oh! *Right*. Erm, you know that little street behind the gazeb—" She stops short, as if she accidentally let something slip. I know damn well about the rumors, the ones about me and that gazebo, but I'm sure as shit not getting into any of that right now. Instead, I stay quiet and wait for her to keep going. "Um, Turnip Lane. My house is at the end of it."

"Great." I nod. "I know where that is."

Instead of getting back on the bike, Olivia simply looks at me. The silence between us seems to stretch all the way to the line of dense trees beyond the ditch, and then she takes a deep breath. "Thank you," she finally says. "For . . . for making Tony leave. And taking me home."

"So you admit to dating assholes?"

She scoffs, her defensiveness sharp like a whip. "I never said Tony *wasn't* an asshole. I just . . . it's not intentional."

"Being an asshole?"

"*Dating* assholes," she clarifies. "I'm not good at this. I-I'm honestly not much of a dater, like, at *all*. But I'm trying to put myself out there, and you happened to catch both of my first real attempts at it. Clearly I'm not having much luck."

I lean back in the seat of my bike, crossing my arms over my chest. "Why are you trying to put yourself out there?"

Olivia looks away, gaze lost somewhere down the road. Her shoulders curl forward in a way that makes me think she's bracing herself for something uncomfortable, and it sends my blood pulsing on some primitive instinct to be alert. "I don't know," she starts. Her teeth rake against her bottom lip, and I zero in on the movement. "I guess I feel like I might be missing out on something, you know?"

I consider her words. Truthfully, I've dated plenty—if you count casual flings and one-night stands. I've never let myself get too serious with anyone because I don't think any of that relationship shit is worth it, but . . . A thought rips through my mind, sudden and blaring and brighter than anything I've felt in a long time. "Maybe I could help," I rush out.

Her face twists into sheer confusion as she looks back at me, and the effect is damning. *Fuck*, the last thing I want to do is make a fool of myself, but something about the idea of Olivia Danvers experimenting with dating puts me on edge. "Help?" she parrots.

"Yeah." I shrug. "Why not?" When she doesn't say anything, I follow up with, "You lookin' for a husband?"

Her brow furrows. "God, no. I'm just . . . dating. Trying to have a little sense of adventure."

I can't help the grin that splits my face wide open. "Well, peaches, you're in luck, because I have a mean sense of adventure."

She shifts her weight to one foot, scrutinizing my face. "Are you making fun of me?"

I drop the grin. "No," I say, shaking my head firmly. "I'm not making fun of you. I'm just offering a solution." Embarrassment crawls up the back of my neck as I try to make a case for this. "Look, I don't want to see you taken advantage of by dipshits like Tony or Trey—"

"Trent."

"Trent, whatever. If you're just looking to get out on the town and have a little fun, I can help with that."

Anticipation unfurls in my chest when it looks like she might actually be considering it, but then something in her eyes flares. "I'm not having sex with you," she says haughtily.

I almost choke on my tongue, the night air brushing against the sweat at my temples. "I never said I wanted to have sex with you. Jesus, woman."

She nods, accepting that answer. "So, a few dates? Just until I clear out some of my proverbial cobwebs?"

"I'm not exactly sure what that means," I rebound. "But yeah, I'll take you on a few dates. Why not?"

Even as I say the words, all the reasons why this is a horrible idea come charging through my mind like a stampede of wild mustangs. I'm the *last* person Olivia should be tying her good name to. If anyone in town knew she was going out with me, she'd never hear the end of it. It's not like I even have time for something like this—lord knows there's enough going on at home. I don't need any distractions, especially a five-and-a-half-foot smokeshow who's already getting under my skin.

But the thought of her spending another second listening to some asshole convince her that she's not worth it is something I can't seem to stomach. I'm not sure why I care so much, but I do.

It calls to mind all the times I may have taken a girl for granted, acting like I was above it all—I hope I never made any of them feel the way I imagine Olivia felt tonight, hearing that bullshit.

"Okay," she finally says. "How many?"

"How many what?"

"Dates," she says.

"Oh, uh, I don't know. As many as it takes for you to feel more confident, I guess."

She nods again, and I exhale my relief. I feel like I'm in school again, trying to pass some obscure pop quiz. "When?"

"I work the bar most nights," I say, "but I'm off Thursday."

She props her hands on her hips. "I work at the café Thursday, but I'll be off around seven?"

"Okay, I'll pick you up at eight."

A smile spreads wide on her face, and it feels like a beam of sunlight shot straight to my gut.

Dangerous, dangerous, dangerous.

I motion for her to get back on the bike. "It's late. I should get you home."

She lurches forward. "Right, okay."

I start the engine as Olivia takes her spot behind me and try not to think about her legs spread wide against my hips or the way she pulls herself close to me. For some reason, being around her these last two nights has sent me into a tailspin, and I know it's time to regain control before I do something stupid.

But then she presses her chest against my back and my mind spins like a top. "By the way," she yells over my shoulder, and I tilt my ear toward her. "I love this bike!"

My chest puffs and I smile like an idiot. I carefully navigate through the back roads of town, lit only by the full moon above and bright stars that feel like prying eyes to what I know might be about to become a treacherous secret, and I bring Olivia home.

CHAPTER SIX

OLIVIA

I finish refilling the last of the salt and pepper shakers just as I hear my mom cry out from the kitchen. "Oh my word . . . *Olivia!*" It's not a happy tone, and it punches right through me.

Dropping the industrial-sized box of salt on the table—and spilling plenty of it in the process—I run through the narrow doorway that leads to the back and immediately find her cause for concern: when I set the coffee to brew a half hour ago, it appears I forgot to set the pot beneath the machine. Dark liquid flows off the long counter, down the doors of the cabinets below, and all over the floor.

"Shit," I mutter.

"Yeah, shit." Mom nods, her fiery red curls swept up in her usual loose topknot. Even at six in the morning, she's a burst of color. "What happened?"

I sigh, looking at her. "I'm sorry . . . I guess I was distracted."

Her eyes soften as they fill with concern. "You okay, honey?"

I plant a reassuring smile on my face. "Of *course*," I practically shout. "I just . . . I didn't sleep well. Feeling a little tired this morn- ing. You know—" I wave a hand, as if I've explained enough.

Her concern only grows. "Would this have anything to do with the letter I found in the office?"

My heart sinks. I'd meant to hide that before I left yesterday—and by hide it, I mean toss it in the kitchen trash where it could be buried beneath all our stinking food waste—but I must have forgotten. "You saw that?" I force out.

"I saw it," she confirms. "But I didn't read it. Honestly, I was just surprised. I didn't realize you'd been communicating with—"

"I'm not!" I interrupt. "I'm not communicating with him. It just . . . it was delivered with the rest of the café's mail yesterday. Total surprise. Like always."

"Oh," she says lightly. "Everything okay?"

I shrug, wondering how a surprise letter from my long-lost father inviting me to his daughter's—my sister's?—wedding can be brushed over as simply *okay*. "Céline is getting married," I explain, "and it seems that my presence would be welcomed at her nuptials."

"Oh," she says again. Her hand moves up to rest on her chest, and regret spears into me. This is exactly why I wanted to bury that letter beneath the mounds of uneaten potatoes and discarded pork chop bones—it kills me to see *that* look in my mother's eyes.

"I'm not going," I rush out. "Obviously I'm not going." As if I'd ever choose to subject myself to the man who'd crushed my mother and caused *that* look in the first place, or any of the other members of his bright and shiny family. Mom had no idea during their year-long love affair that my father had a fiancée waiting for him at home in Charleston, or that, when it came down to it, he was always going to go back.

Unfortunately for him, proof of their relationship was born seven months after he left. When my mom called him the day I was born—what she says was only an attempt to "do the right thing"—I think she'd been holding on to hope that he'd see the light and come running back to finish what they'd started, to *choose* her. But all he'd done was promise to send her some money and explain that, for obvious reasons, he couldn't be a part of our lives.

He'd left her to pick up the pieces of her shattered heart and raise the child they'd created together on her own. And while he made good on his promise to provide some financial support, it wasn't enough. My mother saved every penny she could so she could use it to invest in opening June's Café. It was *her* and this business that had ultimately supported us over the last two decades.

Eventually, my father changed his mind about not wanting to be a part of my life. He must have come clean to his new wife at some point, because letters started being delivered to the café, addressed to me. The first one came around my eighth birthday, and I remember being relieved to learn that this man—my *father* —might actually want to know me. But that first letter was a two-page outpouring of pride for his family in South Carolina, for his three young daughters that he clearly loved very much, and his hope that I could meet them all someday. Instead of feeling any joy or happiness about this newfound connection to him, I was left feeling more abandoned than ever before.

Over the next few years, a new letter came with every passing birthday, each with a new attempt to showcase his dazzling family. Eventually, they slowed to coming only every couple of years, likely because I never wrote him back. How could I? What would I have said that could possibly measure up to his stories of life in that cushy, elegant city with his beautiful French wife and three charming daughters, especially when my life here was nowhere near comparable?

Not that I wasn't proud to be my mother's daughter. The café never made us rich, but it was always enough to keep a roof over our heads and *plenty* of food in our mouths. In my mind, my mother went above and beyond to set aside her own heartbreak and put me first.

And so, to let this . . . *other* family . . . into my life would be to turn my back on the pain and sacrifice she'd weathered my whole life. I couldn't—wouldn't—ever do that to her.

Even if a small part of me is curious.

"You could go, Liv," my mother assures me, as if she somehow read my mind. Even as she says the words, I can see the hurt that's embedded in the crevices of her pale blue eyes. "It might be . . . worthwhile to know them. What do you stand to lose?"

I scoff. "No thanks."

She clicks her tongue, giving me a look like she knows better. But I know she won't press the issue. Not when my resistance is a relief for her anxious heart.

I reach for a clean kitchen towel from where they're stacked near the dishwashing station. "Let me clean this mess up and I'll put on a new pot," I say. "And then I'll make us some omelets before we open, okay?"

She smiles, but it's pulled back, and I can't help wondering how long it'll take before she forgets about this latest intrusion into the safe bubble we've formed around our lives. The last letter I received came at my high school graduation, and it included a check with enough zeros to make me dizzy. Mom saw the envelope first, and even though I'd promptly sent the check back (still without a response), it took weeks for my mom to stop asking about it.

That was four years ago now, and I think we both figured the letters would stop. I mean, this man has already missed out on my whole childhood—what does he have to gain from seeing me now? And what desire could there *really* be for me to attend a wedding for two people I know next to nothing about, simply because the bride and I share a smidge of biology?

Even if I can admit to a little curiosity, it has disaster written all over it.

I press the towel into the mess I've made and look back up at my mother. "It's not worth it, Mom," I say quietly. "It never has been."

After a moment, she nods. "All right, sweetheart. Whatever you think is best."

Much later, when I scoot out the back door after a long day of serving what feels like everyone in town, her words still bounce around my mind. *Whatever you think is best.* I know they're meant to be supportive, meant to grant me the freedom to move forward however I want to. But the reality is I have absolutely *no idea* what's best, because the truth is, if not for my loyalty to her, I probably would have opened the door to this other family years ago.

I wasn't the only kid in Saddlebrook Falls who grew up with a single parent, but there definitely weren't a lot of us. Our conservative town cherished the ideals of a nuclear family, and I spent my youth aware of the father-shaped hole in my life, as wide as a canyon for everyone to gawk at. When I was in elementary school, old Maeve used to stop by our house unannounced with a warm casserole for Mom and me, as if we were in mourning over the inadequacies of our lives. Once, when I was thirteen, Mom just about chased Ron Moore off our lawn when she came home from a Saturday lunch shift at the café and found him cleaning out the gutters.

Sure, it was *nice* of them to worry, but Mom always made sure we had everything we needed, and the extra attention aimed our way felt like that bad dream, the one where you show up to school and realize you've forgotten to put on any clothes. After all the defenses we'd had to throw up, how could I think that taking them down to let the man himself—the one who'd left us in the first place—into our lives would ever be *best*?

My walk home takes me ten minutes, and after locking the door behind me and flicking on the lamp in the living room, I know what I need to do. The fireplace still holds Wednesday's half-charred log of wood from when I'd spent the evening watching *New Girl* reruns with a crisp bottle of Pinot Grigio and a warm bag of buttery popcorn for dinner. It ignites again quickly, and after setting another fresh log in the rack on top of the growing embers, I fish the letter out of my purse where I dumped it on the side table by the door.

It singes in a matter of minutes, until there's no trace of the heavy scrawl that's become the embodiment of my father or the words that never fail to slice me wide open. As I watch the invitation to another life burn to ash, I shove down my disappointment and wipe my tired eyes. It serves me well, I know, to safeguard my heart from men like him. Men who'd think of only themselves when things got tricky.

Oddly, the thought summons a new one—one of Rhett and the absurd plan we made. I'd already been a fool all weekend, so intent on getting out of my comfort zone just to feel something new and exciting. I guess I was successful, because two nights running into Rhett sure made me feel *something*.

My mind snags on his stormy eyes and the low sounds of his frustration. On the smell of his jacket when I wrapped my arms around him on the bike, on the enchanting curve of his top lip.

Anticipation constricts my chest.

And then I do what I can to shove that down too, because feeling anything for Rhett Bennett would be the most foolish mistake of all.

I'M IRRITABLE WITH HUNGER AND A DEEP ACHE HAS been building in my feet all day. I was forced to skip lunch when old man Gerry strolled in with his youngest granddaughter and ten of her friends to celebrate her thirteenth birthday just as nosy Maeve and the rest of Bridge Club arrived for their monthly card game.

I should have been off work hours ago, but Mom's been shut up in the office for most of the day working on admin duties and Teresa—a long-time waitress here and Mom's closest friend—

called to say her sick husband had taken a turn for the worse this morning, and she needed to stay home with him in case things continued to spiral downhill. Rick was diagnosed with kidney failure in the fall, and Teresa has done what she can to be by his side as much as possible.

Despite it only being Thursday, the café was bustling with enough patrons that kept me from having much of a break since we opened the doors this morning. I know I could have asked Mom to jump in and help, but the sooner she gets through payroll reporting and vendor orders, the sooner she can come out and relieve me for the night.

I glance at the clock again, hoping Mom gets through all her tasks and *soon*, just as my stomach audibly rumbles. Taking a quick status check of all the tables in the dining room, I notice Gerry smiling at me, his hand raised in a gentle wave to beckon me over. I smile back and head his way.

"How is everyone doing over here?" I ask when I reach the table. Simone, his granddaughter, beams up at me with a plastic tiara resting on her head.

Gerry chuckles. "I'd say we're doing mighty fine. But I think these girls need some more sugaring up."

Simone and her friends cheer in unison, and I join in with a laugh. "How about some strawberry sundaes?" I ask, arching my brow.

The girls squeal and Gerry's eyes twinkle. He nods in confirmation, and I shoot him a small wink before heading toward the computer to key in their desserts. I don't make it more than two steps before I hear Gerry ask, "Olivia?"

I turn back to face him. "Yes?"

"Isn't it about time you found a nice young man to start settling down with?"

My stomach lurches. His expression is kind, and I know he means well—Gerry is an old man from a much more traditional generation—but if I had a nickel for every time someone in this town has asked about my love life, I definitely wouldn't be working so many shifts here.

The truth is, I can't fathom settling down right now. From my total inexperience in the romance department to my hesitation to trust anyone with my whole heart, I'm not even sure how—*if*—I'll ever get there.

Though, I have to admit the feeling that I'm missing out on something important has been gnawing at me more and more lately. It's a big part of why I've been forcing myself to swipe on the apps and go on dates—I don't want to avoid something important just because it scares me. I force my face to hold its smile and say, "Not yet, sir, but I'm looking!"

Gerry beams. "Atta girl. You know, I was quite the matchmaker back in my day. If you ever need any help, or maybe some pointers—"

"I'll come find you," I insist, backing away from the table.

The bells over the door ring in the harmonic signal of a new customer, and I turn to find a broad-shouldered man dressed in all black walking inside, a cowboy hat atop his mess of dark waves. Shit—*Rhett*. The restaurant quiets as everyone's collective interest narrows on him, and I see the way his back stiffens and mouth falls into a frown. The realization that I forgot about our date swoops through me as I watch him scan the dining room, no doubt looking for me.

My feet bring me to him of their own volition. When his eyes find mine, I see the relief flash through them before they harden into something else. "Rhett," I say in a low, hushed voice. "I'm so sorry—"

"You stood me up."

I shake my head. "No, oh my gosh, no. I've been stuck here all day and honestly forgot that—well, and the other waitress called out sick and . . ." I throw a hand toward the tables behind me. "And things got busy. I'm so sorry."

He simply stares at me. I realize his ears are tinged a bright shade of pink, and I wonder if he's nervous. Or maybe he's just mad after trying to collect me from my house for the date we're supposed to be having only to realize I wasn't there.

"I'm sorry," I say again. "God . . . I should have realized. I should have called."

He cocks his head, considering. "You don't have my phone number."

"No," I agree. "But still, I should have."

His eyes seem to soften as his posture relaxes. Someone at a table coughs, and a low murmuring of hushed voices weaves through the café.

"Do you want to sit down for a few minutes?" I ask, hopeful. "I should be able to get out of here soon, and I'm so hungry I could eat one of Gus's contest pizzas all by myself." Gus offers a free T-shirt and hat to anyone who can eat his extra-large, double-stuffed pizza in one sitting by themselves. It's mostly a thing Mustang's Pizza does for the high school football team, but occasionally others—like Shirley Tucker's eighty-two-year-old grandmother—like to try.

For the record, Shirley's grandmother *nearly* finished it.

A hint of amusement dances across Rhett's face. "Yeah." He nods. "Okay."

I lead him to an empty booth in the far corner of the restaurant, avoiding the gazes of everyone around us—and their gazes are no doubt locked in. Because not only did Rhett Bennett just walk through our door, but he's being seated and staying awhile, and even though I pride myself on minding my own business, this is the kind of big deal people in this town trip over themselves to witness. "Here you go," I say when we reach the table, giving him my best *this is totally fine* smile.

Rhett scoots himself into the side of the booth that faces the wall, keeping his back turned to the rest of the patrons. "Thanks," he says, the corners of his mouth turned down. His eyes are still a pair of thunderclouds, and I'm determined to see them clear.

"Can I get you something to drink? A shirley temple? Oh! We have milkshakes . . ."

"Water would be great."

I nod. "Okay. I'll be right back—and I promise I'll be done here soon."

His eyes seem to come alive at that as they trace across my face. "Soon," he agrees in a low voice. Anticipation for whatever he has planned builds, and I book it to the kitchen.

CHAPTER SEVEN

RHETT

There's nothing I hate more in this world than being the subject of stares and whispering bullshit from Saddlebrook Falls's finest—and when I say *finest*, I don't mean law enforcement, though I definitely don't love attention from them either. I'm talking about the bored and retired gossip peddlers like Maeve Piston and Gerry Thatcher, two of the biggest shit-talkers, who both just so happen to also be here at June's Café.

I feel their attention on me like an uncomfortable sunburn, the steady heat from their gazes blistering against my skin. As a general rule, I do my best to keep my ass out of town so I can avoid this shit. Other than my bar shifts at Wild Coyote, I'm either at home working the ranch with my brothers, or on the slim chance I have a hankering to get out of dodge, I go for a long ride out in the country on my bike or meet up with Colt in another county.

I've been planning this date tonight with Olivia since the moment I dropped her off last weekend, and nowhere in those plans was I here, at her mom's café, in the middle of town square, on what's clearly a busy night. But when I got to her house and

57

found that she wasn't home, I'd been frustrated enough that I couldn't just let it go.

Either Olivia was standing me up, or she'd forgotten about our plans.

Based on the warm flush of her cheeks and the guilt that flooded her eyes when she saw me walk in a moment ago, it's obvious she wasn't trying to stand me up. She looks exhausted from working all day—I don't blame her a lick for forgetting. Still, it's not easy to tamp down the irritation I felt the whole way here at the thought of being fucked with again, and it *definitely* isn't helping to be stuck in this booth like a damn zoo animal for everyone to gawk at.

I should have just pushed for a raincheck and headed home to get a handle on myself, but when Olivia's bright eyes pierced through mine and she indicated that she still wanted to do this, I couldn't say no. Hell, I let her sit me down at this worn table to wait for her.

I've never waited on a girl in my life.

I sit straight and watch the doorway that leads to the kitchen, anxious for her to walk back through it. When she does, I drink her in like the relief she is in this moment, a balm over my spiking anxiety.

"Here you go." She smiles, setting a full glass of water on the table before pulling a straw from her apron. "Want something to munch on?"

I shake my head. "Nah, can't—I have plans with a girl soon."

Her lips twitch, and it loosens some of the tension in my chest. "Lucky girl," she teases.

I scoff. "I don't know about that."

Olivia cocks her head. "Thank you . . . for waiting. And sorry again, about before. I shouldn't be too long."

I roll the straw between my fingers, meeting her eye when I say, "Don't worry about it." The last thing I want to do is pressure her to hurry or make her feel rushed—I'm not *that* much of a dick. Yeah, it's agonizing sitting here with these people around me, but my issues with them have nothing to do with Olivia.

A few years ago, I swore to myself that I'd never step foot in town like this again if I could avoid it—not after I'd stormed my way into the middle of a Sunday church service, still piss drunk from a long night of bourbon and bad decisions. I'd been on somewhat of a self-induced bender to distract from my dad having fallen off the wagon again—Billy Turner, who owns the fig orchard near Wild Coyote, found him in the middle of the street in front of the bar one morning, passed out in his wheelchair—but I knew I was playing with fire, what with all the bullshit stunts I've pulled over the years.

Nobody, not even my own family, has ever understood the real reasons for my bad behavior. It seems easier to chalk me up as a nuisance, and I guess I've let 'em. But the ever-present animosity between my family and the town has always been at the root of it all, and I have a hard time controlling my agitation when I'm exposed to them like this.

I glance at the clock and find it's eight-thirty. The sun set an hour ago, taking with it what little warmth we get this time of year. Temps will fall into the forties soon enough—I just hope the delay in getting to our date doesn't screw up my plans. My heart skitters as my nerves rise. I'm the cocky sonofabitch who offered to give her a "sense of adventure," as if wining and dining and *fun* were just a few of the many things tucked up my sleeve, and now I have to make sure this is worth it for her.

The sound of chairs sliding against linoleum snares my attention and I turn to see Gerry and the gaggle of girls he's with all rising from their table. One has a crown on her head and an assortment of gift bags in hand—a birthday party then. I trace the faces of each kid before landing on Gerry, who's throwing me an obvious glare. My brother might enjoy his company at the bar, but I don't think Gerry likes me much. I sneer back at him and hold his eye contact until he grows uncomfortable enough to look away first.

That's what I thought, old man.

Olivia breezes out from the kitchen again, pressing her hands together in front of her chest. "Thanks for coming in. Happy birthday, Simone."

The crowned girl—Simone—beams. "Thank you!"

I turn my focus back to my water, pulling the straw up to my mouth to take a long pull as I listen to the group leave. Before long, Maeve and her three friends also wrap up whatever card game they're playing and scuttle out of here, and then I'm relieved to see Olivia's mom appear from the back. It's the first time I've ever seen them standing next to each other, and it's obvious they're related. Olivia's features are a much more toned-down version of her mother's. Where June's hair is a bright, natural red, Olivia's is more of a strawberry blonde. June's skin is pale with layers and layers of freckles and Olivia's more olive with a smattering of freckles around her nose and cheeks.

A sudden burst of curiosity about her father rises through me, wondering what he might look like. Whoever he is, I don't think he's ever been around. Maybe my wondering doesn't make me any different from the rest of the busybodies in this town, but I've never found it fair that June and other single mothers get such negative attention when it's obvious the men in these situations are the ones who probably fucked up. For someone to turn his back on Olivia . . .

June ties an apron around her waist as Olivia talks her through each table. I see the surprise in June's eyes when she notices me, head whipping to face her daughter as she no doubt asks what the hell I'm doing here. Olivia's cheeks flush again, a deep rosy bloom, and she responds something low that I have no chance of hearing. She presses a quick kiss to her mother's cheek before disappearing into the kitchen.

June eyes me warily, and while it's precisely *that* look that normally fuels my annoyance with this town, this time all I feel is my chest deflate in disappointment. I don't know what Olivia told her, but I don't like the idea of her mother being worried about her daughter because of me. I'm not an animal, and I'm certainly not out to hurt anyone.

"Okay," Olivia says through an exhale when she reaches my table a few minutes later. "I'm ready!"

Her apron is gone, exposing the tight fit of her blue jeans and sliver of exposed skin above her waistband. I'm happy to see she's added a heavy coat to keep her warm on the back of my bike, unlike the one she wore Saturday night.

"That was quick," I say as I stand, thrilled that we can bail this fucking place.

She nods. "Yeah, I basically told my mom if she didn't relieve me, I was going to pass out from hunger."

I turn to where her mother stands by the back computer and find her keeping a close watch. "Did you tell her you were eating with me?" I ask low.

"No," she says, turning to see the look on her mother's face. "Let's just go, and I can make up something when I see her next." She turns to walk toward the café's door without waiting for my response, and I hurry to follow behind her.

OLIVIA INSISTED SHE DIDN'T WANT TO GO HOME AND change, which ignited my appreciation for the coat she wore to work this morning as we flew down a dark back road. By all accounts, the temperatures haven't been as cold this year as they normally are, but the cool bite that hangs in the air is much harsher when you fly through it at sixty miles an hour.

Reminiscent of the last time she was on my bike, Olivia's arms are wrapped tight around my middle, cheek flush against the center of my back. Her body shakes with high-pitched, near manic giggles as I show off a little on a few empty straightaways, zigzagging back and forth across the road. It's hard not to beam with pride knowing that, even though she's not used to riding on a motorcycle, she somehow still trusts me enough to let herself enjoy it.

We make it to Monarch Saloon in just under thirty minutes, and even from the parking lot, it's impossible not to feel nervous about the low romantic lighting from the exposed bulbs fixed around the building. I've only been here once—to pick up a stranded Colt after the girl he'd brought left him high and dry when she'd seen a text from *another* girl pop up on his phone— but I remember deciding right then, if I ever got the chance, this is the kind of place I wanted to take a girl to.

Olivia and I are both aware of what this is: a date. That was the whole point of what I offered her, isn't it? Still, the way my stomach tips uncomfortably as I rise from my bike is as unfamiliar as it is glaring.

"*Oh.*" Olivia lets out a soft sigh behind me. I turn to find her scanning the property beneath the simple black helmet I brought for her to wear, eyes tracing the decades-old oak trees billowing over and forming a natural canopy over the property, small white lights wrapped around their branches. "This is . . ." Her eyes find mine. "Wow."

My shoulders relax as I reach a hand out to help her off the bike. She tugs off the helmet, strawberry-gold strands of hair falling down her back, and I nearly shudder at the sight. I reach to pull mine off too, replacing it with my cowboy hat. "I hope this is okay," I say, though from the way her eyes widen as she continues to take in our surroundings, I have a feeling she's pleased.

"More than okay," she confirms. "I had no idea anything like this existed around here."

The corners of my mouth tug. "Come on." I offer my hand again, and this time she eyes it for a beat. She takes a long, quiet breath and then slips her warm hand into mine, her skin soft as hell. I've never held a woman's hand before—or, at least, I haven't been the one to initiate it—and I pray to god I don't go clammy with the nerves rioting inside of me. I lead her toward the wide wooden door painted a deep, dark blue and reach out to pull it open for her.

"After you."

Her eyes, speckled in green and gold, burn in the low light above us. "Such a gentleman," she teases.

A burst of heated air engulfs us as we enter the restaurant, smells of roasted meat and garlic lighting me up with anticipation. With everything going on at home, Mom's been too busy with the boys to do a whole lot of cooking. It's been a while since I've filled myself with good food.

Two women wearing matching black dresses wait behind a sleek host stand, and I dip my head in greeting as we approach them. "For two, please."

The shorter one on the left with long blonde hair smiles wide. "What's the name of your reservation?"

My heart sinks. *Fuck.* "Uh . . . I don't have one."

I don't miss how her mouth flattens. Her eyes bounce from me to Olivia before she checks her computer. "Just give me one moment, okay?"

What a *rookie.* Of course this is the kind of place you'd need a reservation for, and my dumb ass just assumed we could waltz in here, no problem. "Please," I nearly beg, the fingers not entwined with Olivia's drumming against my thigh. "We'll take any table you have."

The hostess's eyes rise to meet mine. "One moment, please."

I sigh, nodding. Olivia squeezes my hand, gently tugging me away from the stand. "Hey," she says calmly. "It's not a big deal."

Irritation slices through me, eager to be let out. "They better find us a fucking table—"

"Rhett." Her voice pierces through the rising tide of anger. "No matter what, it's okay. This is a beautiful gesture."

I search her expression for any hint of disappointment, knowing it'll fuel bad behavior on my part, but there's none. She still looks happy, like even if we don't actually make it to a table, it wouldn't sour her experience.

"Sir?" the hostess calls from behind me, and I whip my head around. "A spot just opened up. You can follow me right this way."

I exhale audibly and tip my head back to look at the ceiling, hearing Olivia chuckle behind me. When I look back at her, she's beaming, radiating joy, and I could literally kiss one of the hostess's spiky pointy-toe heels for making this happen. She leads us to a small table for two in the middle of the restaurant—the single, empty table surrounded by others with seated guests. "Here you are." She presses her hand on the ivory linen that covers the table's surface before giving us room to take our seats.

I make sure to pull Olivia's seat out for her—I've been reminding myself to do that on an incessant loop all night, too terrified of forgetting—before seating myself in the chair across from her. The hostess lays two menus down in front of us. "Have you ever been to the Monarch Saloon?"

Olivia shakes her head, still smiling wide like she can't believe we're actually doing this. "No. It's *beautiful* in here."

The hostess lets out a small, polite laugh. "Yes, it might be called a 'saloon,' but Monarch is absolutely a fine-dining establishment. Our food is meant to be enjoyed as an experience, and the ambience strives to support that. Please enjoy your evening—your server will be right with you."

I don't miss the small wink she gives me as she turns to walk away, a knowing smile on her face. I'm not sure what strings she pulled in those few minutes to get us this table, but something tells me she *definitely* pulled them.

Olivia's eyes skim over the menu, her lips twisting in thought as she considers. Even after hours spent on her feet serving others, hair swept back behind her ears and wearing jeans in a place where most people are head-to-toe in designer clothing, she looks like the best damn thing I've ever seen.

CHAPTER EIGHT

OLIVIA

*R*oasted Chicken Au Poivre
    Duck Confit
Wood-Fired Filet
Stuffed Pork Chop

My mouth waters as I read through the entrees listed on the menu—I've never in my life eaten at a place like this. "Are you sure this isn't too much?" I ask, my gaze rising to meet Rhett's.

His brows dip. "What do you mean?"

I look back at the menu. "This pork chop is almost fifty dollars."

Rhett's expression is wicked. "Don't insult me, peaches. Or my wallet. Order whatever the hell you want."

He sounds miffed, and it sends a thrill through me. Something about his gruff communication paired with the clear effort he's putting toward our date is . . . well, it makes about as much sense as him having this idea in the first place. "I should have changed," I mutter to myself.

"Why?"

"I'm wildly underdressed. I'm pretty sure that woman over there is wearing a fur coat."

Rhett's eyes widen as he turns around. "Fuckin' yuppies," he curses.

"Are you against her fashion choice?"

He sighs. "I don't have a problem with animal consumption, or maybe even the use of their hides in a primitive survival sense. But to skin a mink or chinchilla or a fuckin' *fox* in the name of high fashion is where I draw the line."

I can't help but let out a surprised laugh. I'm not sure if it's his defense of animals—although, the way his cheeks flush pink with frustration is something I like very much—or that he isn't afraid to speak his mind, but it's refreshing to be around someone so *honest*.

Our server comes—a middle-aged man with graying hair and a polite seriousness about the process of ordering—and Rhett asks for the filet. I order the pork chop and a glass of wine, handing our menus to the server before he leaves us.

"So," I say, suddenly nervous that it's just Rhett and me now that the food's been handled.

He leans back in his chair and looks at me with a thoughtful gaze. "So," he parrots.

"Tell me about yourself."

He rolls his eyes. "Olivia—"

"This is our first date, right?" I'm not sure where I got the bravery to interrupt Rhett Bennett, but it's still *beyond* me that we're sitting here together, that he actually asked me to do this.

His eyes spark with something dark—there and gone in a flash. "Yeah."

I shrug. "I want the full experience. Tell me something you'd say to a girl on a first date."

He smirks. "'Your place or mine?'"

I throw my napkin at him. "You skeeve!"

His laugh is beautiful and open. I realize it's the first time I've ever seen him do it. "I don't date," he says simply.

"What do you mean?"

"I mean that I'm not sure any of my . . . *interactions* with women . . . would be considered real dates."

My cheeks burn at the insinuation. "Oh." I want to ask him why he suggested doing this with me then, but I decide instead to shift the conversation. "Okay, so give me anything. Pretend I don't know you."

He rolls his eyes. "I'm a selfish asshole who hates just about everybody and, for the most part, wants to be left alone."

I'm stunned into silence. Literally, I cannot even think of a response.

He looks at me with wide eyes. "Shit, sorry. Guess I'm not exactly good at this."

"Um, that's okay. Don't be sorry." After a beat, I ask, "Do you really think that about yourself?"

"What, that I'm a selfish asshole? Or that I want to be left alone?"

"You're not an asshole."

His smile is rueful. "Oh, there's no denying it at this point, I'm afraid."

"I mean, sure, sometimes you act like one. But I think it's with good intentions."

This has him pausing. "What do you mean?"

"You were pretty grumbly at Spurs, but you thought Ivan was yelling at me. And you kicked Tony out of your bar, but let's be real, he wasn't exactly charming. You're rough around the edges and use intimidation when it suits the situation, but so far, I've only seen it used for good. *And,*" I add, a little sheepishly, "you offered to do this with me. Instead of rightfully making fun of me."

"I wouldn't make fun of you, Olivia."

"Exactly my point."

He stares at me. Crosses his arms over his chest. "Most people have no problem thinking I'm an asshole."

I shrug. "Maybe they're wrong. And just because people think it doesn't make it true."

"Hm." He scrubs a hand over his mouth. "What about you?"

"Am I an asshole?"

He barks another laugh. "No. Tell me something about yourself."

I think about it for a second, about Rhett's point-blank response. The swift desire to match his honesty has me speaking before I realize what I'm revealing. "I have a father I've never met who lives in Charleston with his wife and three daughters—my half-sisters. And they want me to visit in the summer. For a wedding," I add, like that detail is important, like I didn't just reveal my greatest secret to this man I hardly know.

He leans in. "You've *never* met him?"

"Nope. He was having an affair with my mom and got her pregnant. Bailed as soon as he found out."

"Damn, that's shitty."

Again, I shrug. "It's okay."

"No, it's not." His expression grows stony.

"It is," I insist. "My life has been . . . fine without him. Good." Oh my god, Olivia, shut *up*. "Great, actually!" Yeah, this is going swimmingly.

He scoffs, but I can tell my stammering amused him. "You've been throwing yourself at literal pests, and then you let me"—he points to himself—"the asshole, convince you to do the same even after I called you out for it. You have a hole in your heart, peaches. Don't pretend it's okay."

Bile nearly rises up my throat at being so exposed by such a quick observation. It unnerves me, for him to think I'm broken. "I don't *throw* myself at anyone, and there's no hole in my heart." The lies easily roll off my tongue, but it does nothing to stop his words from branding into me.

He holds both hands up, palms open in surrender. "I'm not judging. I've just found it's easier to bring that shit out into the open and use it like armor instead of letting it fester and hurt you. I'm not trying to offend, I promise."

Our server momentarily glides back in to drop a heaping glass of white wine in front of me, and I waste no time taking a big gulp.

Rhett doesn't say anything, giving me room to collect myself. "Sorry," I eventually say. "I just . . . sometimes I'm defensive about it all because people look at my mom and me like we're missing something. Like it's obvious, you know? But my mom has always been enough for me. More than enough."

His eyes soften, and he nods. "I get it," he assures. "But her being enough doesn't erase the loss of him, or what could have been." He adjusts in his seat. "Maybe 'loss' is the wrong word, but he's still out there somewhere being a dad to three daughters. Three daughters that don't include *you*." His posture straightens as he studies me, and I feel raw. In the span of mere minutes, he's effectively peeled back my skin to look directly into my insides. "That hurts. And it's okay to feel that too."

"I guess," is all I allow myself to say.

"Whose wedding is it?" he asks.

"Céline. The oldest of the three . . . the only one older than me."

"Yikes." Rhett shakes his head. "Messy."

I sputter out a laugh. "Yeah, you could say that."

"Are you going?"

"Hell no."

"Why not?"

"Because I don't want to." I brace myself for him to see right through it, for more of his brutal honesty.

But instead he just grins, looking like he doesn't have a care in the world about any of this, and I lean into it like a consolation. "Good for you," he finally says, not unkindly. And then he leans forward onto his elbows. "What music do you like to listen to?"

THIS IS THE BEST FOOD I'VE EVER HAD. I'M NOT SURE IF it's the unexpected opportunity to eat something *new* for once that has me nearly licking my plate clean or if it's simply a newfound love of eloquently seasoned and seared pork, but I know I'm going to remember this meal for a long time.

Or, maybe it's the man sitting across the table who's making all of this memorable.

Based on how quickly he had me spilling some of my most inner thoughts about my father, I shouldn't be surprised with how easy the conversation seems to flow—so easily I don't notice the time that passes—but I *am* surprised.

I've heard stories about the Bennetts since I was old enough to start going to school: tales of petty crimes, vandalism, violent fights, and alcoholism. For generations, parents have used the lore around their family as a way to warn children about the repercussions of reckless behavior. Boys learn the consequences irresponsible delinquents like them are forced to face, and girls are taught to steer clear of the bad boys who will chew them up and spit them out for sport.

But whether intentionally or not, the guy in front of me reveals numerous clues that he's not as bad as I've always thought. Rhett is warm and kind and . . . *funny.* But it's also abundantly clear he keeps things tucked tightly to his chest. He is, after all, one of Saddlebrook Falls's greatest mysteries, and with every attempt I make to get a closer look at him, he dazzles me with a distraction.

"What's the ranch like?" I ask.

He forks a piece of steak into his mouth. "It's good. Busy right now, but I love the work."

"What about your brothers?" I brave. "What are they like?"

He eyes me for a beat, then looks back down at his plate. "They're, uh . . . also assholes, mostly." He shoots me a small smile, and I get the sense he's not interested in saying more. Lucky for him, he's saved by the sound of a ringing phone. "Shit," he mutters, pulling it out of his pocket to peer at the screen. I watch as he dismisses it and shoves it back in his lap. "Sorry about—" The phone rings again, and he sighs, shaking his head. "Fuck. Sorry. Give me a sec?"

I nod. "Of course."

He swipes his thumb to answer, pressing the phone to his ear as he stands to make his way toward the lobby. All I hear before he disappears behind the corner is a clipped *busy right now* and *fucking told you I'm done with that shit.*

Apprehension knocks as I pick up my glass to take a sip of the crisp wine. I wonder if it's one of his brothers—perhaps their ears began ringing the moment I asked about them. And then I wonder what sort of "shit" Rhett Bennett might be done with.

It's only a couple of minutes before he ambles back toward the table, dropping his broad frame into his chair. "Sorry about that," he says quickly.

"Everything okay?" I ask, studying his eyes for any clues.

He shrugs. "My friend, Colt," he explains. "He can be a little high maintenance."

I smile in response, choosing to leave it alone. But it's a reminder, I think, that even though this dinner conversation has been casual and open, I still know next to nothing about the man sitting across from me. And while that doesn't scare me, I can't deny the thrill it ignites.

I want to know more, to uncover some of his secrets. To know him in a way no one else does. Maybe I *have* been throwing myself at pests, but something tells me Rhett is anything but. He's a wolf, a brutal and unforgiving force, and I want to know what it feels like to be his prey.

Rhett doesn't say much for the rest of the meal, and I don't let it bother me. We finish our food in a comfortable silence before he pays and escorts me back to his bike, helping me again with the helmet. The ride back to town is much the same, bar the rumble of his engine, and it gives me time to think this all through.

When he pulls up in front of my house and leans the weight of me and his bike onto his strong left leg, I know what I want.

Swinging myself off the leather seat, I wrestle to unfasten the straps of the helmet with numb fingers as he turns off the ignition and does the same before standing to look at me. His eyes are steady and clear, glinting like a flash of metal in the moonlight. His mouth rounds to say something, but I don't give him the chance.

As soon as the helmet is off, I dart forward.

And I kiss him.

I catch the sound of his surprise on my lips, feel the way his muscles grow rigid. For five entire heartbeats, I wonder if I've made a terrible mistake.

But then his arm hooks around my middle to pull me in closer, his other hand winding through my hair as he parts his lips open. And I can't help the violent freefall my heart takes, plummeting off the edge of possibility.

Rhett kisses me back.

His tongue reaches to meet mine, and the feel of it has my mind spinning in endless circles. Pressing my face farther into his, he deepens the kiss with a low groan that I wish I could trap in a mason jar, to open again later and listen to over and over.

I'm no stranger to a kiss—I've had my share. But *none* of them have ever felt like this.

When I finally pull my mouth away, his heart races beneath the palm I have pressed to his chest. I look up to find his eyes burned to ash, and I can't help the smile that nearly splits me in two.

"Next time, I want you to show me more of *you*," I say.

And then I turn toward my walkway, leaving him standing beneath the endless stars.

CHAPTER NINE

RHETT

When I pull up the drive to the main house, the sky is still as dark as it was an hour ago when I woke up. Heavy clouds prevent any traces of the sun's rise over the ranch from breaking through, and a deep sense of foreboding creeps in when I don't see any horses turned out in the corral. A chill winds its way up my spine as I get off my bike because I'm not sure if what I'm feeling is about last night or if it's something I can sense going on here at home.

Either way, my heart sinks further into my gut with every step I take toward the front steps.

Inside the house is warm, but I keep my jacket on and move right through the entry, where I find just about everyone gathered together. Layla stirs what looks like pancake batter in a plastic mixing bowl as eggs fry on a cast-iron pan nearby. Kasey sits at the wooden kitchen table with his head hung in his hands, and Wells stands quietly in the corner of the kitchen carefully watching Brooks pace the wide living room. Everyone's tense, but no one says a word.

Mom must be with Melody—between her and Brooks, they haven't left his wife alone once since she got her diagnosis. Sometimes I wonder how Melody can stand it, to be fussed over so much when all she probably wants is a little peace and quiet. Then again, most people probably crave the warmth of loved ones during a time of struggle. I've just never known what that feels like.

My eyes scout the room again. Dad's nowhere to be found, but I'm not surprised.

"Where are the boys?" I ask no one in particular.

Wells turns his focus on me and his mouth dips in a frown. "Still sleeping."

They must be sleeping upstairs if everyone's here and not at Brooks's. Probably a good thing . . . from the way Brooks looks, he's not in much shape to watch them by himself. Something's clearly happened since I left last night, but I don't have the heart to ask, knowing it's probably not good.

My chest tightens as the familiar dark smoke of fear invades. I turn to head down the hall for the nearest bathroom, eager to splash some cold water on my face, but Kasey's "Where have you been?" sounds from his place at the table.

"Out," I say. I have no interest in sharing anything about Olivia with my family, especially not after last night. Not after she catapulted me into fucking oblivion with that kiss.

I spent hours on my bike after I left her house, hoping to drown out the mental chaos, but as hard as I twisted that throttle, I couldn't shake the feeling that I'd fucked up. Not even after finally calling it quits and finding myself at Wild Coyote where I could hide out in the small apartment above the bar for the night. I tossed and turned for hours, unable to fall asleep as I replayed the moment on a loop. Olivia may have been the one to start it, but I'd damn near melted at her feet from the feeling of her against me like that.

It went against everything I believed about women, which was that I needed to stay far the hell *away* from them. But since seeing her in Spurs last weekend, I was already having a hard time resisting more of her, and now I was wary that Kasey might somehow be able to see it all over me.

He lifts his head when I step back into the living room, his tired eyes straining to glare at me. "That's it?"

I nod. "Yep."

He's probably thinking that I've been up to no good. Sometimes it gnaws at me, the way everyone assumes I'm only made to be reckless and irresponsible. I guess I can't blame them for thinking I take after Dad in that way, and maybe it wouldn't bother me so much if they were right. But they aren't. No one—not Kasey or Brooks or, hell, even Mom—has ever understood the choices I've made or why I've felt forced to make them.

After so long, I guess I don't really care to justify anything.

Kasey sighs, scrubbing a hand across his jaw. "We need to do morning rounds," he says quietly. His eyes are heavy, and it's only now that I notice the bruising beneath them, a clear sign of his exhaustion. He looks at me before tilting his head. "Let's go."

I cast a quick glance at Brooks and watch him stride toward the far wall, his shoulders hunched. He's on edge in the worst of ways, and a knot lodges itself right into my throat with worry. Wells is still watching him too, letting out a quick "I'll be out there in a bit" before pushing off the wall to stand in Brooks's path, his hands out wide to put a stop to his pacing.

Kasey's hand presses against my shoulder. "Come on," he says. "We have a lot to do."

I turn to him and nod, eager to get the hell out of his house.

I follow Kasey through the front door, and as he wraps his coat around his shoulders, I bite the bullet. "What happened?"

He sighs, tipping his cowboy hat down his brow. "Melody spiked a high fever last night, and Brooks took her back to the hospital. Things just keep getting worse for her, and there's not much the doctors are doing other than flushing her full of meds to keep her comfortable. And you know Brooks is dead set on getting her better . . . I guess he got loud enough with a doctor that they made him leave. Gave him a security escort and everything. Told him he could come back after he cooled off."

"Shit." My breath whooshes out of me, fogging the pre-dawn air. Brooks must have been pretty riled up if they made him leave his sick wife.

"Yeah." He nods. "Mom's there with her now, and I'm sure Brooks will head back soon. But . . ." He looks up toward the sky, squinting at the dreary clouds. "I'm starting to think things aren't going to end well, Rhett. I think—I think they're going to get really fucking hard, and we need to do whatever we can for Brooks *and* this ranch."

He looks at me, and I feel it before it comes. The shot he's about to fire.

"We need you here. *I* need you here. And I'll tell you this: the last thing *anyone* needs is you getting into trouble."

"Do I look hungover to you?" I ask.

Kasey does a double take. "No."

I nod. "Because I'm not. I'm not fucking around, Kase."

"Then where have you been going? Just this week, you've been out more than you've been home."

I crack my knuckles and take a breath to stave off the frustration. "What does it matter?"

Kasey takes an assertive step toward me, pointing a finger in my chest. "You think I don't know Ellis is setting some shit up? You think I don't know all the ways you can end up in trouble, Rhett? Most likely either behind bars or *dead*. Whether it's cards or booze or fucking *pills*, I told you to keep your nose clean and stay away from all that shit, and—"

"I'm not doing anything!" I shout. "I already told Colt I'm not going to that game, Kasey. And I haven't touched pills in almost a year. I barely fucking drink. *Jesus*. Whether you believe me or not, I've been keeping out of trouble. You're just always so sure that I'm going to fuck something up—"

"Because you always do," he spits out, his eyes near wild. "Do you know how many times this family has had to save your ass from the shit you cause?"

I shake my head, blood damn near boiling. I can hear my pulse pounding through my ears, and I know that if I don't walk away now, I'm going to do something I'll regret. I don't know how to make him understand that I'm doing my best.

"Rhett!" Kasey calls behind me.

"*Fuck you*," I throw back, heading for the building behind the house that serves as a tack shed and makeshift office for the ranch. Kasey's the one who's been overseeing most of the daily operations lately, but I'm not interested in letting him lead me today.

I check the calendar that always sits open on the desk and see that we have two horses scheduled to come in from a private ranch in Dallas that likes to send us horses for training. The farrier will be here tomorrow morning, which means a lot of prep work to not only get the new horses situated, but also to get the others groomed and ready to be doctored. I bring my fist down hard on the desk, rattling the ceramic bowl of paperclips and jar of pens.

Kasey and I are going to have to work together all fucking day long.

THE WEATHER'S AS COLD AS THE WORK IS GRUELING.

The clouds hang over us until late in the afternoon, finally showing glimpses of the sun when we're about ready to wrap up. My hands are sore from mucking every stall in both barns, and I swear on all things holy I'm going to find some part-time help just so I don't have to keep doing this shit. I'll pay for them with my own tips if I have to. We used to have more outside help around the ranch, but with Melody's growing medical debt, we've cut loose anyone who isn't absolutely necessary— which at this point is only Hank the farrier and the rotation of vets we have on speed dial. But the ranch operation has nearly doubled in the last decade, and it's too much work for only a few of us.

Wells worked both of the new horses that came in, his diligent focus keeping him in the saddle with every attempt to buck him to hell. Layla jumped in to help brush out the horses in the barn in preparation for the farrier tomorrow, but then she disappeared back into the main house to watch the boys when Mom came to take Brooks back to the hospital, and Wells eventually left to open the bar for the night.

I have the closing shift, and I'm thankful as fuck I get to work with Wells instead of the asshole grunting next to me as he lifts a saddle onto its rack. The awareness I feel on the back of my neck tells me he's watching me, so I avoid looking in his direction.

Eventually, he sighs. And I brace myself.

"Look, Rhett—"

I shake my head. "I don't want to hear it."

A horse behind me whinnies, no doubt sensing the tension in the air. "Well, you're gonna," Kasey asserts with a sharp tone. He leans against the saddle rack like this isn't going to be a quick conversation. "I shouldn't have said you always fuck things up. That wasn't fair. Everything just feels so upside down right now and I'm stressed out and honestly a little scared."

My brows scrunch. "Why are you scared?"

Kasey sighs and hangs his head—a mirror image to the way he looked this morning, except now the purpling of the skin below his eyes is more pronounced. "I told you earlier, if things take a turn . . . if Melody—" He swallows hard. "If Melody doesn't pull through, it's going to *wreck* Brooks. And rodeo season starts soon, which means Wells will be in and out of town. Sawyer has another year of school, and Mom and Dad are getting too old to help in any meaningful way."

I can't help the scoff that breaks loose.

Kasey narrows his eyes but ignores it. "It's just you and me, Rhett. Between the ranch and the bar, we have to keep this shit going. I . . . I *need* you to be reliable. And the stress makes me anxious, and I took it out on you this morning and . . ." He takes a breath, eyes locked on me. "The truth is, I'm fucking terrified."

My stomach lurches at his admission. Of all my brothers, Kasey has always stayed closest to me, but it's been out of necessity. His way of keeping an eye on me. For as much as he worries about what I'm doing, he's never shared much about his own life with me.

As frustrated as I am with his lack of confidence in me, I recognize this moment for what it is: a shift in our dynamic. A surge of determination floods my chest, a near desperation to show him that I can be trusted. That I can be reliable.

"We've got this, Kase," I tell him, hoping he can hear that I mean it. "No matter what, I'm not going anywhere. I'm here for this family, okay? I'm here for *you*."

Kasey exhales, his narrowed eyes loosening. He scratches at his nose with a dirty knuckle and then nods. "Okay," he says. "Thank you."

I tuck the stall fork into the corner and start to pull off my gloves. "For the record, I'm scared too," I admit. "For Brooks."

He sighs and shakes his head. "I don't believe in miracles. But we sure as hell need one."

The statement sends my heart pounding.

CHAPTER TEN

OLIVIA

"I need a remake of that chili, please," I shout through the kitchen window where I can see Mark working over the stove. "Without cheese this time."

He turns to face me, his brows pulling together. "Shit, did I mess up the order?"

I shake my head. "No, Maeve conveniently decided she didn't want cheese the moment the bowl hit the table." It's not the first time the old crone has forced us to waste perfectly good food, but where my usual patience runs limitless, I'm struggling today.

Mark rolls his eyes, the silver ring in his right earlobe glinting under the fluorescent lights. "Last week she asked for both cheddar and Gruyere in her grilled cheese sandwich. Is she suddenly lactose intolerant?"

I shrug. "Who knows. Sorry!" I call sincerely before returning to the stack of cutlery that needs polishing. It hasn't been as busy as some Fridays are, but the day has drained me just the same. I'm sluggish on my feet, mind scattered after the way last night ended. I wasn't able to sleep much as my mind spun with what I'd done.

But you don't regret it, I remind myself.

Because I definitely don't regret it.

Kissing Rhett Bennett is one of the most idiotic and reckless things I've probably ever done. Never in my wildest dreams did I imagine I could move with such blatant spontaneity or disregard for consequences, so much so that it would catch someone like *him* off guard. But in a fit of bravery, I'd captured his mouth with mine and changed everything between us.

Okay, maybe not everything . . . It wasn't some sort of declaration of wanting more than he was already giving me. I mean, we *are* technically dating, right? Even if it's just an arrangement and not a real brewing romance, surely a kiss at the end of the night is acceptable. It's not like I brought him inside to ravage him.

I shudder, dropping the spoons back into the ramekin of warm vinegar water and bracing my hands on the counter.

"Liv?" my mother says from the computer to my left, bringing my mind back to the café.

"Yeah?" I hope like hell she doesn't notice the heat crawling up my neck.

She taps at the screen with a delicate finger, sending the kitchen an order before looking at me with a wry grin. "Charlotte just got here—she's at table nine. You didn't tell me you had a date!" Her eyes dance with excitement and my heart skitters.

"Which one?" My hand flies to cover my mouth. *Crap.*

Her eyes flare wide. "Olivia Danvers, what do you mean *which one*?"

I straighten and clasp my hands in front of me, my flush no doubt obvious now. "I've had a couple dates, actually," I explain. "Because I'm . . . dating."

The thrill exuding from my mother is near palpable. But then something dawns on her, her face morphing into concern. "Wait," she whispers. "Rhett Bennett was here for you last night . . ." she says, trailing off.

She'd asked last night, when she saw him sitting in that booth, what he was doing here. *Not* unkindly by any means, but he's never come in to eat before, and I knew it perplexed her. I'd tried my best to brush it off, telling her he was simply helping me with something.

"Mhm!" I nod but don't dare say more. Instead, I rip my eyes away from her and stomp to the booth where Charlotte sits typing on her laptop. I glare at her for nearly a full minute before she deigns to look at me with a wide smile.

"Hey girl," she greets me warmly.

"Since when do you share details of my dating life with my *mother*?" I whisper-yell through clenched teeth.

Her brow furrows. "You've never really had a dating life, so I guess I don't know the rules?"

I roll my eyes. "Okay, no need to offend me further." I lower into the booth across from her. "What did you tell her?"

She shrugs. "Just that we shared a not-so-epic double date last weekend and I haven't seen you since. Pretty harmless, considering you're almost twenty-four and live in your own house and are perfectly allowed to go on dates." She crosses her arms over her chest. "I'm confused why you'd be upset about your mom knowing."

I groan, hiding my face in my hands. "Because Rhett Bennett came here to find me last night after I forgot about our date—"

"*Excuse me!*" Charlotte screeches. "You went on a date with Rhett Bennett?"

"Shhh." I shoot a look around the café, horrified to find that we've not only caught Maeve's attention but just about everyone else's too. "Lower your *voice*, woman."

Charlotte stares at me like I've grown a second head. "Explain."

I pull the saltshaker in front of me so I can twirl it while I answer. "I had plans with Tony on Saturday night . . . Remember Tony? From the app?"

Charlotte nods. "You told me about it on Friday when we were getting ready for Spurs."

"Yep. Well, I took him to Wild Coyote, and Rhett was there bartending and pretty much ran Tony out of the place."

Charlotte's eyes go so round I fear she's going to break a blood vessel. "He *what*? What do you mean he ran him out?"

"He heard Tony make some stupid comments about my profile and butted in, and then Tony tried to stand his ground and it pretty much turned into a pissing contest."

"Oh my god, I'm surprised Tony had the balls. Rhett's like . . . scary."

"He is not," I defend.

Charlotte's mouth curves high. "Okay, so Tony tried to step up and . . . what? Rhett just kicked him out?"

"Basically, yeah. But he made *me* stay until he got off work and then berated me about dating assholes and told me if I was going to date one, to date him."

Charlotte squeals again, and I almost smack her. "Oh my god, this is the greatest thing I've literally ever heard." Her smile is so wide I think her jaw might dislodge from its hinges. "And what happened last night?"

I sigh. "It was so busy here I completely forgot that we made plans for dinner. He showed up looking pissed as hell because he thought I was standing him up. But then when he realized I wasn't, he stayed and waited for things to settle down so I could leave with him. He took me to this amazing restaurant, and oh my god, Char, I fucking kissed him. I can't stop thinking about it," I admit.

"Wait." She holds a hand up, closing her eyes as if savoring the moment. "*You* kissed *him*?"

I nod, biting the inside of my cheek. "Yeah."

"Who are you and where the hell is my best friend, Olivia?"

I can't help but giggle. Because she's right. None of this sounds like me at all. "I know. I mean, it's honestly more of a deal we made than anything else—he's letting me practice dating with him. But the kiss just kind of happened. I'm not sure if kissing is allowed."

She launches forward, leaning her elbows on the table. "When do you see him next?"

I shrug. But then the realization dawns on me: we never made any future plans. I never asked . . . I used up my final moments with him on a kiss. "Shit," I whisper.

She tilts her head. "Did he kiss you back?"

"I . . . I think so?"

Her brows fall. "Olivia, you should know if someone kissed you back."

I think back to the moment, remembering the way his tongue invaded my mouth and the feel of his fingers in my hair, pulling until a bite of pain licked along my scalp. "Yeah," I say, suddenly breathless. "He definitely kissed me back."

Her grin is cheeky. "Bet there's a lot *more* where that came from."

"Char," I whine. "I'm *not* sleeping with him!"

She shrugs, pulling her laptop back in front of her. Charlotte is one of the only people I know who has a remote job, and she brings her computer nearly everywhere she goes on weekdays. "Yet," she says back with a knowing glance.

I roll my eyes again and scoot out of the booth, feeling Maeve's glare burn into the side of my face. Whether it's because she heard every word or because she's waiting on her new bowl of chili, I'm not sure.

In the back, I find the fresh bowl waiting at the service area. As I grab it, I notice my mom through the window standing with Mark, laughing about something as her hand presses to his shoulder. She hides her face in the fabric of his sleeve, and he smiles at her like she holds all his secrets. It's not the first time I've caught them in the middle of . . . something. Mark's worked the kitchen of the café since I was around twelve or thirteen, and I think he's always had a thing for her. But besides these stolen moments in the kitchen, I'm not sure anything has ever happened between them.

I'm not even sure they've seen each other outside of work.

I slink back out to the dining hall, armed with Maeve's new bowl of chili, and delicately set it on the table in front of her. "Careful," I warn. "The bowl is hot."

She eyes me suspiciously under a wrinkled brow. "No cheese this time?"

I shake my head, smiling. "No cheese."

She nods, picking up her spoon and setting her napkin in her lap. She's dining alone today, which isn't unusual for her. I actually think she prefers it over sharing a table with others—better to listen in on the world around her. "You know," she says just as I'm about to walk away. "Those Bennetts aren't to be trusted, dear." Her pale blue eyes meet mine again, studying me.

"Oh yeah? Why's that?" I say, humoring her.

Her expression grows serious. "They're womanizers. All of them." I watch as she lifts a spoonful of chili to her mouth, taking a bite. She frowns at the bowl. "Needs more salt," she mutters.

I point to the saltshaker right in front of her. "How do you know so much about the Bennetts anyway? They don't spend a lot of time with people in town."

She eyes me again, the corners of her mouth still turned down. It makes her look older. Sadder. "They didn't always stay away," she says quietly.

I nod, not quite understanding what that means. For as long as I can remember, they've kept away from anything town-related outside of the Mustangs football team, where most of the brothers have played with varying levels of success. I wipe my hands along my apron, eager to end the conversation. "Enjoy the chili, ma'am," I say with a smile and then make myself scarce.

CHARLOTTE LEAVES ABOUT AN HOUR BEFORE I GET OFF, citing plans with Ivan. He's taking her to the drive-in in Foxborough County to see some new action movie. I happen to know that Char hates action movies, so I'm betting their plans are a little more *frisky* in nature.

The café is still slower than normal, and Mom has been sitting at a table with Luna, who runs the bakery next door, since she popped over to say hello after closing her own doors for the night. I process through all my normal chores: cleaning the soda machine, wiping menus, rolling napkins, and filling the shakers on all unoccupied tables. Teresa is still out today which means I don't have the usual help, but I don't mind. The normalcy and routine of keeping things running here is a comfort I've often found safety in.

I know I'll always belong to this café, just as it will always belong to me and Mom. Someday I'll run it without her, and the surety of that promise is one of the best gifts she's ever given me.

We run out of pepper before I finish refilling shakers, so I wind my way toward the office so I can make a note to order more tomorrow. Pushing through the closed door, I sit at the desk and scan its surface for a pad of sticky notes and a pen, finding both under a pile of papers. Mom isn't the most organized with paperwork—or really *anything*—but despite the chaos of her environment, she runs a tight ship.

I write the note before pulling it off the top of the pad and adhering it to the black screen of the computer monitor, and it's when I quickly scan over the desk again that I see it: a cream-colored envelope with blue handwriting. A letter addressed to me . . . with a Charleston return address neatly printed in the top-right corner.

My mind tumbles as I stare at it. It's not my father's angular scrawl . . . the lettering is more loopy. More feminine. I don't hesitate as I swipe it off the desk, quickly confirming that it's still sealed shut—not that I really think Mom would read something like this—and shove it into the wide pocket of my apron as I stand.

Making quick work of closing out the rest of my tables, I don't even bother to wait for them to leave so I can grab the tips. My mom scoots in next to me at the computer, and I feel the weight of her gaze as she studies me. "You out of here, sweetheart?"

I nod, smiling at her. "Yeah, I'm beat. You need me to open tomorrow morning?"

She shakes her head. "Nah, I got it. I think Teresa will be back in too. Why don't you take the day off?"

I scrunch my nose. "It's Saturday . . . it's too busy for you and Teresa to work alone."

She shrugs. "I'll call in Suzie. She'd probably love some extra cash." Suzie works here part-time, usually on weekday mornings. She's single with no kids, and if she's not working here, she's usually complaining of being bored at home.

"You sure?"

She nods. "You need a day off, Liv. Go sow some wild oats." Her right brow raises as if to drive the point home.

"Ha. Thank you," I say with an eye roll, pressing a kiss to her cheek.

On my walk toward the employee exit, the envelope in my apron seems to burn through my jeans. I do my best to ignore it for now, swiping my purse out of the cubby propped on the wall, and barge out the door into the chilly night.

I need a fucking drink.

CHAPTER ELEVEN

RHETT

For the third time in a week, I'm surprised to see Olivia walk into a bar. Except this time, when I spot the glow of her hair and the shape of her body moving through the crowd, she doesn't have her petite friend or that douchey city boy trailing behind her.

This time she's alone.

And she looks pissed.

Her eyes shine under the bar light and I see it then—the sadness too. Something's wrong. The last two times I saw Olivia in a bar, she wore her usual easy mask of politeness even though she was obviously uncomfortable in both situations. But now she wears her real emotions all over her face, and my heart kickstarts as I think through what I could have possibly done to make her look like that.

As if on instinct, her eyes rise and meet mine, and I'm rooted in place. I have half a mind to rip this bar right out of the floor with my bare hands so I can help close the distance between us, but I swallow back my need to rage at the way she looks and try like hell to exercise a sliver of patience.

"What's wrong?" I say as soon as she reaches the bar. I study her face for any clues, trailing my gaze down her body to see if she's hurt somewhere.

"I need a drink," she rasps out just as the first tear falls.

My thumb aches to wipe it from her cheek, to press into her soft skin like I did last night. But I hold back, aware of the bar full of townies and the fact that my youngest brother is only feet away from me, chatting it up with fucking Boone of all people. So, I simply nod, turning to pull down our best whiskey from the top shelf.

"Not whiskey," she protests.

I don't face her when I say, "Trust me?"

I think she might argue, but then she hums her assent.

I grab a shot glass and fill it. "How'd you get here?" I ask.

"I walked."

I meet her gaze. "Good." I slide the glass toward her. "Drink."

She eyes the bourbon for only a moment before lifting it to her lips, taking it all in one go. I watch her eyes well and her lips tuck into her mouth as she swallows around the burn. And then she sets the glass back down between us.

"Another?" I ask, grabbing a bar rag from the sink.

She shakes her head. "Not unless you want me fast asleep on this bar."

Images of Olivia in *many* different scenarios on top of this bar have me stumbling a step, but I recover swiftly and press on. "Okay, how about wine?"

She peers somewhere behind me, looking at the bottles on the shelf. "You have wine here?"

"Not for anyone else."

Her gaze jumps to me and she swallows again. "Wine would be amazing, thank you."

I nod. And then I tap my finger on the bar in front of the seat closest to the wall, away from everyone else. "Sit," I say. "Please."

When she does, I move to the back office where we keep a couple bottles of Mom's favorite wine for the rare occasions she comes in. She used to be here a lot more—hell, she used to take her own shifts—but it's been a long, long time since I've seen her walk through the door.

She won't miss a bottle.

I bring it back behind the bar, passing Wells on my way. "You good?" he asks, eyes dropping to the wine. His eyes widen. "Is she here?"

"Nope," I say, shaking my head as I walk back toward Olivia. If Wells keeps watching me, I'm not sure. And quite frankly, I don't care.

Olivia waits in her seat, picking at the corners of a cocktail napkin with a frown that makes me uneasy. I pull down a lowball glass and find the wine opener in the junk drawer beneath the POS system, making quick work of opening the bottle and pouring a few fingers of wine into the glass. I have no idea what a normal serving looks like and we don't have actual wineglasses here, but Olivia looks relieved when I push the drink in front of her.

She takes a sip and closes her eyes, nearly moaning. "That's delicious."

I exhale. "Good."

Her eyes lift to mine. "I'm sorry I just showed up like this, I—"

"You don't have to apologize for anything, peaches," I interject. "You can walk through these doors any fucking time you want. But I happen to notice there's a frown on your face, and I'd very much like to know how it got there."

She closes her mouth, pressing her lips together. And then she opens them again to whisper, "I got another letter from Charleston."

Charleston. Where her father and his other family live. "What's it say?" I ask.

She shrugs. "I don't know. I haven't opened it."

"Then what the hell are you cryin' for?"

Her eyes narrow, and I realize I've made a mistake with that little remark. Still, the relief is a thing I can taste. *It's not my fault she's crying.*

"I just mean," I quickly add on, "how do you know it's bad? Maybe it says no one's going to ever bother you again. Or maybe it's a check for a million dollars." I shrug, like it could be possible.

Her face crinkles as laughter bubbles out of her, and I feel my chest expand. "You think?" she asks.

I shake my head. "Probably not, but you won't know anything if you don't open it."

She groans, still smiling, and tucks her face behind her hands.

"Hey," I say softly, pulling her hands away so I can see those hazel eyes. "No matter what's in that letter, you're going to be okay."

She nods and the crease between her brows smooths out. I'm not sure if it was the shot or my words, but I like the way it feels, watching her unwind, knowing I had something to do with it. I watch intently as she lifts the glass of wine to her lips, downing the rest of it in one gulp. "Can I have another?" she asks. "For bravery?"

You're already brave, I want to say. But I keep my mouth shut and pour her another drink. "I'm going to give you some space to read it alone," I say thickly, the words I shoved away lodged in my throat. "But you come find me if you need anything. And Olivia?"

"Hm?" She tips her head up.

"Don't you dare leave this bar without me."

WELLS SEEMS TO SENSE SOMETHING, BECAUSE HIS questions start almost immediately. "Why's Olivia Danvers here?" is the first one that flies out of his mouth the second I walk away from her.

"What do you mean?" I gruff.

He leans back and crosses his arms over his chest. "I've never seen her here before. Is she waiting for someone?"

"How would I know?" I lie.

Wells scratches at his chin. "Huh," he says. And then he grabs two bottles of Miller Lite from the fridge and walks out toward the tables.

Ten minutes later, after dropping a fresh pitcher, I turn to find Wells talking to Olivia. Both of them are smiling, and it grates against my ego—I know damn well Wells loves his girl at home, but the sight of Olivia smiling so freely at another man like that smarts.

I've never felt jealous like this before. Not over *any* woman.

Weaseling my way behind the bar like a chump, I push in beside Wells, looking pointedly at Olivia's nearly empty glass. "How are you doing?"

Wells looks at me hard, confusion rippling across his face.

I ignore him.

"Good," she says with a small smile.

Her eyes look less sad, and I don't think she's been crying. "Did you read it?"

She shakes her head. "Not yet. Wells came by to say hi. Did you know we graduated high school together?"

"Is that right?"

"Yeah," Wells chimes in. "We were just catching up."

I nod. "I think somebody needs help over there," I tell him.

Wells eyes the patrons sitting all around us. "Where?"

I shoot him a menacing glare. "Over *there*."

Wells's head angles as he looks back at me, but then his eyes flit to Olivia before something finally seems to register. "Oh, right." He clears his throat before throwing Olivia a mild grin. "Sorry, work to do. It was good seeing you, Olivia."

"Likewise!"

He walks away, and I turn back to her. "Read the letter."

Her smile shifts into a mock-frown. "You're mean."

I shrug. "So I'm told. You want another glass?"

"Maybe just a *little* one."

I pour her a *little* more wine—only one finger's worth this time—and gently encourage her to read the damn letter before giving her space again.

This time, she does.

I keep a close eye on her as she opens the seal. She pulls out a piece of paper and unfolds it, and I can't see any of the words from where I practically hide around a corner, but it's obvious there are a lot of words written on that letter. Olivia's motionless as she reads, and after what feels like the longest minutes of my life, her shoulders slump and she buries her face in her hands.

I'm moving before a thought even forms in my head.

"What happened?" I ask roughly when I reach her, this time from her side of the bar.

She shifts in her seat to look up at me, a bright smile shining through tears that wet her cheeks. "It's from Céline, my sister," she explains around a hiccup. "She wants me to come . . . to her wedding. And she wrote such nice things."

"That's good. But how come you're crying?"

Her smile slips as more tears well in her eyes. "I-I can't go," she whispers.

"Why not?"

She looks down at her fingernails, taking a moment before she speaks again. But when she does, the words come through a quieter sob. "She wouldn't *understand*."

I wrap my arms around her and pull her into my chest. The lights are so low in the Coyote that it's impossible to make out the space just two feet in front of me, but I *feel* the curious eyes in my periphery. "It's okay," I murmur. "We'll figure it out." Her shoulders shake through silent tears for a few minutes, and then she pulls away from me. Her eyes are swollen and her cheeks are flushed red, and I *hate it*. Hate the sadness seeping from her.

"Can you take me home?" she asks.

I smile. "Of course."

Giving her my arm, I lead her toward the hallway where there's a side door to the smaller lot my brothers and I use for shifts. We pass Wells along the way and I tell him I'll be back soon, thankful he doesn't ask any questions—not after he sees Olivia's face.

We're in front of her little house on the edge of the brush within minutes, but by the time we get there, Olivia's emotions have morphed from sadness into something much calmer. She's quiet as I pull off her helmet and walk her to the door, and she doesn't say anything as she unlocks it and walks inside, leaving it open behind her.

I take a deep breath, watching her linger from the threshold. It's a bad idea for me to go in there—I need to get back to the bar —but the need to trail behind her, to make sure she's okay, is almost overwhelming.

The wooden floor creaks under my weight when I take the first step in. Olivia has disappeared around a corner, and I'm not sure if she wanted me to follow her or not. Hell, I'm not even sure she wants me inside this house . . . but she didn't say good night. And I should at least say good night, right?

I close the door behind me, keeping the chill out. The house is warm. Comfortable. "Olivia?" I call out, scared to death to move any further.

"One sec," she calls back. "I'm just changing real quick."

Blood heats my neck as I hear the unmistakable sound of clothes rustling, and I keep my feet planted right the fuck where I am, rooted to the floor.

I distract myself by looking round the dark room, lit only by the glow of a light down the hall. She has an oversized cream couch tucked into the corner of her living room, perched on top of a light-colored rug. Pink, maybe? There are houseplants every-where, vines running down from the ceiling, tracing along a bookshelf. Her coffee table is made of wood, and it's covered in candles.

When she eventually rounds the corner, she's wearing thick wool socks and a baggy crewneck sweater that skims her thighs. Her smile is loose and teasing as strands of her strawberry-golden hair fall chaotically around her face. She's sexy as hell, and I can't stop staring.

"Do you want to stay?" she asks, voice quiet as she stands right in front of me.

"Do you want me to stay?"

Slowly, she nods, her eyes dropping to my mouth.

I feel it in an instant: the fear. The way it winds through me and tightens with an uncomfortable grip. The way this suddenly feels like I have something real to lose, like I might not have understood the risks when I offered myself to her and now I'm forced to learn the consequences of that impulsivity. But it's not enough for me to back away, to politely wish her a good night and force my feet back out the door.

It makes me *want*. Because I can't remember the last time I had something of my own to lose.

My hands wrap around her waist as I step forward, pushing her against the nearest wall. She gasps, the sound so sweet it spears through me, and I almost lose my mind. Her chest flutters with quick breaths and I want so bad to feel it, to slide my hand up her ribs and over her collarbone. "You've had too much to drink," I say, a reminder more for myself.

She closes her eyes, goosebumps trailing along her slender neck. Her skin is flushed and pulsing. "Probably," she whispers.

My mouth tugs into a grin, eyes tracing down the lines of her jaw, the column of her throat, drinking her in like the glutton that I am. I bend down to press my nose below her ear, breathing in that intoxicating scent. "You're wearing it again."

"Hm?" she hums.

My smile grows, lips brushing against her skin. And then I

force myself to pull away from her, taking a wide step back. "You need to sleep."

Her eyes open again and find mine. "Will you stay until I fall asleep?"

I nod. "Sure. I can do that."

She hooks a finger into mine, gently leading me toward her room. When she reaches the bed, she lifts the covers with her free hand and slips between the blankets but doesn't let go of me. Instead, she pulls me toward her, closer. "Lie with me."

It takes everything in me to breathe deep through the mix of panic and need and growing fear. But I manage to get enough of a grip that I'm able to swallow down the emotion and throw her a smirk. "Be good, peaches," I tease, hoping it doesn't sound like the plea it is.

"Promise," she murmurs, closing her eyes as she nestles into her pillow.

I ease myself over her, curling around her body until my chest is against her back and my knees are hooked into hers. She lets out a deep, rumbling sigh, and I let it wash over me: her comfort. This contentment. Like I've somehow stumbled home after being lost for years. The implication of how good it feels flares and I can't help but feel like, at any moment, a door will slam and I'll realize I'm actually in someone else's house and I've overstayed my welcome.

She's snoring lightly a mere ten minutes later. I skim a single finger down her hairline, careful not to wake her. She didn't mention the letter again, but I have a strong suspicion that it's her mother somehow keeping her from exploring more with her other family. I want to tell her to be brave. To be selfish.

To be happy.

When it's obvious she's out for the night, I press a small kiss to her forehead and pull her covers over her arms before gently lifting myself off the bed and making my way back toward the front door. As soon as I reach it, I realize I don't have a way to lock her in.

Fuck.

The last thing I want to do is wake her up again, but I refuse to leave her sleeping in an unlocked house. If anything were to happen—

A thought hits me, and I wonder if it'll work.

Stepping outside into the chilly night air, I shut her door behind me. And then I pull out my wallet and hope like hell it's still tucked in there . . . I haven't used it in years. But a lockpick meant to open doors can surely secure them too.

When I find the slender piece of metal, I fiddle with the keyhole on her door.

And when the lock finally clicks, I smile.

CHAPTER TWELVE

OLIVIA

I can tell before I even open my eyes that I've slept through most of the morning. The room is bright and warm on the other side of my eyelids, and if the sun's pouring into my room like this, it's already high in the sky.

Taking a quick inventory of the memories I have from last night, I realize the whiskey and wine are the likely culprits behind the sour twinge in my stomach. But my head doesn't pound like I expect it to, which is a small relief. And then I remember the bartender who served me that whiskey and wine, and the letter that brought me to him in the first place.

I quickly open a single eye, squinting against the bright light and wondering if he's still here somewhere. But the house is quiet, and after a sweep around the room, I find nothing beyond my usual furniture and mess of clothes. Stretching the muscles in my arms and legs, I turn over in bed to face the open door that leads to the hall. Something catches my eye on the nightstand by my bed, and I sit up to look.

There's a full glass of water sitting next to the bottle of pain reliever he must have found in my medicine cabinet, and tucked between the two is a folded piece of paper. I snatch it, opening to read a messy, handwritten note on what looks like a gas station receipt.

Be brave. And hydrate.
-Rhett

My heart leaps into a fit of acrobatics as I carefully read the four words again and again. Then I trace along the letters of his name, something a lot like longing winding through me, which I promptly work to tamp down. I close my eyes as visions of him pushing me against my wall come rearing to the surface, knocking a breath loose from my dry lips.

The way his fingers gripped my waist.

The quiet hunger in his silver eyes.

I pull open the drawer of my nightstand and slip the note inside before closing it again with a small thud. Ignoring the medicine—I just need to eat something to ease my stomach—I down the whole glass of water before forcing myself from the comfort of my bed.

The urge to push through my front door to feel the fresh morning air from my front porch drives me to pad down the hallway. It's been so chilly lately that I crave the sun's warm rays against my skin, and my house is secluded enough from neighbors that I'm not worried about my lack of pants.

But the door doesn't open like I expect it to when I twist the knob. It's locked.

Frowning, I turn to the console table against the wall by the door and spot my keys right where I left them. My mom has the only other set . . . How did Rhett lock the door behind him? Is he still here? I crane my neck to peer into the living room and then the kitchen, but I don't see him anywhere.

Definitely not still here.

Anticipation slithers across my skin, an instinctual reminder of who Rhett is and the things he's done. How it might be just as easy for him to lock a door without a key as it is to unlock one. He isn't like anyone else I know, and based on the way I keep baiting him to kiss me, the way he already feels like a high I want to keep chasing . . . I remind myself to be careful.

What if this is just a game for him? I'm also not like most girls he typically . . . associates with. Maybe he's toying with me, seeing how far he can take the inexperienced girl in town over the edge for fun.

Would that even be wrong though, considering we fully discussed this was meant to be practice for me? It's not like I told him I had any physical limits besides sex, and I'm the one who kissed him first. Was it overstepping boundaries, the way he held on to me last night? The way his fingers dug into my skin hard enough it felt like he was struggling to let go?

No, it wasn't.

Hell, I'm the one who marched into his bar last night crying, looking for . . . I don't even know what. Consolation? Advice from a friend? Are we friends?

I groan. This is way too much of a mental war to be waging on an empty stomach. I don't want to overthink this—that was the whole point, to let loose. To have fun.

I turn the deadbolt and push out the front door. I have the whole day off work and absolutely nowhere to be. A rarity, considering I'm almost constantly at the café. It's nice to feel the promise of . . . nothing. At least for a little while, and on what looks to be a beautiful day. Maybe I could hike some of the trails just outside of town and get lost in the brush. Or maybe I could convince Char to come with me to the beach at Scorpion Bay . . .

I close my eyes as the ghost of Rhett's lips brush against mine in my mind.

Be brave, he wrote.

I can do that.

It takes me fifteen minutes to eat something and another

twenty to shower as I oscillate between feelings of anticipation, excitement, and nervousness. I know what Rhett meant when he wrote that note, that it had everything to do with the letter from Céline and nothing to do with him, but I don't care. Not right now, not when bravery feels a little easier with this instead.

I dress in a light pink T-shirt and jeans, pulling on a pair of boots I wear only for concerts or the fair. I'm not really sure what to expect when I get there, but I highly doubt his days consist of lazing around inside on a couch—not with all those horses to take care of.

After swiping on just enough makeup to hide the evidence of my late night, I decide to skip jewelry. Instead, I pick up my bottle of perfume and feel a zing of surprise when my fingers brush over the label—Peach Eau de Parfum. It's an expensive bottle my mother gifted me two Christmases ago. For the longest time, I hardly ever wore it, but in the last few weeks, I've been spritzing some on each morning in part of my attempt to be more adventurous.

It's why he calls me peaches, I realize.

My lips tug, and I catch the giddy smile in my vanity mirror.

I'm pushing back out the front door thirty seconds later with a skipping pulse and a floating stomach, thoughts of Rhett's eyes swirling around my mind.

CHAPTER THIRTEEN

RHETT

*D*espite the low temperatures we've had over the last few days, the sun is warm today, and by mid-morning, I'm burning hot enough that I have to take my jacket off not to overheat. Beads of sweat trickle down my temples and over my jaw as I continue to work through both sides of the first barn, turning out horses to Kasey in the nearest corral so I can muck and feed each stall before the farrier gets here. The ranch feels busier than ever with almost twenty rescue horses currently on the property. There's another half-dozen out at pasture that also need the occasional doctoring, but for the most part, they take care of themselves.

The horses housed in the two main barns are all in various stages of rehabilitation and training, and with only a few of us around to get shit done, their turnaround seems to take weeks longer than it normally would. Some of them are more difficult to move from one place to another, fearful and distrustful of halters and lead ropes and us, but if there's one place a Bennett knows how to practice expert-level patience, it's right here on this ranch.

Horses are a mirror into our own psyche, and I've learned a lot about myself growing up with them. Starting a morning irritable and frustrated only leads to trouble that could turn extremely dangerous, so as much as I love to throw a middle finger up to the world, I know my place at home with these animals. We exist to protect and honor their lives as much as we exist to protect ourselves. At its core, Bennett Ranch is a rescue ranch, and our only focus is making sure the horses that come through here leave happier and more stable than the way they came.

Still, the work is not without its bad days. It's impossible to hustle as hard as we do and not have moments of failure. Last fall, I got too cocky with a mustang and let his training become my own physical release. I missed the signs of his fear masked by his aggression, caught up in my own internal bullshit, and pushed him too far. After we were down and I led him into his stall, he cornered me in the barn and kicked me so hard in the gut I broke three ribs.

I was lucky.

It was the reminder I needed that, regardless of the shit I put myself through, what happens on this ranch has to stay separate. But I still worry—as hard as Kasey, Wells, and I are pushing to keep up with everything, our exhaustion is bound to lead to mistakes. We have to watch each other's backs and keep a careful eye on these horses. Especially the skittish ones.

Layla helps as much as she can when she isn't watching the boys, but she doesn't have the experience the rest of us do. Her instincts are strong and she's got a knack for caring for the colts and fillies we see, but it's not the same as having Brooks's focus and Sawyer's smarts.

"Yo," Kasey calls from the open doorway. I look up to find him poking his head in. "You expecting someone?"

I frown. "No. Just the farrier."

"Hm," he hums, disappearing back around the corner.

Curious, I rest the shaving fork against the wall as I leave the stall and make my way outside, where a sleek gray sedan is pulling up the drive—definitely not the old two-tone Chevy Hank drives.

I move to stand beside Kasey as we watch the car approach, wiping my hands on my dirty jeans. "Probably lost," I mumble.

"Yeah," Kasey agrees.

But then the man in a suit parks and steps out of the car, smiling so big when he looks at us it shows a majority of the white teeth in his mouth. "Good afternoon," he calls out cheerfully, rounding the bumper toward us. He closes the distance about halfway before pausing, throwing a hand up. "Let me guess, Kasey and Rhett, right?"

What the fuck?

"Who are you?" I demand, widening my stance as my mind flips through the Rolodex of people who might try to fuck with us. Kasey straightens next to me, crossing his arms over his chest, no doubt worried about the same. Outside of family and the hands we hire on occasion, no one visits us. Wells is the only one who ever really had friends hanging around, but that shit stopped years ago.

The man somehow smiles wider. "My name is Stuart," he says. "I just have a few questions about the ranch I'm hoping you can help answer, and then I'll be right on my way."

"It's not for sale," Kasey says flatly.

Stuart's eyes widen. "Of course not! The ranch has been a Bennett birthright for over a hundred years. I assure you, I have no interest in seeing a change in ownership."

How the hell does this guy know so much about our family? "What is it we can help you with, Stuart?" My tone is a little harsher than intended, but I don't really give a shit.

"I was hoping William might be around?"

Kasey stiffens as Stuart, who has the audacity to look over my shoulder, scans the grounds for evidence of my father. I haven't heard anyone call him William since I was a kid, and this guy sure as fuck isn't going to find that man anywhere near the barn or horses.

"He's not," Kasey says simply. A clear door closed.

"Right." Stuart nods. "I figured as much. A shame, to be sure. Look, as William is the current acting trustee of all Bennett family assets and operations, it's imperative that I speak with him as soon as possible. Do you know when might be a better time for me to come back around and see him?"

I snort. "It'll be a cold day in hell when William is ready for any sort of meeting with you."

Stuart's eyes narrow, but there's something that flares to life in his expression. Something . . . triumphant, like he's got the best hand at the table. I don't like it one bit.

"Do you have a card?" Kasey asks.

"Oh, sure!" Stuart reaches into his suit jacket to pull out a black card with white lettering. "That's my cell phone there, and my email is also listed beneath if that's easier."

"Great," Kasey mumbles. "I'll, uh, reach out soon."

Stuart nods, that ridiculous smile shining bright again. His comb-over doesn't so much as bounce when he turns on his heel and marches to the passenger side of his sedan.

It's not until he's all but disappeared in a cloud of dust that Kasey speaks again. "Fucking hell."

He's turning the card over in his hands. "What is it?"

"He's a fucking lawyer."

HANK AND HIS USUAL COLLECTION OF FARRIERS-IN-training arrive not long after our unwelcome visitor, forcing Kasey and I to set aside whatever the hell just happened. Wells, who'd spent the morning mucking through the second barn, pulls out the large stereo we keep shelved in the office and sets it up on the back of an unused trailer bed, plugging it in with an extension cord that winds along the ground from the open office door.

It's tradition on the ranch to have a little fun on farrier days, cranking old '90s country music as we all work together to get as many horses as we can in front of Hank and his team by the day's end. The music and casualness of what could easily become a stressful process seems to settle many of the horses, and as many of them as there are—and as few of us—it doesn't matter if fun is the last thing any of us feel like having. We owe it to the horses to keep things light today.

Kasey and I help Hank and the others set up the portable forge and anvil outside the first barn, careful to keep both far enough away from the hoof stand so we don't spook the horses. Most of them are back in their stalls, but we kept the first few in line for new shoes in the nearby corral for easy access. I push through the gate and hook a lead rope to Pistol's bridle, gently leading the huge paint horse out where Hank waits.

I catch a glimpse of Mom trailing a sullen Brooks out of the main house in the distance. She throws us a small wave before following him to his truck so they can no doubt head back to the hospital. Brooks doesn't so much as glance our way. Minutes after, Layla appears on the porch surrounded by the boys. Liam beelines it down the steps with excitement splashed across his face. Noah follows, forever shadowing his big brother, especially around the ranch. Where Rooster goes, Bruiser follows.

James is the only one who hangs back with Layla, his small hand wrapped firmly in hers. My chest tightens at the way his little brow furrows as he takes in all the extra people around, no doubt nervous from the commotion. He's had the hardest time being away from his mom. There's a level of uncertainty wrapped around Brooks's family, and I know the pressure of it increases with every day that Melody isn't home and healthy.

Liam and Noah eye Pistol curiously as they approach. "Is that a new one?" Liam asks, eyes tracing along the horse's muscled hind.

I shake my head. "Nah. He's been here almost two months."

"Are we riding today?" Noah asks, a hopeful gleam in his eye.

I smile, shaking my head again. "Not today, Bruiser."

"It's farrier day," Liam tells him, glancing toward Hank.

"You boys gonna help or what?" I ask.

"Yes!" Noah shouts, pumping his arm toward his hip.

I laugh and look around, spotting Wells heading into the barn to ready the next wave of horses. "Why don't you go find Uncle Wells in the barn, yeah? You can help with halters."

Noah nods and takes off like a rocket, but Liam hangs back with a determined expression. "I'm not a kid anymore, Uncle Rhett. I can do more than hunt for halters."

My smile slips, and I look him up and down. To be fair, the kid is almost twelve years old. My brothers and I were already learning to ride the wild ones at his age. But I know Melody would never forgive us if one of her boys got hurt—especially without their dad here to keep a close eye on them.

Still, they've been through their share of shit lately, and there's plenty of us around to watch them. Liam deserves this. "All right." I nod. "You listen to me real good then. These horses are *not* playful. Most of them want to be anywhere else but here because they don't know how good it is here. Not yet, anyway. When you lead them, you have to be confident. You can't be scared or show them weakness or they'll see it as their chance to hightail it. And Rooster, if I have to chase one of these horses down because you let him go, I'm gonna be real pissed. Do you understand?"

His eyes flare wide, but he does his best to keep his expression schooled. The boy's tough—I've gotta give him that. "Yes, sir," he says with a nod.

"All right. Why don't you walk Pistol here over to Hank, and I'll get the next one ready."

Liam takes the lead rope from my fingers and looks at Pistol, clicking his tongue. And then they're on the move. Liam's shoulders square as his attention stays focused on the horse beside him, and a swell of pride burns through me. Liam and his brothers are the ranch's next generation, and I want so badly for them to have an easier time with it than my brothers have had.

It helps that Brooks is a much better father than ours has ever been.

Liam and I work together to rotate horses out of the corral and over to Hank while Noah and Wells bring more horses out of the barn, and the next hour runs as smoothly as we can hope for. Kasey takes the lead on making sure everyone has what they need, checking in with each station as the horses' hooves are trimmed and fitted with new shoes. Layla keeps a close eye on little James, who runs along the lengthy fence that separates this working part of the ranch from the wild pasture beyond, stopping to ogle at two mustangs who peek out from behind a cluster of trees in the distance.

More than once I catch Wells looking at Layla like she's the sun, and it twists something in my chest every time I see it. Brooks used to look at Melody like that, but now he looks at her with so much pain and longing it nearly crushes me. I wish I could tell Wells to jump out of that saddle, to pull on his ripcord and get out of that mess while he still has his heart intact. But he's always been a stubborn one.

Can't really blame him for it—most of us Bennetts are.

When the sound of an engine snakes through the wind, we all look to find another approaching car weaving up the drive. This time, it's a car I recognize—one that sends my pulse into a frenzy.

"Hey, Kasey!" I holler, keeping a close eye on the moving vehicle.

"Yeah?" He walks up beside me, and I can hear the *What now?* in his voice.

"I got this one," I say quietly. "You got Liam?"

I feel him look at me, but I can't get myself to face him. To show him what might be written all over my face. "Sure," is all he says.

And then my feet are moving.

CHAPTER FOURTEEN

OLIVIA

I push open my car door and sputter out a cough from the cloud of dust that surrounds me, an embarrassing beacon of my sudden arrival. My nerves quickly tip from moderate to severe as I risk a glance to the crowd of people and horses collected out past the large white house in front of me, next to a matching structure I'm guessing is a barn.

In an impulsive fit of Rhett-induced bravery, I found myself driving here, probably the one place in Saddlebrook Falls I've never actually been, and now that I've made it, I'm questioning my own sanity.

If it weren't for the fanfare of my arrival, I'd quietly slip back into the car and turn right around. As it stands, nearly every pair of eyes is on me, so I know there's no going back. I may have made a monumental mistake in showing up here without so much as a heads-up, but I have to see it through.

Tucking my ring of keys into the front pocket of my jeans, I keep my head down as I make the climb up the worn path that cuts from the drive to the side of the house and beyond. The house itself is something out of a storybook, with its beautiful front columns and wraparound porch. The shrubs that flank either side of the front walk bear no flowers this time of year, but I can only imagine the colorful bulbs of various species that will adorn them come spring.

A tire swing hangs from a massive tree to the right, the long sweeping branches shading much of the ground against the high sun. A long wooden fence stretches far into the distance, separating the yard around the house and the corral up ahead from the wild land on the other side. I wonder how far the ranch goes—it seems endless in every direction except the one I came from.

For a place wrapped up in so much town lore, it's not at all as scary as I once thought it might be. Quite the opposite: it feels like a well-loved *home*.

I take a deep breath, inhaling the scents of grass and horse and wet dust, and force my gaze toward the group ahead. My eyes immediately land on Rhett, his face twisted in confusion beneath his black cowboy hat, and I force a smile. "Hey!" I call out.

He's walking toward me, and the tips of his boots graze mine in only a handful of heartbeats. "Olivia?" he says, like he's not sure if I'm really here.

"I'm so sorry," I rush to say. "This sounded like such a good idea in my head and now I realize how intrusive it is for me to just show up here like this—"

"Are you okay?" he cuts in, carefully scanning me up and down in that way that he does, like he's looking for a reason I might need him. Like he's ready to take aim at whatever spills out of my mouth.

"I'm fine," I assure him. "Thanks for getting me home last night. For . . . staying."

His eyes soften, a smile playing on his lips. "How are you feeling?"

"Great," I say. "I got your note."

He balances his weight evenly on both feet, crossing his strong arms over his chest. Unlike most of the others behind him, he doesn't wear a jacket, and my eyes trace along the corded muscles of his forearm. "Yeah?"

I nod. "You said to be brave. So I . . . I guess I thought I'd come here and see what you were doing today." My gaze flits back to the horses behind him. "But you're obviously busy—I really didn't mean to interfere with your work or anything."

He tilts his head and looks at me, as if seeing me for the first time. "You wanted to see what I was doing?" That smile keeps playing on his lips, a secret that burns somewhere in the space between us.

"Yes." Another wave of embarrassment nearly pulls me under.

He turns to look at his brothers and I follow suit. Wells is curious beneath his dirty backward hat, not all that different from the way he looked at the bar last night. Kasey's expression is a little harder to read, but something tells me he's not happy about me being here.

Rhett pivots to face me again, his smile widening in a way that says *fuck it*. "It's farrier day," he says, like I know what that means. When I don't say anything, a quiet chuckle escapes him and he tilts his head toward the barn. "Come on."

FARRIER DAY, IT TURNS OUT, IS *FUN*.

Between the whinnying horses, the hammering of steel, the smell of the forge burning, and the music that plays from an old-school stereo perched on a trailer bed, it's a coordinated dance of overstimulation that feels comforting in a way only the café has ever felt. I slip right into the rhythm and movement of it, focused on every quiet instruction Rhett gives me as I give the horses a wide berth.

I've never been this close to such a large animal, but everyone else here looks like they've been handling them their whole lives. Even Rhett's nephew—Liam, I soon learn—collects them from where they wait in the corral and guides them confidently to the farrier for new shoes.

I'm not exactly surprised to find Layla Hayes here. Not after learning she moved onto the ranch with Wells after coming home from NYU last year—a piece of gossip that swirled through the café with a level of gusto I hadn't seen since the town gazebo burned down. But it *does* surprise me to see an honest glimpse of what ranch life is like for her, the way she happily chases the smallest boy around in well-used boots stitched with yellow flowers.

When Layla and Wells started dating so soon after the tragic death of her years-long boyfriend (and Wells's best friend) Jason Moore, it was like the threat people believe the Bennetts' wield became stronger. As if Wells had somehow worked some conspiratorial outlaw magic to snare Layla to him. Nosey Maeve, in particular, presented new warnings to any single woman in town: stay away from a Bennett man or they'll bound your life to theirs on this ranch.

Rumors of all the illegal things the Bennetts are up to out here have been as cemented in our history as every important town tradition. But to be here now, to see an honest day's work playing out right in front of me, I have a hard time believing anything nefarious is actually happening.

Eventually, Rhett is pulled away by a blonde woman with the farrier's logo embroidered on her polo, and I hang back with Liam. I've *definitely* noticed the way the woman has kept a hungry blue eye on Rhett all afternoon, so it's hard to fight the urge to watch him with her now.

But every time I give in, I find him focused on the horse in front of him, or on a clipboard that gets passed around, or on his quick conversations with Hank and the team working in tandem with each other.

It's hours before the last horse is finished, when everyone lets out a collective whoop and claps, and I can't absorb the feeling of it fast enough. I'm sweat-slicked and dusty, but I feel like I was a part of something real. Something important.

Rhett makes his way toward me, his black collared work shirt ripe with sweat and just as dusty. His face is flushed, hot and bright, like he's wrangled the sun and swallowed it whole. Liquid pools of silver hook into my marrow and tug me toward him.

"Hey," he drawls, the low rumble of it like the engine of his bike. I want to feel the shape of his voice vibrate against my skin.

"Hi," I say back. A chilly breeze winds between us, cooling the skin on my face, but the heat of the day still smolders beneath my jacket.

"Rhett," Kasey calls from outside the barn. "You got Champ?"

He turns and nods with a silent thumbs-up, and Kasey disappears back into the depths of the barn. I look at the lone horse left in the corral, his golden back stretching wide beneath the late afternoon sun. "Can I help?" I ask.

Rhett gives me that slow smile that I'm growing more and more addicted to and dips his chin toward his chest in a nod. "You confident enough to lead him in yourself?"

I look at the horse again, taking in the depths of his dark eyes. His hair is near-white, the opposite of Rhett's coloring in almost every way. I'm tempted to ask if the horse is nice—some of them today were pretty resistant to being handled—but I have a feeling Rhett wouldn't ask if this could turn dangerous.

Then again, everything about Rhett always feels a *little* dangerous.

I push open the wooden gate into the corral and slowly walk toward the horse, careful to stay in his line of sight so I don't spook him. "Hey, Champ," I murmur. "I'm just going to bring you back inside, okay?"

The horse chuffs.

When I get close enough, I offer out my hand for him to sniff. He leans his head forward and brushes his nose along my fingers before straightening again with a regal posture. I smile, taking another step forward to glide my hand over his shoulder. "Good boy," I whisper.

Once I'm sure he's not going to attack me with his teeth or squish me with the sheer force of his muscle, I grab hold of the rope slung over his back and turn toward Rhett. To my surprise, Champ takes two sure steps, edging closer to my side.

We walk together back through the corral, to where Rhett waits at the open gate. "He goes to the second barn." He points to the twin white building that stands about ten yards beyond the first, and I steer Champ toward it. Rhett closes the gate behind me and then trails closely behind, but he doesn't intervene or give any further direction.

When we approach the second barn, Rhett jogs ahead and opens the last stall gate on the right. I guide Champ toward it, and he eases himself in without any drama. I watch with rapt focus as Rhett removes the lead rope and bridle, leaving Champ's face bare before us. "He's beautiful," I say, awed.

Rhett angles his attention on me. "So are you."

I whip my head to look at him.

The right side of his mouth lifts. "Your bravery," he explains, though for what I'm not sure. For leading Champ? For being here at all? "It looks good on you."

My cheeks heat with a burning eagerness that, until now, I've really only felt with crushes back in school. But even that doesn't hold a candle to the way this spears into me like a sharp craving, a *need* to feel Rhett's hands on me again. To feel his body pressed against mine the way it was last night. Which . . . is a problem, considering I *specifically* told him sex was off the table.

I think of the way the gorgeous farrier-in-training looked at him, the way it felt like she *knows* him in ways that I don't, and I can't help the question from spilling out of my traitorous mouth. "Do you sleep with the staff around here often?"

Rhett's eyes widen in utter surprise, his mouth parting and

rounding like he wants to rebuke my words. But then his lips press together and his eyes shine with a new wave of curiosity. "Are you *jealous*, peaches?"

"No." I shake my head dumbly, like a petulant child.

But then my mind spins, picturing him meeting her later. Giving her the kind of *date* that I suddenly want to beg for.

He grins as he shifts to lean a shoulder against the stall wall. Champ's long face pokes over the gate, nose ruffling Rhett's waves beneath his hat.

"No," I say again. Firmer.

"Tell me what you're thinking," he orders. Calmly. Like he's requesting my middle name.

My own stubborn hackles rise to meet his and I decide to push back. "I was considering whether I'd made a mistake."

"A mistake?"

"In keeping sex off the table."

Satisfaction swells at the way Rhett's jaw sinks toward the ground, a fumbled "*Jesus*" leaving his gaping mouth.

"You wanted to help me, right?"

And there it is: his hunger. The storm of it engulfing the gray of his irises. "Olivia."

"So I was thinking," I continue, "that maybe you could."

His eyes are dark with intent, focused on my lips. "Help you with what?" he asks, urgent, his voice husky and shapeless in the way it moves through my skin and bones.

"Maybe you could teach me," I whisper, not quite sure of myself or this thing ricocheting between us.

He hangs his head, eyes squeezing shut. I've unarmed him. Stunned him, even. It captivates me, makes me feel like I'm floating.

A smile ghosts his lips when he lifts his face again. "Teach you?"

I nod. "Yeah. I mean, you're a . . . man," I say, not so expertly.

"And you know what men like. So teach me. Teach me how to be what men want."

A low laugh vibrates out of him, amusement sparking in his eyes. "As profound as that idea might be, I don't think I should be the one teaching you what men want."

I narrow my eyes. "What does that mean?"

"I'm just saying. The kind of guy you'd want to have like *that* . . . I doubt he'd share my tastes."

My cheeks are *radiating* heat. "The kind of . . . I'm not sure what that means," I say haughtily. And then I take a breath. "Look, I just . . . I missed most of the fun part of being young. Being reckless and messy and naive and . . . I want to get some of that back before it's too late. Sex should have *always* been on the table." It's not the whole truth, but it's the first time I've let myself admit out loud all the things I've been starving for.

Any trace of humor is gone from Rhett's expression, but he doesn't say a word as he waits for me to go on. "I want to be messy, Rhett. I don't want to be careful. I want to have stories to tell someday, because right now, I feel like I have nothing of my own."

He lets out a slow breath, looking back down at the floor between us. Like I might burn him alive if he keeps looking at me. "I get it." He nods. "I do. But I'm a whole 'nother level of messy, peaches. And I'm a little worried it'll be too much for you."

I scoff, rolling my eyes. "I'm not scared of you." His eyes flare at my blunt response. "All I'm asking is for you to teach me how to be desirable. How to please a man."

He rubs the scruff of his chin with the back of his knuckles before he shakes his head. "I can't teach you how to be desirable," he says firmly.

"Why not?" I ask, thankfully only vaguely aware of how desperate it makes me sound. But it isn't desperation I'm feeling.

Something on his face changes, sharpens, as if he's considering something. And suddenly I *am* desperate—desperate to know what he's thinking, if there's a chance he might actually say yes. I'm about to ask again when he takes a step toward me, moving until he's crowding into my space and pushing me back against the wall.

His broad chest brushes against mine, and my stomach somersaults from the feel of it. Two pale gray eyes move across my face as he leans in closer . . . so close I think he might be about to kiss me. My heart fully stops beating as I brace myself for it, praying to god my breath is still fresh enough from the mint I had hours ago.

He's close enough now that his nose lightly grazes mine, eyes caught somewhere on my mouth or my jaw, but he stops.

"I can't teach you somethin' you already know," he rasps. "You asking to be desirable is like asking how to fucking walk. You are *already* masterful. Trust me."

I close my eyes at the feel of him so close to me. "You think I'm desirable?" I ask through a shaky breath. Want scuttles up my spine as my stomach swoops.

A low sound escapes him, raw and grating. "Yeah, peaches," he admits. "You could say that." His eyes drop to my mouth and flare. "But you're asking for the wrong things."

I swallow down my nerves. "I am?"

He nods. "You shouldn't be asking how to please a man. You should be asking how a man could please *you*."

I nod once, mind going blank as I watch his pupils dilate, and I decide to take the bait. "How can you please me, Rhett?"

He groans and reaches a hand out, covering my throat. His thick fingers are warm as they flex around me, but the pressure is light. "You have no fucking *idea* how much I want to please you."

Something hot lurches in my stomach.

He takes another step into my space, forcing me to move backward against the hard, wooden wall, crowding me with that broad chest. When he lifts the tangle of rope in his hand, the end of it traces up my arm and I shiver. "Tell me to stop," he murmurs.

I shake my head, defiant. But I don't trust myself to speak.

He clicks his tongue. "You can't possibly want this, peaches."

"I do," I argue, eyes tracing the curl of dark hair against his temple, leaning into the foreign feel of his hand wrapped around my neck.

His mouth bends into a grin that shines right into my chest. Our eyes lock, and I feel my breathing shift as my heart pounds. He simply looks at me. *Studies* me. And it leaves me feeling so exposed I'm sure my clothes have caught fire and burned to ash.

"You want this?" he drawls in a voice like velvet, his smile turning wicked. "Now you're going to get it. But not here . . . let me take you somewhere."

It's a threat that snakes around my consciousness, tangling with hope. When I nod, he leans in to brush a soft kiss to my cheek. And then he steps away, pulling his hands off my body.

The loss of him nearly sinks me to my knees.

I nod as I brace myself with a hand against the wall behind me, eager to go wherever he'll take me. Eager to get more of *this*. My body feels hollow, void, without him. "Yes," I sputter out. "Please."

His eyes darken, the shadow of a sharp blade. He closes them briefly as if to steady himself. "*Fuck*," he mumbles, and my heart gallops. When he looks at me again, there's a promise in the way his eyes hold mine. One that I grip onto for dear life. "Let's go."

CHAPTER FIFTEEN

RHETT

Olivia heads home to shower and change with a promise to be ready in an hour. Anticipation is a ravenous monster inside me, and my mind spins around the thought of her getting ready for *me*. I might have kept up a confident front in that barn with her, but the truth is that everything about her makes me feel wildly out of control.

I mean, goddamn, the woman flat out asked for *sex*.

It takes some convincing to get Wells to cover my shift tonight —he worked last night, and I know he wants to spend some alone time with his girl after Mom gets back home and can take the boys. But I think his general curiosity about whatever the fuck he thinks I'm doing with Olivia wins him over.

I try to make quick work of my own shower, scrubbing myself raw in my cabin to get the sweat and dirt off of me. I'm hard the *entire* fucking time, mentally creating and cataloging every single thing I want to do with her. Every position I want to see her in.

Knees spread wide on all fours, baring herself open for me so I can get a nice, *long* look.

Hands bound high above her head, her loss of control so sweet.

The way her hair might skate across bare shoulders, chin tilted up as she kneels for me. Eager and hungry as I slide into her mouth to see the shape of me swell through the outside of her cheek.

I wonder, *badly*, if she's just as stubborn and argumentative with the rest of her body as she is with that mouth. How hard I might be able to push her. If she'll let me break her the way I want to, if her desires might match mine.

Careful, I warn myself. Olivia isn't some random kinky woman I found in a bar.

She's warm. Soft. Pure.

I need to take *care* of her. To show her how fucking special and good she is. She's the first person who's ever looked at me like . . . like I'm a human being who fucking matters. And the last thing I want to do is ruin it. To prove her wrong.

Hazel eyes shine bright in my mind, looking up at me with so much of that trust I know damn well I don't deserve.

I don't even realize I'm pumping myself until I'm already coming.

OLIVIA BARRELS OUT OF HER HOUSE LIKE A BAT OUT OF hell, and my amusement splits my face open in a wide grin. Her hair is mildly damp, her cheeks flushed, and I do my best to memorize every detail as she springs forward down the front steps, nearly knocking her head against a plant that hangs from the overhead beam.

"Can I put this in one of those bags?" she shouts over the bike's engine, holding up her purse. I nod, shifting my leg so I can open the one on my right because the left one holds our food. She tucks her purse in next to the backpack I've already shoved in, and then stands to look at me with a rushed smile. "Thanks."

If she's nervous, she doesn't look it. She looks . . . happy.

"You ready?" I ask, eyeing the orange dress she wears beneath a white denim jacket. Its skirt is going to be hell for her on this bike, but the image of it has my blood pumping.

"Yep." She takes the second helmet from my hands and buckles the strap beneath her chin. And then the weight and warmth of her surround me as she assumes her position on the seat behind me.

We take off down the road in front of her house, turning at the first stoplight. I open the throttle and send us soaring down the long stretch of open road as Olivia's arms squeeze tight around me. In the minute or two we stay like that, life feels as damn near close to perfect as it's ever felt.

Soon I'm slowing us back down, easing carefully off the shoulder and into the dirt lot that stretches far in the distance, surrounding a chain-link fence that circles the water tower reaching into the sky. Olivia's lips ghost my ear, testing my restraint as she asks, "What are we doing here?"

"You need to eat." I push out the kickstand with the toe of my boot and lean the bike on it, turning off the engine. Olivia climbs off, looking around, her hair a mess of gold beneath the stark black helmet. I stand and reach for her wrist, pulling her to me. *Look at you*, I think, on the verge of voicing the words.

Her smile is soft, her eyes bright, and I have to push down the sharp impulse to do something with all this want. *Not yet*, I add as she patiently lets me unfasten her helmet and pull it off. *But soon.* "Is there an invisible restaurant?" she asks. "Maybe a gateway to Narnia?"

I roll my eyes, resting both of our helmets on the seat before pulling out the canvas bag of food. "What planet do you live on?"

She laughs. "Your imagination is sorely nonexistent, isn't it?"

If she only knew how savage my imagination has been. "We're going up there." I point to the large tank that holds the town's water, a chipped red *SF* painted in thick strokes across the middle.

She faces the sky, propping a hand over her brow to shield against the dying sunlight. "You're joking, right?"

I smile. "Nope."

Thankfully, she follows behind me as I lead us toward the steel ladder. "I thought we were . . ." Her voice trails off, dropping somewhere in the loose rocks beneath our feet.

"Fucking?" I ask.

I don't need to turn around to know I've made her blush. "Well . . . yeah. Are you an exhibitionist or something?"

My hard laugh surprises me. "Or something," I say, turning to look at her when we reach the bottom of the ladder. "You haven't eaten all day, and after our last date you said you wanted me to show you more of myself. I guess what you saw today at the ranch is a big part of it, but there's also a lot of other things about me no one really knows, not even my family. I figured I'd feed you in one of my favorite places before we . . . move on to other things."

I'm right: her flush stretches from her neck to her cheeks. And it's beautiful. She looks from me to the ladder and frowns. "Are we going up?"

"Yep." I move out of the way, giving her access to go first.

"What if I fall?" Worry bunches between her brows.

"I'd never let that happen," I say. And I mean it. "Plus, the ladder is caged, so even if you slip a little, you're really not going anywhere."

The look she shoots me is full of daggers, but then she's moving to hook her palms around the rung at eye-level. She takes a deep breath. "You're gonna have to live with it if I die, you know."

I shake my head. Smack her ass. "Get up there."

She yelps and laughs. And then she starts to climb.

I make sure to stay only a couple rungs below her so that if she *does* somehow manage to fucking fall and the cage around us doesn't break it, I will. She must realize how safe she is because she climbs with confidence, even as the ground beneath us gets smaller and smaller.

The caged chute opens through the floor of the five-foot balcony that wraps around the whole water tank, and Olivia clears through it with ease. "You know we're trespassing, right?" she asks, pointing to a sign bolted to the railing as I climb onto the balcony behind her.

I give her my best smirk. "Highly doubt Sheriff Joe is pulling any kind of surveillance on this thing. I've been up here probably a hundred times and never run into anyone."

She eyes the bag still clutched in my hand. "What did you bring?"

"Hungry?"

She nods. "Starving."

"Ranch work will do that to you."

"I mean, if you call hanging out with your cute nephew and petting a few horses 'ranch work,' then, yeah, I get why it's so hard."

I laugh. "We like to pretend it kicks our ass, but really it's just cuddles and kids."

"And here I thought it's where all that muscle was built."

I cock my head. "You like my muscles, peaches?"

She rolls her eyes as she sits on the floor of the balcony and dangles her legs over the edge. "I think we've established that I do."

I sit next to her, try *hard* to pretend like that doesn't light up every nerve ending inside of my body. "Here," I say, handing her a burger.

"Where did you get these? The only burgers we have in town are from my mom's café."

"There's a greasy hole-in-the-wall in Foxborough I like."

She eyes me. "You went to another county to get *burgers*?" I nod. "Why didn't you just get them from June's?"

"I would bet at least ninety percent of your meals are from

that café. And when I take you on dates, I want to make sure you actually enjoy the food. Plus, as a general rule, I try to find what I like in places that *don't* exist in Saddlebrook Falls."

I watch her take a bite, see the pleasure of it splash across her face. "Oh my god, this is so good." She takes another bite, this time bigger, and it leaves a smear of mustard on the corner of her mouth.

I swipe it away with my thumb.

Put it in my mouth.

Her eyes track the movement, but she shakes her head as if to clear it. "You really hate Saddlebrook Falls, don't you?"

I shrug, turning my attention to my own burger, unwrapping the paper around it. "The history between my family and this town is long as hell and pretty fucking messy. But yeah, I guess you could say that I hate it. Or at least what the people in it have done to us."

"What have they done?" she asks, genuinely curious.

I can't help the anger that flares. It's always *right* there, just waiting for the tiniest reason to ignite. "Those sons of bitches have been trying to dig my father's grave for *years*, Olivia. People have wanted to see him—us—fail, for as long as I can remember." My thoughts trail to the lawyer this morning, the unease on Kasey's face. I have half a mind to think it might be something Mayor Moore is up to—he's been trying to chase us out of town since he was elected, even when his son was Wells's best friend. "Look. Bringing me into your life in any public way is something you won't be able to take back when shit hits the fan. And trust me, it *will* hit the fan. People around here hate me too. It's bad blood that runs both ways, and I don't want to see you get caught up in shit that has nothing to do with you."

"I don't care what people think, Rhett. I only care about the truth."

"What truth is it that you're looking for?" It comes out harsher than I mean it.

She shrugs. "You haven't exactly been a real likeable guy."

I scoff. "Understatement of the century."

"Well, then you can't be mad that people have opinions."

My gaze snaps to her. A light breeze dances through her hair, her face glowing in the sunlight that remains. She's a force of nature. So brutally honest in the way she effortlessly calls me out.

I like it. More than I should, probably.

I tilt my chin toward her burger. "Eat."

She smiles like my attitude doesn't faze her. I watch as she lifts the burger back to her mouth and then I do the same.

It's quiet between us for a while. But the urge to explain myself eventually becomes unbearable, so I try again. "Bennetts aren't exactly known for being warm and fuzzy—especially the men. We've had the ranch for six generations—Liam and the boys will be the seventh. My brothers and I grew up when our grandparents were still running things, and my grandpa was tough. He babied Wells a little bit—I think he got softer in his old age—but the rest of us learned how to work really hard pretty early on.

"My dad, though—" I stop. Wait for the rush of frustration to pass, and then force it back down. "My dad took the ranch over when I was nine, and it was like a bomb dropped on the way of life we'd always known. Where my grandpa was strict, my dad was ruthless. He was already pretty deep with a drinking problem, and things derailed fast. My mom used to be good friends with some of the women in town—Mayor Moore's wife was one her best friends actually. But my dad would prowl around town like he owned the place, like the ranch and the bar were some sort of proof of his superiority. And it didn't help that he was drunk all the time. Her friends eventually stopped seeing her."

Olivia watches me, patient. Gives me the room I need to find the right words to explain something that feels so complicated.

"When I was thirteen, my dad competed in a rodeo—it was normal for him. Another way for us to make money. But he was wasted when he got in the saddle that day, cocky in thinking he could handle a bronc in that state. He was thrown off in the first three seconds, and he didn't move out of the way fast enough before the horse stomped over his back. His spine was shattered and he lost the use of his legs. Brooks and Kasey were still kids, but they were forced to step up and run the ranch. To train all the horses that came in. And my mom had to take over working the bar. Constantly facing people who'd essentially abandoned her. And my dad just . . . kept drinking, and he became more miserable than he'd ever been.

"I guess somehow I figured out that if I could get people to talk about me, they wouldn't talk about him. It *wrecked* my mom, the way people spoke so poorly of her husband. The way they laughed at him. And I just couldn't—I couldn't see her hurt like that anymore. So, I started doing stupid shit. Fights at school. Drinking a lot. Causing scenes I knew would fuel the gossip. And it worked, for the most part. People still talked about him now and then, but mostly, they were talking about me. It's . . . it's how the gazebo happened," I admit.

Her eyes flash wide in surprise.

I throw her a half-cocked smile, like it's not a big deal. "Everyone thinks it was about a girl who stood me up." He shrugs. "There *was* a girl, I guess. And she *did* stand me up that night, but I was already three sheets to the wind looking for trouble, because I'd found out earlier that day that my dad got caught stealing from the hardware store. He was arrested and everything."

"Rhett," Olivia murmurs, a look of agony on her face.

"I'd been sulking in the dark in that gazebo, and at some point, I dropped a bottle of whiskey. It shattered on the floor, spilling everywhere, and . . . I guess I wanted to see the whole thing burn."

She squeezes her eyes shut, blowing out a breath. "You were . . . suffering."

I nudge her shoulder with mine. "Hey, none of that. I've

made my bed. Done plenty of shit to hurt the people around me. And I can't lie and say I never enjoyed it." I take another bite and chew. Watch the tops of trees sway yards below us. "No one ever cared to help us. Like, sure, my dad was an asshole. *Is* an asshole, even sober now. But my mom is one of the kindest people you'll ever meet, and we were all just kids, you know? But no one wanted to help. We almost lost the ranch. Almost couldn't make ends meet. Even had to borrow from the devil a few times to stay out of the red." I decide *that's* not a truth I'm willing to share right now. Maybe not ever. But whether Kasey realizes it or not, there's a reason I started playing cards with the Rustler boys.

"I'm so sorry," she whispers. "That must all be so hard."

"I'm not looking for you to be sorry, peaches. But I guess it's good for you to know who you're dealing with before things go any further."

She takes the last bite of her burger and rubs her fingers free of crumbs. "I know who I'm dealing with," she says after she swallows, giving me a wry look.

I chuckle, and it feels good. "Have to say, I was surprised when you showed up today."

Her expression falters. "I really should have called."

"You still don't have my number," I tease. "I'll give it to you today. And for the record, I'm glad you came. But that note I left you was more about your letter than it was about me."

She stays silent. I don't miss the way she turns her focus to the ground far below.

"You want to talk about it?"

"What's there to talk about?" she asks. "It was a really nice letter from a half-sister I've never met, who for some reason wants me to be there for her wedding. There's just no way I could hurt my mom like that though. I've gone *this* far in my life without knowing my father and I . . . I guess I thought once I became an adult, his attempts to communicate would end. I thought it was all based out of guilt, anyway. He has this whole other family, you know? But Céline kept saying how hopeful he is, and I don't know. I don't know what to do with that."

I bunch our trash together and toss it in the bag, pulling out bottles of water for both of us. "What does your gut say?"

She looks at me. "All roads lead to this hurting my mom."

I shake my head. "That's what your brain is telling you. What does your gut say? Your heart? What do you *actually* want?"

Her gaze moves to her bent knee. "I want to understand. I want . . . I want to see what they're like. For myself."

I nod. "Perfectly acceptable, *normal* response. There's nothing wrong with you wanting to know your family, Olivia." I reach my hand toward her and tug on a piece of her wind-blown hair so that she looks at me again. "Your mom will understand."

She blows out a breath. Like she's come to the same conclusion, but she's still scared.

I push myself up to my feet. "Come on," I say, holding out a hand to pull her up.

Her eyes track up the length of my arm, a slow smile creeping along her lips as she palms my wrist. "Is this where we move to the 'exhibitionist' part of the date?"

I help her up to her feet and give her a smile that spells trouble. "I'm not *opposed* to fucking you in public, but I have another bag of tricks in mind."

CHAPTER SIXTEEN

OLIVIA

I trail behind Rhett up the narrow staircase behind Wild Coyote, listening to each step creak as we climb. A spark of anticipation catches when I see a closed wooden door at the top of the stairs, and my focus zeros in on the simple black knob.

When Rhett reaches the top, he turns around to face me over the shoulder that bears the strap of a dark backpack, his gray eyes glittering with the reflection of the wall sconce beside him. He doesn't say anything, and it prompts me to ask, "Is this where you bring all your girls?"

He smirks, but the curve of his mouth slips away just as quickly. "You'd be the first."

I don't believe him for a second.

"I need you to understand something," he says quietly. "You can leave at any time. You can . . . *stop* this at any time, if you—"

"Rhett," I say.

But he keeps talking. "Tell me that you will. If you need to." His tone is insistent. "Tell me that you'll stop this and *leave* if you need to. I'll take you home, no questions asked, and we can never talk about any of it again."

I nod, mouth dry. "I will. I promise."

His stare lingers for a lifetime before he turns back to the door, unlocking it with a small key he produces from his pocket. I follow him inside, the smell of warm spice and stale dust enveloping me—it's like stepping into another world. The apartment is a small studio, with a kitchenette and bathroom to the right and a bed shoved into the corner on the left. The blankets are rumpled, clearly recently slept in, but the room is cold.

It *looks* lived in, but it *feels* empty. Deserted.

Rhett must see the question on my face. "My grandpa had it built on top of the bar decades ago. I think he used it to sleep off the late nights he spent working downstairs." He shrugs. "My family never really used it. But I started sleeping here on and off a few years ago."

"Why?" I look around, eyeing the sheer curtains that hang from the single small window, embroidered with roses. The knotted hardwood floors creak with each slow step I take. It's beautiful but ghostly. The cozy warmth I felt at the ranch—even outside the big beautiful house—doesn't seem present here.

I find Rhett staring at me, face unreadable. "It's quiet" is all he says. "Do you want a drink?"

I nod, nerves spiking as my gaze catches back on the bed.

Rhett swings the bag he pulled from the bike off his shoulder, dropping it on a narrow dresser pressed up against the wall. He unzips it and pulls out a bottle of whiskey and a single plastic cup.

After pouring about a shot's worth into the cup, he hands it to me. And then he leans against the wall, a picture of patience, and waits.

My fingers tingle as I tip the cup to my lips and drink it all in a single swallow.

His mouth twitches, eyes sliding down my neck.

"Another?" I ask.

He shakes his head. "That was just to calm your nerves. I can feel your heart pounding from over here."

"Oh." I smile around the burn in my throat.

He pushes off the wall, bottle still in hand, and closes the distance between us in two long strides. "My turn," he says, still eyeing my throat. He lifts the bottle between us and I think he's going to drink straight from it, but then he tips the neck of it in my direction and whiskey spills over my bottom lip and chin. Down my neck. Into the front of my dress.

And then he's *on* me.

I barely register the thud of the bottle before his hands grip my hips, *hard*, pulling me toward him as he bends to lick me chest to chin. Lapping the whiskey off my skin with a low, rumbling groan. He sucks against me with wet lips, chasing open-mouthed kisses with more of his tongue, and I fucking *melt*.

Dropping the cup to the floor, I lift my hands to his face, tunneling my fingers into his thick, black waves as he buries his face in my throat. His grunt is sharp as he finds my lips, and I swear he wants to swallow me whole with the way he licks into my mouth.

He pulls away, heart flying against mine. "Breathe," he orders. And I suck in air, completely unaware that I'd been depriving myself of it. His eyes dance across my face, and he looks . . . almost panicked. "I don't . . . I don't normally kiss on the mouth," he says, voice low. Shaky.

I nod, careful to hold attention to the words. "Okay. We don't have to—"

I'm cut off by another searing kiss, one that has us both pressing further into each other, desperate for something to hold on to. He pivots to pin me against the nearest wall—his favorite place to trap me—and I open my lips to let him in, hearing the deep groan that climbs up his throat as his tongue slides against mine again. His hands are flighty against my body, quick flares of pressure before release as they travel to new places, like he's not able to get what he wants fast enough.

My stomach swoops with something silky as my ribs tighten.

No one has ever been this desperate for me.

Or this *rough*.

He must finally regain control over the operation of his hands, because they coordinate together and curl around the backs of my thighs, lifting me until our waists align. I wrap my legs around his middle, squeezing tight, and barely feel the loss of direction as he moves us.

It's not until I feel myself falling that I gasp out my surprise, my shoulders hitting something soft before the rest of my spine follows. I open my eyes and find myself on the bed, angled a bit diagonally. The scent of clean linen and lilac surrounds me from the soft comforter, and it settles some of the raw emotion. Rhett's standing over me, eyes roaming, chest heaving. "Do you trust me?" he asks, raspy and unfocused.

"Yes." I don't even blink. I think it surprises him, but it's hard to tell for sure because he's reaching for the backpack. When he pulls the rope out, a replica of the one attached to Champ earlier, my body bursts with pleasure. I sigh out a breathy whine, a sound I've never heard from my own lips.

He smiles. "You want this." It's not a question, and I don't give him an answer. When he bends himself over me to steal another kiss, I whine again as the rope drags up my knee. Glides along the inside of my thigh.

"Rhett," I whisper, closing my eyes at the scratch of it against my skin.

He rumbles out something I don't quite catch, lost in the trail the rope is blazing up my leg. He drags the end of it higher, over the hem of my dress, my ribs, until it dangles along my throat. Collecting both wrists with his free hand, he moves them high above my head and then uses the rope to fasten them to the iron frame of the textured headboard. While he works, I take in the detail, the intricate carvings of horses and cowboys giving chase.

Once he's satisfied with the knot, he stands to his full height and looks at me, pleased. His eyes catch mine and he asks, "Is this okay?"

I'll admit, a *small* trace of fear winds its way through me. But it's not Rhett—not at all. I've just . . . I've never been in a position like this, at the mercy of someone. I don't know what comes next, having zero frame of reference for what to expect. And his words from earlier come creeping back in.

I'm a little worried it'll be too much for you.

Is this what he'd meant?

But if I'm really honest, I can also admit that nothing has ever excited me more. It's what drives my eager nod. To whisper "Yes please" in a way that reveals my desperation.

He hooks his hands behind my knees and yanks until the rope pulls taut and my hands hang suspended in the air half a foot above the mattress. Dropping to his knees, he shoves my dress up around my waist and skims his fingers over my underwear, tracing along the whirls of lace. "So pretty," he mumbles before pulling them down my legs.

My cheeks burn hot at the way he looks and looks and *looks*. I've never had anyone so blatantly absorb my body like this, the thoughts rushing through my mind oscillating between blinding lust and heady regret. I study his face carefully, looking for any sign of what he's thinking, but all he does is look at me.

"Rhett," I plead.

He closes his eyes, takes a minute, and then asks, "Are you real, Olivia?"

The question hangs over us, too bright to look at directly. My mind spins as I try to form an answer, but he lets me off the hook when he leans forward and *licks*.

I yelp, instinctively pulling against the rope. But his knot holds true, and when he cups my ass to press his face deeper into me, I'm completely defenseless against his mouth's assault.

"Rhett," I gasp, frantic. No man has ever done *this* to me before. I have no idea what I'm supposed to be doing. "I don't . . . I don't know—"

He stops immediately, his mouth leaving my body. "You don't like it?"

"*No*, I do. I really do." My words sputter through shaky breaths. "I just . . . I've never—"

"Ah," he rumbles, understanding. A dark smile transforms his face. "Olivia, any man worth a damn will give you pleasure in all the ways you want it." He darts his tongue out for a long, languid stroke, and the rope tugs once more. "He won't stop until you get it, no matter how long it takes or how hard he has to work for it." Another lazy stretch of his tongue, this time circling around the bundle of nerves that has me bucking off the bed. "I'm going to help you find all the ways you like to be pleased. We're going to learn together."

And then he lifts my hips, burying his face into me.

I'm a boneless, mindless mess of flesh and bones, so devoid of thought that there's no agency over the curses and shouts that flow from my mouth, no regard for the bar full of people—including two of Rhett's brothers—right beneath us. The way he works me is an art form, his unhurried licks and sucks winding me higher and higher until I feel like I'm floating outside my body. I start to flutter, clenching around nothing, so wound tight with a desperate need for *more* so I can crest the edge of this cliff and fucking fly.

"Be good, peaches," Rhett tells me, feeling my tension. "Don't come. Not yet."

I suck in air as frenzy takes over. He must not understand that I *can't* come, that he's playing my body into a crescendo that it can't reach without just a little more . . .

It's not until he whispers a soft and filthy "Good girl,"

plunging a finger in and curling it to wield the first wave of my orgasm, that I realize he's been toying with me on purpose.

I'm still soaring when he stands, when the words leave his glistening lips. "I want to fuck you, Olivia, and I want to feel you when I do. I don't want to use a condom." His voice is assertive and strong, but the question in his eyes is real. "Can I fuck you the way I want to?"

I'm not capable of much thought at the moment, but something about his words still snags. "Does that line always work?"

His eyes sharpen. "Line?" he asks, shaking his head. I watch his intense focus scan along my ribs. My thighs.

"You know . . . with other girls."

Something fractures through the light shining in his eyes. "It's not a line, Olivia." He inhales sharply, wrapping a warm hand around my shin, dragging it higher. "I might want to fuck you bare, but don't think for a second it's not another first for me."

A *first*. Maybe he's really never had a girl up here before. The weight of that truth prickles along the base of my neck. He's going to respect my answer either way—I know it without a doubt. But I *want* to give him this. To see him come as undone as he's making me feel, especially if he's trading some of his firsts for mine. It's not like I'm not on birth control. I tilt my chin up and stare right at him. "You can fuck me however you want to, as long as you do it right *now*."

His pants are off in under ten seconds and he's on me in another two. His nose grazes along my jaw as he inhales deeply. "You smell so good. You know that?"

"Peaches," I say, smiling. Happy to tell him I know.

I feel him grin against my cheek. A small nod. "Peaches." He bites into my neck when he pushes into me, barely making it inside an inch before there's simply no more room. "*Fuck*," he hisses, utterly, *painfully* still, panting against my collarbone.

My pulse skitters beneath his lips.

"I don't—I'm not—" I babble before Rhett shushes me, pressing a warm finger hard into my lips.

"You can take it," he murmurs, the soft tone of his voice a clear offset from the second hard thrust he spears into me, slipping in another inch. I think I might rip in half from the delicious pressure of it, at once painful and *impossibly* magnificent. He kisses me sweetly, tenderly, before he rolls another hard slam of his hips. "You can take me, can't you?"

On the next thrust, I cry out.

Again. Another inch.

"Tell me you can take it."

A tear slips out the corner of my eye, and I'd be embarrassed if I wasn't mush-brained. As it stands, all I can do is mumble out a half-hearted plea for more, needing to feel him deeper.

Rhett kisses me again, lips wrapping around the hinge of my jaw. "Such a good girl," he murmurs. "So sweet."

Hearing his praise a second time sends me into another dizzying spiral. I come around him, mouth wide in a silent scream. He presses more soft kisses all over my face: my eyelids, my nose, the corners of my mouth. Tender and rewarding and so pure.

He doesn't give me much time to come down from it before he pulls out and flips me over, the rope biting into my wrists as it makes a full twisting rotation. His knees bracket around mine and close my legs together, and I'm almost scared this is over. But then I feel the head of his hard length nudge against my ass as he palms both cheeks to spread them wide before settling himself between them.

And then he *spits*. Wipes his saliva over himself. Over me.

He starts to move again, thrusting—not *inside* me, but between the fleshy muscle of my ass. His fingers sink deep into my skin as he works himself over and over again. I concentrate on the way he grips me, pushing himself between my cheeks as his hips rock forward with every thrust. The sounds of his breaths turn sharp and wild as he seems to blow a lid off his need, chasing a release that's right there for him to find.

"You're so pretty, peaches," he says somewhere above me. I can't see anything from this angle, but I feel *everything*. "Your skin, I can't—"

He grunts, his movement sputtering as if he's surprised himself, and I feel his release paint the length of my back. He drops his forehead between my shoulder blades, his weight settling over me, and it takes him several long minutes to regain control of himself. Before he's able to move, to breathe with a steadier rhythm.

His fingers wind through my hair as he works to calm himself, gently brushing it along the tops of my shoulders as his lips press against my spine, and my skin ignites in a riot of goosebumps from the featherlight feel of it. Eventually he pushes off me, pulling the end of the rope loose from where it's anchored to the bed. And then he grabs a washcloth from the bathroom, drowning it in warm water.

The way he uses it to clean me up is almost reverent. Like he knows I can hardly think straight, let alone make the necessary moves to help myself. When he's done, he pulls his boxers on and curls himself around me underneath the covers, scooping me closer into him. I almost laugh when I realize that, besides the loss of his jeans, we're both still nearly fully clothed. "Do you feel this?" he asks, lifting my palm to his chest, pressing it against two buttons of his shirt. "My heart beats so fucking fast for you, Olivia, I feel like I'm dying."

I can't help but smile, hiding it beneath his bicep. "Mine beats fast for you too," I whisper, closing my eyes.

It's the last thing I remember before I fall asleep.

CHAPTER SEVENTEEN

RHETT

Olivia sleeps for a little over an hour, but it's not enough time to settle the stampede roaring in my chest. I keep myself as still as I can, feeling her breathe against me, watching a strand of hair fly away from her rosy lips with every exhale that leaves her pretty mouth. Her cheek is pressed deep into my bicep, and it's probably been a little too long since I've had any feeling in my left hand. But I can't bring myself to move her.

I'm terrified of what happens when she wakes up.

Instead, I trace my gaze along her auburn-tinged lashes. Memorize the constellation of freckles splashed across her face. I can't see her wrists from where they're pinned between us, but my pulse grows unruly every time I think about the way they looked bundled in that rope. I wonder if they're marked with what I did to her. It sets me off all over again with a deep, uncomfortable worry that I went too far.

When she eventually stirs, I stop breathing altogether. I've never done . . . *this*. Never let a girl I fucked fall asleep next to me. Never fucked one in my own bed to begin with. So I have no idea how to handle what comes next or the frenzied insecurity that I might have royally fucked things up with her.

Gold-flecked hazel eyes blink open in front of me, and I sink into them.

"I fell asleep," Olivia says, voice sleep-rough.

"Yeah." I brush the pad of my finger along her cheek, only vaguely aware that the numbness in my other arm is starting to become painful. But I still don't care. "I'm sorry," I say, rolling my lips.

Her eyes widen, flitting back and forth between mine. "For what?"

"I was too rough with you."

She sighs, her eyelids falling closed. She keeps them closed, even as she smiles. "No, you weren't."

It's the first trace of potential relief. A softening in the pinch between my shoulder blades. But I've been winding myself so tight since she fell asleep, it's not enough to really ease the worry. "Olivia—"

"It was perfect," she says, like it's fact. "It was *perfect*, Rhett. Exactly what I wanted." She leans forward to kiss me, slow and lazy. And then pulls herself up and over me, the weight of her hips pressing against mine with a pressure that calms my racing heart. "I liked the way it made me feel. I . . . I liked you rough." Her voice is clear and honest, and it sends a rush of heat up to my ears.

I almost can't fathom it—that this sweet and soft girl, this beautiful angel, would *like* the way I want to fuck her. I slide my hands up her thighs, under her dress, and rest them around her waist, watching her face for any trace of worry. For any sign she might just be telling me what I want to hear.

But I see the way her cheeks flush and her lips part as she watches me just as closely. "I don't want you to be careful with me," she whispers. "What was it you said earlier? Oh . . . right." She smiles. And then she sets her hooks in. "How *else* can you please me, Rhett?"

It's enough to sit me upright, slotting her down into my lap with my grip at her hips. Her calves stay buckled beneath her, giving me the leverage I need to keep her right *here*. Right with me. "This wasn't a good idea," I tell her.

She frowns beneath a studious brow. "Why not?"

I watch the words leave her lips. Watch the shape of them change with every syllable. "You're already wrecking me," I admit. And then I lean down to capture those lips with mine, to give her more of something deep and dark that I've never given anyone before: my hope.

Wrapping her arms around my neck, she pulls me closer, her nails pressing into my back. My mind blanks when she sucks my tongue into her mouth before releasing it, following with a harsh bite to my lower lip. I know it for what it is, the permission she's giving me. The trust.

I make quick work of getting her out of her dress, yanking it over her head and throwing it to the floor next to the bed. Her smile is lazy and bee-stung, and I can't stand to be away from it any longer than I have to. "I meant it when I said I don't normally kiss on the mouth," I whisper, tracing her top lip with my finger.

"Why?" she asks, taking my finger into her mouth.

Fuck, this girl. "Because it means something . . . something more than sex and fucking. It means something to me." Her eyes brighten, and I kiss her again, hoping like hell she understands.

She struggles to work the buttons down my shirt, distracted when my hands cup the shape of her breasts, pinching her nipples in tandem with the pulse of our mouths. Eventually, she gets frustrated and pouts against me, my shirt fisted in her palms, only half the buttons free. I smile down at her so wide it hurts. And even though I can't shake the feeling that this is wrong, that someone like her is far too good to be true for someone like me, I can't deny her a single thing.

This might be a casual fling for her, nothing but a fun future story to tell, but I'm suddenly finding myself in so deep there's going to be no way out but through my own ruin.

I rip the front of my shirt with a hard pull, sending buttons flying across the room, and Olivia tips her head back to let out a booming laugh. With one hand settled against her spine to brace her weight, I keep my focus fastened to her face as I slide my free hand up her body, blazing a trail from her navel through the center of her chest, until I reach the expanse of her delicate neck. Wrapping my fingers around the column of her throat, I give it a light squeeze before bending down to pinch her nipple between my teeth, soothing over it with my tongue. Her laughter turns into a throat-deep moan, and I memorize the sound. Engrave it somewhere far inside my brain.

When she pulls herself upright, her eyes are dark. Urgent. "I need you," she says, and I can't fucking *breathe* with the way she's looking at me. She rises up on her knees so I can push my boxers down my thighs, her palms skimming up my chest as she settles herself back down. Her fingers tip over my shoulders as she shoves the ruined shirt down my arms. When I'm free of it, I hold her tight, the warmth of her bare skin against mine a whole new level of vulnerability.

We stare at each other as she positions herself over me, slick enough to ease me in a quarter of the way herself, her fingers turning white where they sink into my arms. My groan turns into a swear, and I keep my eyes glued to hers, the feel of her near-blinding. When it's clear she can't move any further, I tuck my arms under hers and position one under the other at her nape, angling for better leverage. "Relax," I order.

She nods, her swollen lips parted as she heaves a breath in. I watch with rapt fascination as her face twists in a beautiful mix of pleasure and pain when I thrust up into her, simultaneously pulling her down onto me. It nearly gets me all the way in, forcing me to hold still before I accidentally end this for myself far too soon.

She's so fucking beautiful, so wonderfully perfect, that I ignore the warning bells and press small, quick kisses up the length of her jaw while I hold her in place. It's too intimate, but

I've thrown caution to the wind all night; there's no sense in stopping now. "Again?" I ask when I get my bearings.

Her forehead rests against my chin as her breathing runs wild. When she nods, I smile, letting go of her briefly so I can push her hair out of her face. She's already pulsing around me and I know it won't be long before I get to see the way she shatters. With my next thrust, she cries out, the sound sharp as it cuts through the silence. I wouldn't doubt it if someone could hear it from downstairs, but I don't give a fuck at the moment because she's coming, her body tensing, hands fisting into my skin as her eyes squeeze shut.

My god, she's stunning.

"You're so good at this, you beautiful girl," I murmur, licking up her neck. Her body squeezes mine with an orgasm that lasts for several long moments, her nails ripping into my skin and drawing blood. It's the way her eyes roam over me, glassy and sated, that sends me over my own edge. One more thrust, *one more* flexing reach into her body, and I have to quickly yank her off of me as I come all over her thighs.

The sight of it makes me fucking feral.

This time, as I clean us up, I know we can't end up back in bed tangled together the way I want to be. It's getting late, and we both have early mornings. Still, it's really damn hard to stop myself from tucking her back against me and holding on to her with everything I have, scared of what happens when I cut her loose from the cocoon we've wrapped ourselves in.

It's even harder when I give into temptation and push her against the wall in the stairwell on our way out. My mouth scorches a blazing trail up her jaw as her breath hitches, one leg lifting high to wrap around my waist. It takes sheer will to pull myself away from her, to stop myself from throwing her over my shoulder and marching right back into that apartment.

I keep one arm stretched behind me on the bike, hooked around her back to hold her close to me the whole ride back to her place. It cuts deep to watch her walk through her front door alone, but I don't trust myself to follow her. When I pull the bike back onto the main road and point it toward the ranch, I wrench the throttle open and fly on the high of everything she is and every new part of me born from it.

THE HIGH DOESN'T LAST LONG.

On Monday, Melody comes home from the hospital—but it's not because she's doing any better. The doctors decide she's stable after breaking her fever, and then tell Brooks there's no good enough reason to keep her under their observation, much to his frustration. She's transported back to her temporary room in the main house with the help of two nurses who set her up in the hospital-grade bed that definitely cost more than Brooks could afford.

The ranch paid for it, like it's been paying a lot of her medical bills, but I don't have to look at the books to know business isn't going to cover things for long. We're already struggling to stay afloat with Sawyer gone and Brooks distracted. Wells entered his name in a few small rodeo circuits this spring, hoping to earn the first-place prize money to help, but the first one is still over a month away.

Colt must have developed a weird level of telepathy because he calls me again Monday night, trying to convince me to go to their upcoming card game by again flaunting the obscene amount of money up for grabs. I have to admit—it's more than enough cash to take care of things around here for a good long while. But I know in my gut it's not worth the risk.

Money like that is a felony. A long sentence behind bars.

Brooks grows restless and impatient the more uncomfortable Melody becomes. She's made it clear to everyone that she doesn't want to live sick. Doesn't want her boys to have a sick mother, to see her like this. On Wednesday, when her oncologist comes by to check in on her in the late afternoon, things get worse.

"How long, doc?" she asks. Kasey and I stand together in the hallway, quietly looking in through the open door. Her face is so goddamn pale it twists tight in my stomach.

"Not long," he confirms, eyes kind. Patient.

"Will it hurt?"

The doctor shakes his head. "No, Melody. I'll make sure it doesn't."

Brooks bursts from his chair, eyes wild as he looks at his wife. "Do not quit on me, Mel," he nearly spits. "You're not fucking dying, do you hear me?" He turns to face the doctor. "Do you hear me!" he shouts. "You keep her alive!"

Dr. Hawthorne's face remains stoic yet solemn. "I'm afraid this is no longer a matter of *if*, Brooks, but *when*. Melody is presenting with multiple-system organ failure. Her body is not responding to our efforts to eradicate the cancer, and it's only a matter of time before she succumbs to it." Melody closes her eyes as the words wash over her, but she doesn't cry. "I'm so sorry, to all of you," the doctor continues. "Sincerely. I wouldn't wish this on anyone."

The sound that rips from Brooks's throat is guttural as he launches himself at the doctor. Kasey and I burst through the door and hurl ourselves at him before his fists can make impact, pushing him back against the wall of the room. "No!" he screams, eyes filling with tears. "Help her, dammit! Fucking help her!"

"Brooks." Melody's voice cuts through his terror. He turns to her, utterly broken, and climbs onto the bed to wind his body around hers. Like if he can just hold her tight enough, he might be able to stop what's happening. He might be able to keep her here far longer than her body is giving her.

I don't have the stomach to see that look on his face for a second longer. Pushing past Kasey, I flee out of the room and then leave the house altogether.

The hours I spend on my bike do little to settle the panic.

I'm keyed up through my whole shift at Wild Coyote, anxious for a distraction. It used to be so easy to turn all of this off with booze, but now all I want to do is drown in Olivia, to lose myself in the heat of her touch. With her, I don't go numb. With her, it feels more like white-knuckling the reins of a racehorse as we approach the edge of a cliff—scary as fuck, but . . . different. *Good* different, I think.

Being known by her doesn't feel like a threat. It's almost a relief, even with the deep unknown of it all. She's a beacon of light I want to cling to when the demons threaten to pull me in with their claws. Still, her presence in my life is a whole 'nother tornado of worry that threatens to sweep me up when work isn't busy enough to distract me from it. I haven't heard from her since dropping her off Saturday night, and I'm sure she's probably still processing everything that happened, but the urge to show up at her house grows every hour that my phone stays quiet.

When I first proposed this hasty plan to unofficially date her, I had no fucking idea I'd trip into something this deep. If anything, I thought it was ridiculous: *me*, suggesting I could somehow positively support her dating life. But it pissed me off to see her with the losers she was going out with, and I guess I just thought I could be a better version of them. That she deserved a little more of an effort.

Turns out I'm greedier than I thought I'd be.

CHAPTER EIGHTEEN

OLIVIA

Avoiding my mom becomes an intricate dance—especially with it being a slow week at the café—but I'm having a *really* hard time finding the confidence to talk to her about the wedding. I've thought about continuing on like nothing's changed, pretending I have no interest in going to Charleston or meeting a whole group of strangers I happen to share a bloodline with, but after allowing myself to admit what I wanted with Rhett over the weekend, it feels like I'm burning with a newfound need to be honest about this too.

Still, the fear of Mom's reaction scares me more than anything. I'm so worried she'll feel like I'm choosing my father over her, which isn't the reality at all. Every time I catch a glimpse of her long red hair floating somewhere back in the kitchen, my heart stops in a panic. I spin on my heel and bail, convinced she'll see the truth of my feelings written all over my face if I let her look too long. When she's out on the floor or rooted in front of the POS system talking to Teresa, I find a reason to be in the kitchen, pulling out more napkins or making small talk with Mark while he works on a meatloaf special that smells amazing. I move through every shift carefully, ensuring I never end up alone with her. But if she senses anything wrong with me, she doesn't make it known. She's calm and graceful as always, her easy smile bestowed on every patron who walks through the door.

Today the café is so slow after lunch that I decide to break out the Valentine's Day decorations to keep myself busy. The holiday is still technically a couple weeks away, but people around here love getting in the spirit of—well, *any* spirit, really—and it's the perfect distraction. Charlotte, who's been working from the far corner booth all afternoon, eyes me with an arched brow as I unravel a giant pink heart made of tinsel.

"You have something you want to share, Liv?" she asks.

I throw her a look. "Do *you*?" I've hardly seen her in weeks since she's been spending a majority of her time at Ivan's house. Their relationship is trapezing from *casual* to *serious* really fast, but I can tell it makes her happy. Even as she rolls her eyes now.

She rises from the booth and stretches her arms over her head before meandering over to check out the box of decorations. When she pulls out a roll of red streamers, she nonchalantly mutters, "Ivan asked me to go to Florida with him for Valentine's Day weekend."

I gaze at her. "A romantic *vacation*?"

Her brows pinch. "Do you think it's too soon?"

"How the hell should I know? The furthest I've gotten in a relationship is all the campaigning Shawn did to ask me to prom." Shawn was in my senior year math class. He was definitely cute but super timid, and mixed with my overall lack of confidence with boys, nothing between us ever stood a real chance at amounting to much. He was my first kiss though and, later, *almost* my first time . . . but his intense nervousness sort of shut the whole thing down before it ever really got anywhere.

"What if he murders me? What if I end up on an episode of *Dateline*, my body lost at sea?"

I shrug. "Not the worst way to go—you've always wanted to be famous. And a mermaid."

She swats my shoulder, laughing.

"Honestly, Char, if he's making you happy, just lean into it. Take the chance. He seems to really like you."

"What about you?"

I think about Rhett and everything that happened in that apartment four days ago and have to work to fight a blush. "He's . . ." I say, not knowing how to finish the thought. He's kind and warm? Sexy as hell? He knows how to work my body better than I do? "He's good."

Char gives me an incredulous look, like she knows I'm holding out. "Good?"

I sigh, looking around before making eye contact. "We had sex," I whisper. "Twice."

The roll of streamer drops from her hand, wheeling across the floor until it runs into the leg of the table the mayor's wife currently occupies with two other ladies from town. "Shit," she mumbles, running to pick it up and apologize to the women before coming straight back to me. "Spill," she directs, her eyes bright with excitement.

Laughing, I try to explain as honestly as possible so she doesn't get any wrong ideas. "I sort of asked him to," I say. "After we kissed, I guess I decided if he was going to let me practice . . . *things* with him, I should take advantage." The words taste bitter as they leave my mouth, but I'm not about to tell Charlotte how thoroughly he'd dismantled me in that apartment, both with his body and the things he'd said after.

"And he was happy to oblige?" she asks, wagging her brows.

Shame burns the back of my neck. "It wasn't like that," I quickly say. "It was . . . really nice. Thoughtful, even."

The look on her face morphs into something rooted in confusion, and I can't blame her. "Rhett Bennett was *thoughtful* with you?"

I nod. "He . . . cared about my experience."

She smiles, a knowing gleam in her eye. "He fucked you good, didn't he?"

"Charlotte!"

"I mean, it's Rhett Bennett! If there's anything he'd be good at when it comes to women, it'd be delivering memorable nights in bed." She leans forward. "I want to know *everything*."

My cheeks burn hot and I'm suddenly sweating. I should be comfortable telling my best friend all about my night with Rhett —lord knows she spares no details when she's dishing about her own sexcapades. But something about sharing the way he was with me, simultaneously dizzyingly rough and tender, feels cheap.

I had to hide small bruises that wrapped around my wrists under an oversized sweatshirt the next day for work. And that's not counting the half-dozen sprinkled fingerprint-sized marks he'd left around my thighs . . .

It feels wrong to give details about something I'm not even sure I fully understand for myself. The way the marks he left on my body don't scare me. The way I *liked* all the things he did to me, how it made me feel powerful when he lost control. The way he held me afterward and told me that his heart raced . . . I had a hard time believing that would be normal for him.

Then again, do I really know him? Maybe it's part of the reason everyone is so quick to warn girls about the Bennett brothers. Maybe he's just playing with me and I'm naive for falling for it.

I sigh. "Another time," I mutter. "I need to get back to work."

Charlotte's gaze skims over the decorations at my feet, picking up on my hesitation. "Okay." She nods, a coy grin still plastered to her face as if to tell me my lack of desire to spill my guts about the whole thing won't deter her for long. "Sure."

When she eventually leaves to meet her parents for dinner, I'm still battling the onslaught of thoughts about Rhett and the things we did. At least it's enough to drown out the worry about

Mom and Céline and anything else I could possibly be bothered about.

I finally make it home around seven, immediately opening a bottle of wine I'd saved in the pantry. It's too chilly to enjoy it on my front porch where I normally like to decompress, so instead I decide to pull a warm blanket over my lap on the velvet couch that takes up most of my living room, a candle lit on the coffee table in front of me throwing off a calming scent of jasmine. For the most part, I think it's nice to live alone, to find reprieve in the quiet space that surrounds my little bungalow. But there are nights like tonight when a loneliness takes root, seeping through the cracks of my long-worn armor, and I wish for someone to sit with. To share all of these fears and dreams and *thoughts* with.

I'm about to call it a night just before nine when the unmistakable sound of an engine rumbles outside the house, somewhere in the distance. It gets louder with every heartbeat that passes, and soon mine is flying behind my ribs as I whirl to peek through the shutters of my front window. I'm stunned to find Rhett pulling up the drive like a black knight right out of my deepest, darkest fantasies.

I have the front door open before he even makes it to the porch. He tugs off his helmet to reveal a tired face, eyes worn and the skin around his mouth heavy. "Rhett," I breathe.

His mouth curves just enough to make me shudder. "Peaches."

"What are you doing here?"

He begins to say something before thinking better of it, his lips sealing shut with a tight press. His eyes bounce between mine before he eventually shrugs, his jaw tight. "Is this okay?"

"Of course! Come in." His broad frame slips into the house. Where a cowboy hat normally sits on his head, unruly black waves stick to his temples in a disheveled mop. "Are you okay?" I ask, worry spiking as I take in the slow way he moves into the living room, where I urge him to take a seat.

"Yeah." He nods. But I don't quite believe him.

"You don't have to work tonight?"

"Already off. It was slow."

"The café too," I say. "I'm glad you came."

The corner of his mouth lifts as he looks around the room. He's already seen my house, but the way his eyes trace the furniture and scattered plants, it feels like the first time. "Yeah?"

I nod. "I . . . we didn't say when we'd see each other again, and I—" Oh god. I already sound clingy.

His eyes move to me, something dark pulsing behind them. "You thought I wouldn't stick around after that?"

"Not exactly." I force a smile. "I just didn't know when I should try to reach out." He'd given me his phone number when he brought me home after . . . well, *after*, but I couldn't bring myself to use it.

"You can reach out whenever you want to, Olivia. Anytime."

The words warm my cheeks. "I guess that's part of all this, huh? Learning the ropes on how to communicate."

His eyes pulse with that icy heat. "Guess so," he agrees.

It becomes more and more obvious that something's wrong. His hands are clenched in his lap, the hard set of his jaw sharp enough to cut glass. "Are you really okay?" I try again.

This time, he blows out a breath. "It's been a really hard week," he says quietly.

I lift my hand between us, braving a touch. The rough stubble of his cheek scrubs across my palm, and his skin—he's *freezing*. I frown.

An idea hits me. "Do you trust me?"

His eyes flare. Whether he realizes it's the same question he asked me before we went inside that apartment, I'm not sure, but his answer is almost as quick as mine. "Yes."

I smile. Bite the inside of my cheek. "Stay here. Give me a couple minutes."

I don't wait for him to respond. Moving into the small bathroom in the hallway, I work to draw hot water in the tub, lighting the three candles I have spread around the bathroom. It takes about ten minutes to fill, the water hot enough for traces of steam to cling to the cold mirror above the sink.

When I steal a glance back out to the living room, I find Rhett's head tilted back against the top of the couch, his eyes closed. There's a low dip in the corners of his lips, proof of whatever it is he's fighting through. It makes my heart ache. "Rhett?" His eyes snap open and he turns to face me. The moonlight paints half of his face, leaving the other half shrouded in shadows, and I see it then: the dichotomy of who he is. "Come here."

I watch as he rises, long limbs and hard lines. He moves to follow me into the bathroom where the warm bath waits, eyeing it curiously. The surface of the water holds a layer of bubbles and, well, I may have gone a little overboard. "For you or for me?"

My heart pounds. "For you."

He hums, the sound rumbling in the space between us. Winding my palms up his chest, I push off the work jacket he wears so well and unbutton the shirt beneath. He doesn't help, but he doesn't move away either. He watches me closely, and I feel the heat of that gaze like a physical touch.

When I work the shirt off of him, I reach for his pants. The silver of his eyes darkens to near black, a heated counterpart to the ice I saw out in the living room. "Sometimes I feel like the world is pressing down against me," I tell him softly. "I've always tried to figure out where that feeling comes from. Maybe it's the expectation for how the rest of my life is supposed to look? Pressure to make sure my mom knows how thankful I am for everything she's given me? I'm never really sure . . . but it makes me feel heavy, like gravity's pulling me into the floor and I can't stand straight or breathe fully." I give him a half-hearted smile. "I learned a long time ago that baths help. The warm water—it feels like a hug. Like an assurance, you know?"

It takes a bit of effort to push his jeans down the thick muscle of his thighs, the weight of his stare burning the crown of my head. When I've got them wrapped around his ankles, he lifts each foot, one at a time, and lets me pull them completely off. I stand again, reaching for the hem of his boxers. "Is this okay?" I ask.

He swallows, the apple of his throat dipping. Nods.

I take them off quickly, fighting the rush of heat that I know snakes up my chest and neck. "Get in," I say when he's bare, nodding toward the tub.

"Will you join me?" he asks, voice rough.

My belly swoops as heat sinks inside of me, a throbbing ache I feel everywhere. "Okay."

Rhett steps into the tub, carefully lowering himself into the water with a low groan as I slip out of the sweats and T-shirt I have on. He holds out a hand for me when I step toward the tub and I take it, letting him ease me in with him. I settle between his long legs, resting my back against his chest as the water rises around us from the space our bodies create.

I try *really* hard not to take inventory of all the places our skin touches, especially not after he wraps his arms around me to pull me closer to his body, the tops of his arms skating under the swell of my breasts. "Tell me something real," I murmur, desperate to keep him with me, to not lose him to the dark corners of whatever's going on in his mind. It's obvious something is looming over him, a storm cloud threatening to burst, and if he tells me what it is, I might be able to help.

I feel the way his shoulders slump. The way his body seems to sink further into the water. "Sometimes," he says, so quietly it's almost a whisper, "I just don't know what the point of anything is."

"What happened?" I ask more forcefully.

He sighs. "I don't want to talk about it. Not right now."

Disappointment spears through me, but I push it aside. "Okay," I say. "Would you rather I distract you?"

His grip around me tightens. "How do you plan on doing that?"

I hike my shoulders in a shrug. "Maybe you can tell me how you learned to . . . do what we did."

He stills for a moment and then he lifts his arm to trace warm, wet fingers along my skin. The scratch of his chin grazes the nape of my neck. "What we did?"

"You know what I mean."

He smiles inside the crook of my neck and it feels like the first taste of relief. "Some experience," he admits, voice thick like honey. "Paying attention when I try something new. Not being afraid to try in the first place."

"Hm," I hum, mind spinning at the easy confidence he exudes.

Be brave, he wrote to me only days ago. That small piece of paper I now covet.

"Tell me what to do," I whisper. "Tell me how to help, how I can do things the way you like."

A long moment stretches out around us and I begin to think he's going to pretend the words didn't leave my mouth. That he might go back to hiding in his own head. But then—

"Touch me," he murmurs, his breath heating the skin of my neck before his hot mouth presses to my temple. "I want you to touch me, peaches."

I squeeze my eyes shut as goosebumps race across my skin. "How?"

His chuckle is dark and gritty. "However you want to. You can't possibly go wrong."

I lean forward, turning to face him as water sloshes back and forth between us. Even through the clouds of bubbles that ripple along the surface, I see the expanse of skin and long, muscled limbs beneath. He watches me with only half the grin I know he can produce, his eyes pure smoke, and yet . . . there's still a void that sings along my senses.

I think back to our conversation on the water tower, to all he's endured, carrying so much of the weight of his family's struggles. Holding space for all the hate and vitriol everyone spews at them in a fight that he never belonged to in the first place. I'm not sure when, exactly, it happened, but I want him to know that I *see* him. And not just the version he shows the rest of the world, but the shades that lie within that are honest and careful and kind.

I watch his gaze move down my face, to my neck, my chest. His eyes linger there for a while, and my heart gallops with the strength of a full stampede with every second that passes. Reaching through the water, I lightly wrap my hands around his legs at a spot just above both knees, easing them higher with a pressure soft and teasing. He lets out a sharp exhale as the pads of my fingers whisper along his skin.

His eyelids fall, dark lashes fanning across a sun-kissed face. And I think I might remember him, picture him like this, for the rest of my life.

It's the heat of the water and the sparking energy between us that sends a tentative hand between his legs, where he's already hard. I trace the length of him, watching as his jaw clenches and brows knit. When I wrap a firm hand around him and tug, he hisses out a low "*Fuck*" as his eyes open, catching mine.

"Does that feel good?" I ask, tongue dry as I tug again.

Rhett's eyes flash, pupils blown wide. Every cell in my body narrows its attention to my hands and what they're doing. To the muscles clenching along his face and neck and the blazing confidence I feel at the sight of it.

I nearly yelp when his arms suddenly burst around me, hands gripping tight, and then he's lifting me up, stepping out of the tub as water streams off both our bodies and onto the tile floor. His mouth is rough on mine, teeth scraping against my lips as he moves us out of the bathroom toward my room. Toward the bed.

He sets me down and breaks his mouth away from mine to lie

in the center of my mattress, his still-dry hair spilling across a dusty pink pillow. "Come here," he rasps, holding out a hand.

But I can't stop staring at him.

I've never wanted sex like this, never wanted to feel someone move against me so badly. The need nearly buckles me. The cut of his jaw and the dip of his throat. The steeliness and strength and power that swirl together in the pools of those moon-like eyes. His calloused fingertips roughly dragging along my skin while the hard lines of him meet the soft curves of me.

The way his need pours out and collects in my heart, a chemical reaction that will inevitably bind the memory of him to my skin and bones forever.

And that's just it. This thing we're doing . . . it's changing me.

"Olivia." He says my name quietly, like it's a secret. Like it's the answer to a question he's held for such a long time, and now that he has it, he wants to be *so* careful. My hand rises to meet his, still warm and damp from the water, and he pulls me to him on the bed until I'm on top of him, knees bracketing his ribs. His eyes devour me, hands settling on my waist. "I don't think you understand how much you turn me on."

My throat tightens.

"Your golden hair, the freckles on your face. The way the light brightens the flecks of amber in your eyes, like sunlight through the trees. Your skin . . . god, Olivia," he rumbles, low and gruff. "Your *skin*. It drives me fucking insane to stop myself from touching you as much as I want to."

My mind tumbles over the words. But I have no time to respond before he's lifting me off his stomach. Pulling me up toward the headboard, so that my legs rest around . . .

Oh *god*.

There's no time to process what's happening before one large hand catches both my wrists, pinning them behind my back as his first lick spreads me open. There is nothing careful or teasing about the way he tastes me, his tongue greedy and cruel in what feels like a claiming, like I was made for him to do *this*. Made for him to feast from, to drown in. The sensation is at once too much and not enough as my hips writhe, the intense pleasure edging along painful.

A low groan rumbles out from him, vibrating against me, and I buck against the feel of it, lifting myself up with the strength of my thighs when the pressure of it all becomes too much. But he clamps me back down against him with a heavy arm, his teeth nipping in warning before another long stroke of his tongue blinds me. Forced to take the pleasure head-on, it doesn't take long before the tension snaps and I scream as I fall apart around him.

Still, he doesn't stop. One orgasm quickly tips into another and I swear I'm going to lose my mind if he doesn't let me catch my breath. "*Rhett*," I beg. "Please."

The arm he uses as a band around my lap relaxes, and I reflex up and off of him. There's a sharp inhale and a chuckle beneath me. "Come on, peaches. You can give me one more."

But I'm a boneless heap.

I look down at him to tell him so, but there's a grin tugging at his wicked mouth, a gleam in his eye that's been missing all night. "I don't think I can," I say, chest heaving.

His grin only grows wider. "How 'bout you take over, then?"

"What do you mean?"

Rhett releases his hold on my wrists and wraps his hands around my waist again. As easily as before, he lifts me off of him and scoots me back to his hips, the impossibly hard length of him caught right between my legs. Right where his mouth just was. His eyes fasten there, wide and gluttonous, as he slowly glides me back and forth over him.

When he speaks, his voice is hurried. "You're going to ride me like you mean it, peaches. Because you do, don't you? You want me to be inside you?"

I nod, breathless.

"Say it," he orders.

"I want you inside me," I mumble, wholly focused on the friction and heat growing, despite being sure I'd had enough. Turns out I might be as insatiable as he is. I squeeze my eyes shut as the tension in my belly grows taut.

"You're so fucking wet. I bet you're soft enough to take me even deeper this time, don't you think?"

The warmth of his hands disappears and the rocking stops. I almost whine from the loss of it, opening my eyes to find him studying me. "I want you inside me," I repeat, firmer this time.

He winks at me . . . *winks*. "You know what to do."

But . . . do I? I've only been on top one other time in my life and it was short-lived—and *not* because I'd rocked his world.

Rhett must see the hesitation on my face because his eyes sharpen. "Olivia. If you're somehow worried about getting this right, trust me when I say you could probably just *breathe* on me and I'd come harder than ever from it."

The words blaze through me like an inferno—enough to tame my insecurity, to grip him softly before shifting over him. The sound he makes when I sink down around him catches in my own throat, and the pinch of his jaw as he watches my body move lower is enough to fill me with the deep gratification I'd almost lost hold of. To see the proof of the effect of this—even when he's not the one in control, not the one *taking*—blooms within me like a wildflower.

When I can't possibly take any more, I roll my hips experimentally, finding the movement somehow eases Rhett in farther. He groans again, and I'm . . . enraptured. Utterly fixated on the feel of being stretched around him like this, on the sounds he makes from the way I move. I roll again, coming alive from the sensation, from the pure joy of it.

Rhett's eyes shine bright as he looks at me, and I fall deep into his stare. I love the way he has no problem doing what he wants with me, the way it somehow still feels as much *for* me as it is for him. And now . . . now I understand how chasing my own pleasure can also drive him toward his. How it can be possible, with trust and communication, to create a physical dynamic that brings us both to the edge of sanity.

He makes no move to hold me in place like he's done before, but his hands begin a light pursuit along my skin as I shift and tilt my hips. When one curls around my breast and squeezes, I nearly lose it. But then he gives my nipple a well-timed pinch as I sink down again, rolling his hips up to meet mine, and I *shatter*.

He does his best to wait, to let me keep rocking as I ride the wave of pleasure, pulsing around him and gripping tight. But soon he can't stop his own release from barreling through him, the pressure of his hands on my waist squeezing hard as he pulls me off of him, just as he starts coming. I fall to the bed next to him, utterly spent, and watch his release with fascination.

It takes both of us a long, long while before we can move again.

WHEN I WAKE THE NEXT MORNING, EARLY ENOUGH that the light streaming in through the window is still a mere whisper, it takes only seconds to realize he's gone.

CHAPTER NINETEEN

RHETT

The ranch is most peaceful in the mornings, when the sun's only a golden glow in the eastern sky and cold dew clings to the foliage in the trees, dampening the air. When the tails of horses swish against a quiet wind and birds start singing to each other across the pasture. My family's land is a living, breathing thing of beauty, and to see it in the early light of dawn like this is to be silenced by it, to be made still.

Most folks go to church for the religion I find right here on these grounds, or in the corral or outer pastures. Within the very hearts of all the horses we work with and connect to. I don't need some ancient book or pastor to teach me about the honor of a man or what it takes to make a good life—the proof is all around me. If my father hadn't spent so long tarnishing the Bennett name —if I hadn't followed down that same path—maybe the rest of this town would benefit from learning what we do here. Maybe if they understood the power that exists in all this wild beauty, they wouldn't spend so much time bucking against us.

They wouldn't call us heartless, because the truth is there's so much heart in all of this. More heart than I ever thought I'd be capable of, that's for sure.

Sometimes I regret my actions on the days I let the hard shit win. As much as I hate the divide that exists between my family and everyone else, I know damn well I've contributed to it. Much more than any of my brothers. Hell, there've been so many times I've wanted to shoot out the damn sun for how cruel life has been to my family, our land stuck in a town full of people who fear us. But despite it all, we get to call this magical place home, and I know deep in my soul that we're lucky.

It's no surprise I'm the first one to the barn this morning after not sleeping at all last night. My mind was way too busy to find any real rest as worry and guilt and shame rear themselves harder and harder with every passing day. Olivia, it seems, is the only comfort I can find . . . That damn girl is sinking into damn near all my thoughts. It's the biggest con in the world to feel as safe as I'm starting to feel with her, but she's the first person who seems to really give a shit about me.

Showing up at her house last night was a risk—one I shouldn't have taken. She deserves a hell of a lot more than my sorry ass, and I had no business darkening her doorstep with the rage and sadness I'd been carrying. Brooks hasn't left the house—hasn't left Melody's room—in four days, and I can't fucking stomach to think about what comes next. Just like the doctor predicted: Melody's health is rapidly declining. She sleeps most hours of the day and can't keep anything down. Her body is deteriorating faster than any of us could have anticipated, and Brooks is out of his mind with fear. I should be ashamed of myself for spending the night with a girl when my brother is suffering.

Maybe Kasey was right to think the worst of me.

I know I need to get a hold of myself and keep my focus on my family. It's not just Melody—money is dwindling, there's too much work to keep up with, and I have no fucking idea how to save us. We can't hire hands around the ranch with all the money we're spending on hospital bills, and we can't make money faster without more hands. The bar is doing just enough to keep us afloat, but it's not nearly enough and it won't last long.

"Mornin'," Kasey mumbles as he comes to meet me at the fence line overlooking the endless sprawl of green grass around us. An Appaloosa mustang stands proud by a copse of aspens in the distance, a wild mare Layla named Stardust years ago. A quick glance at my brother proves the exhaustion I know he's fighting: his face is still swollen with sleep, the purple beneath his eyes darker and darker with each passing day.

"Morning. You see Brooks yet?" Kasey's been checking in on our brother first thing each day, reminding him that he's not alone.

Kasey nods. "Just left from her room." He doesn't say anything else, but he doesn't need to.

I blow out a breath, not sure what there is to say. I've been avoiding the main house since the doctor came to see Melody. It only deepens my shame, but I've been honed to cut into the enemy, not to tend to the emotional needs of the people I defend. I wouldn't know where to start. But Kasey . . . Kasey will be who gets Brooks through.

After a beat of silence, he pulls an envelope out of his back pocket and shoves it into my chest. "Read this."

Even through the exhaustion, it's hard to miss the worry in his eyes. "What is it?" I look down and see the envelope's already been opened. Addressed to William Bennett with neat, black handwriting.

Fuck.

"That lawyer . . ." Kasey starts, but I'm already yanking on the folded piece of paper from where it's tucked inside, tilting it toward the still-warming sun so I can make out all the words.

It's a . . . summons. Words that look a lot like what happens after someone gets arrested. "What does this mean?" I ask, face bunched in confusion.

Kasey shrugs. "I don't know. Mom said it came yesterday. Dad hasn't seen it yet . . . I have a feeling it ain't good."

I read through the letter a second time. It's a bit different than the court orders I've received in the past after some of the stupid stunts I've pulled, but it's just as blunt and demanding. From what I gather, it seems that the little pipsqueak lawyer has called a meeting with our father, the date and time set for next week. There's also a lot of jargon I don't understand, language about the ranch deed and an inheritance trust, and I have a looming feeling that Kasey's right—this isn't good.

"Looks like good old Stuart is trying to force that meeting he wanted."

"Yep," Kasey nearly growls.

"You gonna tell him?" I ask.

He sighs. "I was hoping you'd talk to him with me. He's always been a little more open with you."

I almost fucking laugh. "Open in his blatant dislike of me, maybe." If Kasey only knew the shit our dear-old-dad has put me through.

But the words have Kasey's head snapping my way. "He doesn't dislike you, Rhett. He just . . . he doesn't understand you."

I snort, doing what I can to tamp down the fire growing in my chest. "It has nothing to do with *understanding*, Kasey. And if it did, I'd say that *he* of all people should be the one who fucking understands. He doesn't give a shit about any of us—never has." I hold up the letter from the lawyer. "I have no idea what this is about, but if it means we need to rely on Dad to make something right, I hope to god there's a way one of us can do it instead." Anger thrums uncomfortably through my veins as I push the letter back into his hands.

Kasey just stares, considering my words. "Look," he says after a long moment, "I hear you. I know you and Dad have had your issues, and lord knows that man has never been particularly good to us. But whatever this is, if it's a threat to the ranch, we need to put on a united front. Without Brooks, it's up to you and me to figure this out, to show these suits that no one fucks with our family or our land and gets away with it."

"You want to play dirty?" I ask carefully.

Kasey's eyes are hard and unyielding. "If it comes to it, if we need to. We do whatever it takes to protect what's ours."

I look back out at the horizon, at the sun now fully glowing in the sky. "You think Dad knows what it means?"

He shrugs. "I don't think that man knows his ass from a hole in the ground. But if there's something to learn about the land trust, he'd be our best option. Or Mom, but you know she'll want him to know if it involves him. If we have to dig out records from the office, we'll do it. I'm just hoping he can save us some time, because we don't have much of it."

I nod, staying silent. Kasey's right . . . If our father can shed any light on whatever that letter's about or who this asshole Stuart is, we'd be better for it. But I've worked hard to never put myself in positions where I have to rely on him for anything. I don't like the feel of it, the power it gives him. Eventually, I relent. "I'll go with you to talk to him."

Kasey shoves the letter back in his pocket and leans against the fence next to me. "Thank you," he says quietly.

"You all right?" I ask after a few beats.

He shakes his head. "Nothing's all right, Rhett. Nothing. Most times I can see the way through, but right now, it feels like we're in the middle of the ocean, taking on water faster than we can throw it back out."

The words are like a knife to the heart. I clap a hand on his shoulder, gripping him tight. "We'll get through whatever comes," I promise. "We always do."

But even as I say the words, I wonder if I'm lying.

"Can I ask you something?" Kasey hedges.

"Shoot," I rumble.

"You and that girl . . . Is there something going on?"

My stomach plummets. I had a feeling the question would be coming at some point, especially after she showed up at the ranch. I'm honestly surprised it's taken this long for someone to ask. "What girl?" I try.

His eyes narrow. "You know what girl."

I sigh, knowing I'm about to have a real hard time hiding the truth: that I'm beginning to wonder whether it's possible. If I could . . . be *meant* for someone. God, if someone like Olivia could be meant for me. It's foolish, I know. There's no way in hell I could deserve her, but still. "I don't know," I admit. "I . . . I thought it could be something casual, but I think I'm in a little over my head."

Kasey's eyes widen in surprise. "Oh shit," he lets out through a rush of air, and I want to walk away from this conversation. "You *like* this girl."

I roll my eyes, impatient with the way he's looking at me. Irritated with my own truth. "Yeah, well, it's not going anywhere, so don't get your panties twisted up about it."

He frowns. "Why not?"

I throw him a hard look. "Kasey, look around. You think it's a fucking good time to get caught up in something like that?"

He doesn't answer right away, but when he does, it's low. "I think it's about time we see some good, Rhett. And since when have you ever been the one to truly let yourself get caught up with a girl? I don't think I've ever seen you like that with one." He takes a breath, scratching at the back of his neck. "You don't get to decide when the good shit comes, but if you don't grab it while you can, you'll lose it. *Trust* me. I think . . . I think if you like her, you give it everything you have."

I blow out a breath, feeling my stomach tighten uncomfortably. "I can't," I let out.

Kasey's eyes grow harsh, and it almost feels like he's . . . *disappointed.*

"I can't. Not when Brooks—"

"Rhett," he interjects. "There's plenty of bad around us right now, we both fucking know it. You finding a slice of good to enjoy doesn't make you any less of a man when it counts."

He walks away before I can say anything else.

CHAPTER TWENTY

OLIVIA

$\mathcal{I}$ have the morning off. My shift at the café doesn't start until late afternoon, and I spend the first few hours of the day utterly restless in my own skin. There's a worry coiling tight in my chest, an unease about the way Rhett was so obviously lost inside of himself last night. And the way he left me this morning . . . this time without a note and almost no indication that he'd even been here at all, completely unlike the last time he'd left me sleeping in my bed.

If it weren't for the still half-full tub of cold water in the bathroom, I might have thought I dreamt the whole thing up. But the sight of the tub knocked through me like a bowling ball. Rhett *had* been here last night, had kissed me and held me and pushed his body into mine in more new ways that I want to hold fast to, but there's a sinking feeling in my gut, a gnawing concern that he's struggling even more than I realized.

I just don't know what the point of anything is.

The words had been raw and honest, and the weight of them . . . it'd been enough to thread through me and pull tight. I'd wanted to loosen the tension of them, to remind him that he was good and safe and trusted. I'd wanted him to have a little reprieve from the dark corners of his mind, and while I don't regret a second of it, I'd be lying if I said it didn't hurt a little to wake up alone.

Eventually, I wrestle my energy toward an impulsive plan to talk to my mother about Charleston. I figure I can play it safe enough . . . Rhett's right, I *do* want to go. I want to see these people for myself and make my own determinations about their potential place in my life, and though I'm still extremely nervous about hurting Mom in the process, I think I can navigate a conversation strategically enough to feel out what she might think.

I was barely nineteen when I moved out of the house I grew up in: a dainty cottage at the head of a cul-de-sac that sits just off the main road in town. Less than a five-minute walk from the café, it's where Mom settled shortly after she bought it. And while I've always known I wanted to stay in Saddlebrook Falls and take over the business someday, I've also wanted to slice out my own brand of autonomy.

Still, I love going home. It's the house that built me—built *us* —into the strong, independent women we both are today. Where Mom taught me about kindness and perseverance and where I learned that, no matter what, I could always take care of myself. I didn't need a traditional nuclear family dynamic to be genuinely happy—I had her, and it was enough.

As I pull along the front curb now, it's hard to take in the navy-blue trim and shutters against the bright splash of red gardenias and not ache for all the ways Mom made sure we had a good life. I picture our silhouettes in that big front window, dancing to Shania Twain—or, on a rare, cruel day, Alanis Morrisette—in our matching terrycloth robes as the sun bled along the horizon, a cold glass of white wine clutched in Mom's hand and a lukewarm peppermint tea wrapped in mine.

I mean it when I say we've always had a good life. Despite the worry and needling and *judgement* from neighbors all around us,

I never felt like I was missing a single thing without a father. It's a truth that winds through me now as I stare at the front door and find the bravery for a conversation that revolves around the man who left us.

Sighing, I pull my key from the ignition and push open my door. The cool morning air bursts across my face and sends a shiver through my limbs—it's gloomy today, the sky heavy with what looks like an impending rainstorm. Pulling my denim jacket tighter around me, I climb the wide brick steps up to the front door.

Inside, the house is warm and full of the familiar scents of vanilla candles and lavender laundry detergent. It's a small two-bedroom, not much bigger than mine, and smells always had a way of seeping through the entire house. There's a fire roaring in the hearth, warming the living room, and I notice two white ceramic mugs set on the coffee table in front of the couch, the label of a teabag hanging from each lip.

Two mugs, I realize.

I didn't tell Mom I was coming by this morning—I never do. I've always just walked through the door like I still live here, and she's never given me a reason to think I shouldn't. But the sight of those steaming mugs, the crackling fire behind them, it all sends a jolt of awareness through me.

I don't think my mom is alone.

Something clatters in the kitchen, and I hear her bright laugh crack through the quiet of the house. A low murmur trails behind the sound, and my feet are moving before my brain catches up to what's happening. Turning the corner around a yellow-painted wall, I find my mother perched up on the center island in a dazzling green pajama set patterned with frogs wearing pink dresses in various poses. Her red curls are unbound and spill across her back and in front of her right shoulder, and her cheeks are flushed and bunched with a wide, beaming smile.

And standing against the counter across from her is Mark.

Mark who, to my surprise, is *without* a shirt.

Only a pair of loose black sweatpants wrap around his hips as he works over something sizzling on the stove. His hair is ruffled and sticking up at odd angles and his face is still etched with sleep. It's painfully obvious that this is the aftermath of a sleepover, and based on how comfortable Mark looks in this kitchen, I'd guess it's not the first time.

"Mom?" I turn to look back at her.

Her gaze snaps to mine, brows arching high as a smile lifts her mouth. The surprise in her eyes is evident, but there's no trace of the frantic edge that comes with being caught. Unlike Mark, who looks like he might shit a brick with the way he startles.

"Lovebean!" Mom exclaims, jumping down from the edge of the island and moving toward me with her arms stretched wide. She pulls me into a tight hug, her wild hair pressing into my face, and I can smell the traces of Mark's spiced cologne in it.

"Good morning," I say around a short laugh, checking out the country gravy Mark's got simmering in a pot. A baking sheet of fresh biscuits cools on the counter and, despite the unbelievable awkwardness of this moment, my mouth waters. "Special occasion?" I ask pointedly.

Mom shrugs. "Nah."

I nod, taking this all in. "Right."

"You hungry?" Mark asks, looking a little worse for wear as sweat seeps from his temples. He's totally freaking out but trying so hard to act normal.

"I didn't mean to interrupt." I wave at the food. "I can come back—"

"Oh, nonsense," Mom retorts, reaching into the cabinet for a third plate, but Mark stops her with a gentle hand.

"I should actually be going," he murmurs, eyes bouncing to me before resting back on her. "You two enjoy breakfast, and I'll see you later?"

Mom hesitates with a long look and then she nods. "Okay,

yes. Later." The words are a promise, and I have to hide a smile in the crook of my shoulder.

Mark gives me a sheepish look on his way out of the kitchen. "Sorry you found out like this, kid," he says, a pinch of regret between his brows.

I pat him on his bare shoulder. "Nothing to be sorry about." I hope he knows I mean it.

Mom and I wait for him to grab his shirt and a few other items from down the hall, from her *bedroom*, while the shock of it still blares through me. He presses a chaste kiss to Mom's cheek on his way out and says he'll see us both at work.

When the front door shuts behind him, I turn to stare at my mom.

"What?" she asks, smiling through another shrug.

I burst out laughing. "How long?"

She has to think about it. "Short answer? A few months. But the long and more complicated version is the last decade, on and off."

"Mom! Why didn't you tell me?"

"Oh, honey," she tuts. Her golden eyes pierce mine, made bright by the splash of red that frames her face. "I wanted to keep you safe from it."

"Safe? Safe from what?"

She shakes her head, holding her hands out around her. "From the uncertainty and messiness of love."

"Mom, I'm a full-grown adult woman. I hardly think you need to worry about how your love life impacts me. I'm not even that surprised—I've seen the way you and Mark look at each other. But . . . I didn't think you'd actually take the plunge. I thought you never wanted to be in love again."

She clicks her tongue, leaning a hip against the edge of the counter as she crosses her arms over her chest. "I didn't, you're right. For a long time, I didn't. I was jaded and naive about the control I thought I needed to have over my life to feel safe. Turns out, love sometimes creeps in whether you mean for it to or not. Mark's been trying to lock me down for years, and until very recently, I've been too scared to let him. I actually think, more than anything, I've been scared to admit to *you* that I was wrong."

"Me? What do you mean?"

"Oh, honey, I think I messed up with you in a lot of ways."

I frown. "How?"

She takes a moment before speaking again, her forehead bunching in that way it always does when she's thinking something through. "I was so vocal with you about all the ways I'd been hurt. I wanted you to have my story about your father because I thought it would help you someday. That you might learn from my mistakes." She wipes a finger over her bottom lip before saying, "I should never have put that on you."

"Mom," I say around an exhale.

"Let me finish," she insists. "I think it felt like your story as much as it was mine, to tell you of the kind of relationship that brought you into the world but that also left us alone to face it. I just wanted to keep you safe from all the ways I opened myself up to hurt. I never wanted you to experience anything like it, so I made sure you knew what it was.

"But . . . I think I messed up, Olivia. I didn't realize that I was forgetting to tell you about love itself. How, unbound by the flawed humanity of the two people in it, love is a beautiful, shining beacon of *everything* good. It's something to strive for, not shy away from. I forgot to tell you that despite the hurt we caused each other, I don't regret falling in love with your father because it was one of the best years of my life. Sure, it didn't work out. He wasn't the right one in the end. But there was bravery in trying, and all these years I spent ashamed about the experience only proved my own cowardice."

There are tears running down my face when she finishes, but I'm not sure when they started falling. The words are everything I didn't know I needed to hear: the permission to do something different, the bravery that it takes.

Be brave.

Rhett's words—and now, my mother's.

"Well," I say on an exhale, more tears stinging in the corners of my eyes. "I guess since we're being honest, I have something I need to tell you."

Mom's eyes widen as they trail down my body, like she might be able to find some clue of what I'm about to tell her. "Are you okay?"

Another tear spills over, gliding down my cheek. The proof that all she cares about is *me*. "Yes, I'm just—I've been afraid of hurting you."

Her eyes close tight, a smile lifting from the corners of her mouth. "Baby girl," she whispers. "Try me."

So I do. I tell her about Dad's last letter again, and then about the next one from Céline. About how, against my best intentions, the soul-deep need to meet them and explore this part of me is bleeding out of my heart, and I know I would *regret* not going to Charleston. And then I say the thing that scares me most.

"I was hoping you'd come with me."

At this, I see her flinch. Evidence of a crack in her steely armor. She looks at me, mouth pressed tight, but says nothing.

"I . . . I just want you there with me when I face them. Not even *there* there, like you don't have to stand next to me or anything, not if you don't want to. But I was hoping you'd make the trip with me so that at least—at least I know I have you close."

I watch as her eyes shine and soften, shoulders sagging beneath her wild hair. And I hope it means she understands this is for me, not for them. My heart thunders when her mouth finally parts to say something. "Would they even allow it?"

And I see her worry for what it is: that old wound, the fear of rejection from the very same man behind all of this new hope.

"I'm prepared to ask. And if they say no, I'll understand of course. I don't want to cause issues for them, but . . . they say they want to get to know me. And I want to give it an honest chance, but that means knowing *you* too." More tears spill down my face, but I don't wipe them away. "They might share my DNA, but *you* are my family. You're the sole reason I'm the woman I am today, Mom, and if they want to know me, they need to know you too."

"Oh, honey," Mom blurts, charging forward to wrap her arms tight around me. "Of *course* I'll go with you."

I hold her just as tightly, just as close. "If they aren't okay with it, I won't hold it against them. But I *will* let it all go. I want to know them, Mom, I do. But I want it to be real, even if it's a little messy. If they aren't okay with that, then I don't want it."

"I'm so proud of you, Olivia," she says, breathing in deep. "I'm so damn proud of the woman you are, and honored that I have a chance to learn from you too."

I squeeze my eyes shut, soaking in the pure and honest love that only a mother could give. I don't know why I ever doubted that we could handle this, but I'm so thankful I was brave enough to try.

CHAPTER TWENTY-ONE

RHETT

It's been a few years since I last braved the stairs of the main house, since I've let myself acknowledge how small the climb still makes me feel, like I'm a man trapped inside the constraints of a boy's fear-addled body. With every creak of the steps beneath us, deep reminders of that old panic spike as I trail behind Kasey, hell-bent to knock down whatever walls I'd planned to hide behind for this meeting.

When I was a kid, my brothers and I did what we could to avoid the second floor of our home because of who was always up here, waiting for every opportunity to cut us down so he could feel big. The main house of the ranch, big as it is, holds a total of seven bedrooms: three downstairs and four upstairs. Brooks and Kasey—as the oldest—got to choose their rooms, so both of those lucky bastards had the luxury of sleeping downstairs. The rest of us, bound to our lesser privilege dictated by the order in which we were born, were forced to keep rooms upstairs, next to our parents.

I used to fight like hell for the spare room my mother kept on the first floor for guests, knowing if I could just move down there, I'd get some relief from the anxiety of being so close to my father while I slept. As a bunch of wild and reckless boys, we spent most of our daylight hours outside playing and learning the ways of the ranch. But in the hours between dinner and bedtime, when Dad did the heaviest of his drinking, the slightest disturbance to his peace often led to terrible consequences.

Once, when Sawyer was no more than eight or nine, he'd woken in the middle of the night from a bad nightmare and came running to my room. I tried like hell to keep him quiet as he told me all the ways his little mind was playing tricks on him in the dark, and eventually I helped shuffle him back to bed. It wasn't until he was tucked in and half asleep again that I heard movement from my parents' room on the other side of the wall—not the gentle movements of my mother, but the rough scraping and groaning of my father.

Quickly beelining to my room on silent feet, I thought I could make it back inside and avoid any issues. Unfortunately, I wasn't quick enough, and the firm hand that shoved me into the wall was cruel and unrelenting. I'm not sure if it was nights like those that created the specific way my father sought to terrorize me, or if that came later, after I started to get into more trouble in school. But I always had a strong suspicion that he reveled in those opportunities to get me alone so he could blow off a little steam, and I don't think anyone else in my family knew or understood how lonely it was. Brooks and Kasey had each other, and Sawyer and Wells were almost just as close. I was the odd man out, the one with a darker mind full of secrets and pain. My brothers had their asses handed to them too, no doubt about it. But the way Dad treated me . . . it was something different. Something more rotten and cold.

When I finally got old enough to inherit a cabin, I left that childhood bedroom of mine and never once looked back at it. When Brooks eventually had the boys, Mom swapped out my old furniture for bunk beds and toys, and the room became theirs to use for sleepovers with her on nights Brooks and Melody got away for themselves. I used to worry about them being up there, but

Dad's become a recluse in the last decade and hardly comes out of his room for anything. Plus, even if he still might holler and grumble about things he doesn't like, the wheelchair he's in stops him from using that brute power the way he once did.

I remember how thankful I'd been when he had that rodeo accident. How terrible it felt to look at my mother's face back then, twisted with so much despair for her husband, and still feel such *relief*.

My chest tightens as Kasey reaches the top of the staircase, turning left toward the one place I promised myself I would never willingly go. The sound of a TV bleeds through the door, the strongest proof of my father's existence that I've seen in months. Kasey raps his knuckles against the door three times, and for a moment that seems to stretch, nothing happens. I hold my breath and silently pray that he's not in there, even though we both know he is.

My heart sinks when the sound of the TV disappears and a rough "Come in" sounds from somewhere far behind the door.

Kasey pushes it open and there he is: Bud Bennett.

For a man somewhere in his mid-fifties, he looks at least a decade older. His once-dark hair, as dark as mine, is full of so much silver it's shocking. He's nestled in a heavily cushioned recliner, the fabric stretched around the armrests threadbare and shredding. A folded wheelchair is perched against the wall closest to him—hardly used these days other than to get himself to the bathroom and back. I think it's been months since Dad's actually left this room.

I was thirteen when he competed in his last rodeo, the one that left his body broken and shattered. Kasey had just started competing in a few youth circuits in East Texas, and I guess Dad thought he could dust off his old rodeo chaps and take a wild bronc for a spin. Back in his prime, Dad and his brothers would ride anything just to prove they could. And on that sweltering summer day in June, he'd had more than enough whiskey in his coffee to feel confident with his draw. To feel like he was capable enough of straddling the wide shoulders of the meanest horse at the event that day.

His alcoholism only got worse after the accident, and life at home was difficult for us all—especially Mom. But he's been sober almost five years, his longest stretch yet. It does little to make up for all the years his drinking made life hell—especially since he still doesn't do anything to help with *anything* around the ranch—but I guess life's given him plenty of pain to deal with.

I can't tear my eyes away from him now. For all of my avoiding, he still yields such power over me. I want him to see me for the man I am, for the man he forced me to become. I want him to see that he couldn't break me like life broke him. And with the way he glares back at me, a rush of sensation up my spine says he just might fucking know it.

Kasey's the one to finally break the silence. "Dad," he says in a low voice, bringing his hands to his hips as he looks around the room. It's relatively clean thanks to Mom, but even the small open window doesn't settle the musty weight of the air around us. "How are you?"

My father's eyes finally break from mine as he turns his focus to my brother. I can't help the exhale that pours out of my nostrils in relief. "Dandy, son," he answers with a smart-ass tilt of his lips. Like he's in on some joke that we're on the outside of. "It's a beautiful day to be alive. Now, to what do I owe the pleasure of you two finding a reason to visit me today?"

I roll my eyes. Always with the fucking games.

Kasey, though, stays in control. "We were hoping to ask you a few questions about the ranch," he says matter-of-factly. "About the land trust."

This catches my father's attention. "The trust?"

Kasey nods. "A lawyer stopped by last week looking for you. And then we got a letter in the mail. A summons."

Dad frowns. "What's the lawyer's name?"

"Stuart Brown."

"Don't know him." He shrugs, like that's the extent of what he can do for us.

"What do you know about the details of the land trust?" Kasey tries.

"Not much to know," Dad gripes. "The land is ours."

"Cut the bullshit," I say, a little louder than intended. Dad's smokey eyes find mine again, and I see the welcome challenge in them. "There's a lawyer who is looking for you about the ranch. There's gotta be a fucking reason. Did you gamble the deed at some point? Make enemies with another ranch? What about your brothers—would they try and take it?"

A flicker of something cold registers on his face before he tries to hide it. His gaze falls to the carpet beneath his socked feet and he takes a deep breath. "My brother, Huck . . . he's always been a jealous man. Especially when it comes to this ranch."

"What do you mean?" Kasey asks quietly.

Dad lets out a humorless laugh. "He was always the serious one. Smart with books and money, not great with instinct or the horses. But he didn't care much about the animals. He just wanted the business. Wanted to sell us all out and turn the ranch into some stupid tourist trap. And if he'd been born first, I'm sure that's exactly what he would have done. Luckily for everyone, I was."

I snort, shaking my head. It's not news to us that the eldest Bennett of the brood inherits the bulk of the ranch and operations, something Brooks has been preparing for his whole life. The rest of us will profit from it, more so if we stay on and work with him. He doesn't officially take over until our parents formally retire, and I've done nothing over the years to hide the fact I think Brooks should ask Dad to do just that.

We'll always make sure Mom is taken care of, whether Dad's running the ranch on paper or not. But I think Brooks has wrestled with guilt about making that move, especially with Dad's disability. He has his own complicated relationship with Dad, since Dad had a pretty long stretch of sobriety during Brooks's formative years. They . . . *bonded*, in ways I never got the chance to. Kasey benefited from those good years too, I think. It's what makes it so hard for us to understand each other when it comes to our father.

"Huck knows I'm in a chair," Dad says. "He's probably looking for a way to weasel his grubby hands in."

Kasey frowns. "But . . . Brooks is next in line to take over."

Again, something flashes across my father's face, and it looks a lot like fear. "Despite his inability to gain control of the ranch, Huck's done pretty well for himself. Last I heard, he'd built a little empire out in Dallas. But he was always scheming under my nose, getting himself nice and cozy to Mayor Moore and Sheriff Jones with his dream of what this place could be and what it could do for the town."

And he never thought to mention a threat like that? Fucking figures. "What does any of that matter if Brooks is taking over?" I demand. "I mean, there are five of us . . . there's no shortage of successors."

The bedroom door creaks open behind me, and I whip around to find Mom walking into the room. Her eyes bounce around at all three of us as a grim line sets in her mouth. And then she moves to stand behind my father, resting a hand on his shoulder. "You're here about the letter?" she asks Kasey.

He nods before looking back down to where Dad sits in front of her.

Mom surprises us both when she, too, turns her attention to our father and says, "I think you need to tell them, Bud."

My eyes snap to hers. "Tell us what?"

Dad sighs, and the sharp heat of anger coils through me like a venomous snake. "Four generations ago, there were . . . *rules* created around how the ranch transitions to the next generation.

The oldest child has the right to it by default, as you boys know. But there are stipulations about the inheritance, old bylaws that we have to adhere to about who can rightfully take over." He fidgets with a wrinkle in his pants, pressing the pads of his fingers over it to smooth it out. "I'm fairly certain the Bennett line has always possessed its share of recklessness, because one of those stipulations exists to make sure the one who inherits the property is supported as best as possible."

"What does that *mean*?" Kasey barks out.

Dad looks right at him when he says the word. "Marriage."

Silence falls over us again as we consider what he means. And then Mom chimes in again. "Your great-great grandmother saw the flaws of her husband and knew, if left to his own devices, he would have run the ranch into the ground." She gives Dad a knowing look. "She was a fierce old woman who forced few of her own opinions into the details of the inheritance trust when it was created.

"She believed that any firstborn Bennett—man or woman— who wanted to take over the deed would need the structure of a life partner to be successful with the weight of responsibility the ranch entails. Marriage, in every sense. It also ensured that new generations born into the inheritance would be raised in a nuclear family setting on this very ranch.

"Traditions were different back then. And while your father and I have never cared about what your futures look like, who you choose to love or how you choose to love them, we *are* bound by the rules of the trust. I personally would love to take a red pen to some of the nuances of it, but as the woman of this household and your father's wife for almost forty years, I can understand where the old bird was coming from. How our marriage has kept the wheels on the track over the years."

We all know what she's not saying: when Dad was too drunk or angry or miserable to be responsible for anything, Mom kept things moving. Kept us boys on track.

Something still doesn't make sense. "Brooks is married," I say to no one in particular.

It's when Mom's eyes meet mine again that I understand.

Holy fucking *shit*.

"You boys best find a good lawyer," Dad grumbles. "If your brother loses his wife, it's possible he loses his shot at the ranch."

"And you never thought to fucking tell us?" Kasey shouts, the sound of it startling even me. Kasey can be a mean son-of-a-bitch when he needs to be, but I've only heard him raise his voice on very few occasions. "You've *known* this—you both have—and you never thought to say something?"

Mom flinches, raising a hand to cover her mouth. She looks at him with the current of her own anger that's even rarer than Kasey's shouting. "Melody is still alive and breathing down those stairs," she scolds. "Forgive me if I'm still holding on to *hope*, son, that Brooks doesn't ever even have to know about this. That death might look at his wife and decide to *move on* instead of taking her. Don't you dare think for a second that this isn't an impossible situation for *all* of us, but if I'm protecting anyone's heart right now, it's theirs."

I believe her. That, in due time, we would have all learned about this from her together, and then *faced* it together. For Brooks. So why the hell aren't we getting that time? "How would Huck know?" I ask. "About Melody? Say you're right—that this is about her. How would Huck even know?"

Dad's gaze warps into something cold and menacing. "I'd wager either the mayor or the sheriff knows."

"It doesn't matter how they know," Mom says softly. "Our poor girl's dying. We're not going to turn it into some dark secret."

"But if someone put this family in jeopardy—" Kasey starts.

"*Enough,*" Mom interjects with a tone I haven't heard since I was a kid. "We *will not* turn on each other. No one could have predicted this because none of you knew what was at stake. That's our fault." She wipes her hands down the front of her shirt. "Right now, our immediate focus needs to be on Brooks and his family. Do you understand me?"

"Yes ma'am," Kasey relents.

She looks at me, and I give her a small nod. "Yes ma'am."

"Good. Now call that bastard and push the meeting. Try to buy us as much time as possible."

Kasey dips his head low and turns toward the bedroom door. But I look at my father. "You need to get a grip."

He looks at me through thick, furrowed brows. "The hell you say to me, boy?"

I square my shoulders. "You need to get a grip on yourself and get the fuck out of this room. This ranch needs you. Your *son* needs you. It's about time you stopped letting us fight every fucking battle that comes *your* way and started doing something to help."

I'm surprised when he doesn't say anything to argue. He doesn't so much as show a single sign that he's heard a word I said. I throw Mom a pleading look and then turn to follow Kasey out of the room.

CHAPTER TWENTY-TWO

OLIVIA

Now that the truth is out about my mom and Mark, I catch them *everywhere*. On Friday morning, I walk back into the kitchen looking for table seven's breakfast order and find Mom sidled up to the flattop stove, flipping sausage patties while Mark rubs her shoulders. On Saturday, I open the office door to exchange some cash only to find them sucking face like teenagers up against curfew, her straddled in his lap in the desk chair.

I'm honestly not even sure they noticed me since they didn't make any moves to stop, not even after I mumbled a quick apology and skirted away, utterly mortified. When Mark shows up to work Sunday donning a purpling hickey the size of a golf ball, high enough on his neck that he can't hide it with his uniform, I drag Mom into the walk-in fridge for a little chat.

"You two need to cool it," I demand, wrapping my arms around myself to keep warm against the frigid air.

"Cool what?" she asks, completely aloof and unconcerned. Her curls are barely contained in a bundle on top of her head, a colorful-patched smock hanging from her shoulders. I have a feeling Mark isn't the only reason for her good mood. She moves through the café on light and airy feet, as if no longer held down by the weight of all the things she was undoubtedly worried about before our conversation.

"Mark has a *hickey*, Mom. It looks like he ran neck-first into a tire iron."

Her eyes spark with quiet amusement. "Honey, we're just happy."

"You can be happy without gyrating all over him around the café," I insist. "Or are you so lost in the *throes* of him that I need to sprinkle a box of condoms around to make sure you're protected when the mood strikes?"

"Oh, we don't use those." She waves a hand to brush off the thought.

"Mom!"

"Let me bask in the hazy chaos of love, sweetheart. Maybe you should find some of your own?" She laughs as she pushes open the door to saunter away like none of this is a big deal. And I suppose it's not, because she's happy, and I'd take her happiness over anything—even if it means I have to scrub my eyeballs of all that I witness between them every day.

It makes me think of Rhett. Of all the ways I'd like to get lost in *him* throughout the day in quiet, stolen moments when no one's looking. I let myself wonder if we could ever have the same kind of open affection, but then promptly shut the thought down. He's still such a mystery to me, and after he left the other morning without so much as a word, I've been feeling more and more insecure about whatever it is that may or may not exist between us.

Sometimes I notice the way he looks at me, like he's just as startled as I am about the way he feels, and I wonder if his world is just as off-kilter as mine when we're together. Like what we're doing is changing the very shape of us, even though it's not at all what either of us were after. But then other times . . .

Other times I wonder if I'm just a naive girl with a stupid

crush on an emotionally unavailable bad boy. If I should protect my heart while I can and *run*.

I've been trying to hold out, to let him seek me out first. It's only fair, right? After slipping away in the dark? Though, I guess he was the one who showed up on *my* doorstep that night. Maybe it's my turn to make the next move.

Doing my best to shuck away all the uncertainty that holds tight beneath my ribs, I make it through my shift relatively unscathed from any further catastrophes where my mother and Mark are concerned. But Mark's good mood is just as noticeable: as the dinner rush begins to wane, I find him in the kitchen working on an assortment of desserts.

"Whatever you're doing, keep doing it," I say through the expo window with a smile. "It smells amazing."

Mark's grin rises as he turns to look at me, wiping his hands on his long apron. "I've got something up my sleeve just for you actually."

"Oh?" My brow arches. "Bribery?"

His laugh is loud and booming, and it makes my chest squeeze. "Yeah, something like that." He lifts a pan and tilts it for me to see, and I almost melt.

"Cheesecake!" I squeal, looking from the yet-to-be-baked delicacy to Mark's warm face. That single hoop earring sparkles as he pivots to set it back down. "You remembered."

He shrugs. "You used to ask for one every birthday. Not hard to forget the way you nearly swallowed it whole every damn time."

It's true—it's always been my favorite. I don't remember when or why I stopped asking for it, but it pierces into me that he hasn't forgotten. I look at him again and take in the worn backward hat he uses to keep his hair out of his face, the laugh lines embedded around his eyes and mouth. He's been around so long that I think I forgot to appreciate how *good* he is, how good he's always been to Mom and me, to this café. "I'm happy she has you," I tell him. And I mean it.

His eyes shift back to mine, his wide grin slipping into something softer. The sincerity that wraps around us is nearly palpable. "I'm happy I have *her*, Olivia. Thank you for being okay with it."

I throw him a smirk that, in my mind, is equal parts playful and dangerous, but probably only makes me look constipated. "Break her heart and I'll break your face."

He laughs again, but I see the way his eyes shine. "I'd hope so."

I have to wipe my own eyes when I turn to head back out to the dining floor.

A few hours later, I'm marching under the scattered streetlights of town square with a to-go box full of cheesecake and a train of thought stuck back on the sticky tracks of Rhett Bennett.

My face burns from the cold night air, but despite the cold, I hardly ever drive to work—I love having the walk home to unwind and shake off the day. It'd been a relatively easy dinner shift: Gus Romano brought in his mother who is visiting from Florida, and a group of parents from the school district's PTA met for a couple of hours, discussing fundraising opportunities over plates of hot roast. Nosy Maeve didn't make her usual Sunday night appearance, but according to old man Gerry— who'd stopped by to say hi to everyone after picking up a chocolate pie from Luna's bakery next door—Maeve was busy hosting bunco at the library.

I have to admit, her absence was a welcomed reprieve—especially after she called the Bennetts womanizers the last time I saw her.

I wonder if Rhett's working tonight at the bar. For a heartbeat

I consider dropping by to see for myself, but my feet are sore from being on them all day and . . . what if he's not even there? If he's not, one or two of his brothers surely are, and after showing up at the ranch unannounced, I'm sure they'd have questions that I don't even know how to answer.

Still, despite feeling a little foolish, I miss him. My mind has traced over thoughts of him every night before I fall asleep, how his body felt against mine in the bath and, later, in my bed. And I worry about the darkness in his eyes—the way he'd seemed distracted.

I *do* have his phone number, I realize, and I *still* haven't used it

. . .

I'm barely through my front door before I'm scrolling to find his name in my contacts, pressing the call button with an eager finger. He answers on the second ring, and my heart does a triple backflip.

"Hello?" he says, voice gruff through the phone. It sends a pulse of desire through every nook and cranny of my body.

"You answered," I declare, hoping the cool evenness of my own voice at least hides a little of the effect he has on me, even from afar.

"You called," he says pointedly, and I can picture his uneven smile as he says it.

"I wanted to check on you. See how you're doing."

"That so?" he asks, voice lowering. There's some background noise, and it doesn't sound like he's home.

"Sorry, are you busy?"

"Uh . . ." He trails off for a beat. "No, just give me a sec." There's some chaotic rustling and a bang. I hear something that sounds a lot like *fuck off, Boone,* and then after a few more moments, he's back. "Okay, I'm good now."

"Are you sure?"

"Yep." His voice is so deep it sounds almost dangerous. "Why?"

I laugh. "It just sounds like you're at work."

"Nah. Well, okay, I am. Was," he corrects. "But now I'm upstairs."

"Oh, in your kinky sex dungeon?" Flashes of that ghostly apartment come alive in my mind, and I fight a blush thinking of the rope he used to tie me down.

"Mm," he rumbles. "You think it's kinky?"

"Isn't it?"

He laughs. "I like that it is for you. Damn, now I'm going to have an even harder time not thinking of you when I'm up here."

"What is it for you?" I press, ignoring the way his words swoop through me. "I remember you said you liked the quiet."

"Yeah, I do," he agrees. "I guess it's a home away from home? My cabin at the ranch is hardly cozy. No curtains on the wall, not much food in the fridge. And . . . it's where my parents lived before they took over the main house. I was pretty little when we left it, but I remember they weren't the best days. Hard memories, I guess. I feel lighter in the apartment. Always have."

I nod, understanding. "I'm sorry."

He snorts. "What do you have to be sorry about?"

I give myself a second to muster up the words. "For all the shit you have on your plate. That you feel like you have to hold it all in. I was . . . I was worried about you. The other night."

He sighs. "I know. I shouldn't have just shown up like that."

"No, no. I'm glad you did. I always want you to show up when you need a friend."

"A friend?"

"Aren't we?"

"Hm." A pause stretches out between us and I hear faint rustling on the other end of the line. "Maybe."

I want to throttle him. "Be honest, Rhett. Are you okay?"

But he doesn't answer. "Can I ask you something?"

I sense the shift in his tone, imagine the hard set of his jaw. "Of course."

"There's some shit going on at home. My brother's wife . . . she's sick."

I set the box of cheesecake down on my counter in the kitchen and spin to stare at the far wall. "Brooks's wife?"

"Yeah."

I swallow. "How sick?"

"It's not good," he says.

"Shit," I whisper. Liam and his brothers flood my mind, and my chest squeezes. No wonder Rhett looked like he was being pulled under the tide.

"I guess that answers my question." He exhales. "You didn't know?"

"Of course not," I say quickly. "How would I?"

He sighs again, and this time I hear the relief in it. "I'm sorry. It's somehow gotten out and . . . I didn't know how big the story might be. In town, I mean."

Understanding sinks in. "I haven't heard anything about it. How would someone know? Did something happen?"

"It's a long story," he grumbles. "Someone might be trying to take the ranch from us."

Oh my god. "Can that happen?"

"I sure fuckin' hope not."

The Bennetts have had that ranch for *generations*. How could Brooks's wife being sick lead to something like that? "Is there anything I can do to help?"

"Just . . . just keep talking. This is nice. How was your day?"

My heart aches with the way he changes the subject so quickly. But I don't want to push too hard, especially not over the phone like this. "Good," I say. "I talked to my mom. About Charleston."

"Yeah?" He sounds genuinely intrigued.

"Yeah. I told her I want to go to Charleston, but that I want her to go with me."

"Well, look at that. That's a damn good idea."

"I thought so," I say, smiling again.

"How'd she take it?"

"Surprisingly well. But after catching her indisposed with our chef, I think she was probably willing to hear anything I had to say."

"No *way*. June Danvers? With the *chef*?"

A laugh bubbles out of me, loud and bright. "I wish I could say I was surprised, but I've sort of been on to them for a while."

"Stirrin' up a town scandal—I'm impressed," he says. "Good for her. Everyone deserves . . . well, that."

So do you, I think, and it helps me brave the question. "Can I see you again soon?"

A pause. "You miss me, peaches?"

My face burns hot, and I'm thankful he can't see. "Maybe?"

He chuckles. "What are you doing tomorrow night?"

"Working." I frown. "But . . . you could come in?"

I doubt he'd want to, especially knowing there's a threat to the ranch and potential gossip about his sister-in-law. Which is why I'm surprised when he says, "That sounds good. There's some stuff I need to work on at home, but I'll let you know when I'm done."

I smile. "Sounds perfect." But there's something else I need to say, something that burns on my tongue. "Hey, Rhett? We *are* friends, you know."

"Yeah?"

"Yeah." I nod. "This isn't just about . . . experience. At least not anymore. I promise I'm a good friend, and . . . I guess I just want you to know I'm here for you. For anything you might need. You don't have to be alone with it all."

He sighs, and I hate that I can't see his face to read his expression. "Just so *you* know, I don't exactly tie my *friends* up in my bed, peaches. Though, I bet Colt would love it." *Colt*—I've heard him say that name before, though I can't place it with anyone from town. "But I hear what you're saying, and . . . thank you. I hate to say I don't think I'm a very good friend myself, but for what it's worth, I'm here for you too."

I lean back against the wall and catch my grin in the entryway mirror. "Yeah?"

A dark chuckle. "Yeah. Turns out I have a thing about you smiling."

He's . . . *flirting,* I think. A foreign emotion spills through me, crisp and bubbly, like a bottle of champagne popping open. It floods my senses, distracts me from the conversation until he's speaking again.

"Don't tell anyone or I might lose my edge."

I laugh. "It'll be our little secret," I promise. And I mean it. But a sudden want for *more* tears through me so violently, I feel it sting like kerosene in the corners of my eyes.

"A secret between friends," he murmurs.

When we hang up, I stare at my phone with a pulsing ache in my chest, guilty that I ever second-guessed him or his intentions with me. He *does* need a friend, and despite what he believes about himself, this soft and vulnerable side of him matters. More people should know about it, should care about him. I want him to know he doesn't need to hide behind a mask, that his deeper layers deserve to be seen.

Tomorrow, I think. When he comes to see me at the café. I'll make sure everyone in that building knows how happy I am to see him.

CHAPTER TWENTY-THREE

RHETT

The day starts as normal as any other: a late-winter sunrise that bleeds oranges and pinks across the horizon, the whinnies and chuffs of horses in the barn as we move in to clean their stalls, the firm grip of the saddle between my thighs while a young stallion lets out his restless temper. We don't have any new horses scheduled to come for a few weeks, and it's a break we all need. Kasey takes the morning to catch up on admin work in the makeshift office while Wells and Layla take turns brushing and tacking the horses before letting them loose in the corrals.

Melody's even having a good day—one of the best in weeks. Other than our meeting with Dad, I've mostly stayed away from the main house to give Brooks and his family the space they need to feel and process what the doctor had said on his last visit, but I almost wonder if he'd been wrong as I watch Brooks help her out to a rocking chair on the front porch where she can enjoy some fresh air. She's pale and skinny and she looks tired as hell, but she's smiling, and it breathes hope into me.

Especially as I catch the way Brooks beams at her.

Liam and Noah are at school, but James doesn't start till September, so Mom brings him to the long driveway to help him practice riding his bike. It gives Melody a chance to see him sun-kissed and happy, and there's so much pride and love in her face as she watches him fight his fear of falling. By all accounts, it's a damn good day—the kind where peace swells and a steady calm takes hold, giving nothing to indicate the way it'll end.

I suppose it's no surprise when my thoughts turn to Olivia. Sometime around early afternoon, I catch Wells draw in close to Layla, sharing something that's just for her. She tips her head back and laughs, open and carefree, and my chest tightens. I imagine an alternate reality where I take Wells's place and Olivia takes Layla's. Imagine the light of the sun on her face during golden hour, when the sky explodes into a roaring fire. I picture her hazel eyes watching me with tenderness and trust, and it lights me up.

I'd be so careful with her, so opposite of everything I've ever been.

I'd do anything to show her how much she's beginning to mean to me.

Christ. I dig into my eyes with both thumbs until the pressure becomes painful. A few nights and a damn phone conversation with this girl and I'm already planning an entire fucking future, one that plants her smack dab in the middle of it.

"You good?" I hear Kasey call over the distance, and I look to find him in the open doorway of the tack shed, eyeing me with concern.

"Yeah," I holler back. And then I tilt my head toward the house where Brooks and Melody sit, and watch Kasey do the same. When he looks back at me, he's grinning. "It's been a good day," I add, just loud enough for him to hear.

He nods. "I see that." He gives the porch another quick look before his grin grows, then he shakes his head and disappears back inside.

I wonder if he's thinking the same as me—that maybe we can still be okay.

The kernel of hope inside my chest only grows as I finally

head to my cabin to wash off the sweat and grime from the day. I have a lady to see, a smile to earn, and it might be my guilt over leaving her the other night while she slept or just the progression of my own tumble into the unknown, but I've never been more excited to get out the door and see someone in my life.

It's when I finally jump on the bike and make it out of our driveway that I notice the dark clouds in the distance. There's no mistaking the storm they're going to bring, and it's the first hint of the changing tides. I almost wonder if I should turn around to park the bike in the shed and borrow Mom's Suburban, but I don't have it in me to wait any longer.

I make it to June's in less than ten minutes, instantly noticing another problem: the sheriff's car is parked in the front row of the café. For a few long minutes, I sit on my rumbling bike and stare at it, trying to figure out what the fuck I should do. Seeing Sheriff Joe is the last thing I need. I don't want to give him any damn reason to heckle me the way he loves to do. But I want to see Olivia *more* than I want to avoid him, so with a harsh exhale to blow the frustration from my lungs, I back my bike into an open spot and turn off the ignition.

The café is a warm relief from the dropping temperatures outside. I scan the dining room, the anxiety I always feel in town spiking harder than usual, and I deflate a little when I don't spot Olivia. I do, however, lock eyes with our town's finest, still dressed in his dark uniform after a day spent protecting Saddlebrook Falls from our overzealous senior community and maybe a stray cat or two. I watch him rise from his chair, an instinctual alarm clearly tripped from my mere presence. He angles himself toward me, mouth tipping up with a spiteful grin as he takes the first step away from his table where he's eating dinner alone.

But then Olivia bursts through the swinging door from the kitchen and I forget about everything around me except for her golden hair and the freckles that splash her cheeks and the way her mouth breaks out into a surprised, uneven smile that shakes my whole world. I'm paralyzed by the force of the way she moves, my boots rooted to the ground in front of the café's door, unable to do anything but watch her close the distance between us. This sweet girl, who makes me *feel* and *want* and *hope*, moves toward me with determined, confident steps, and I brace myself for her.

"Rhett," she says through a crooked smile. It's one I haven't seen before, and my pulse leaps.

"Peaches," I breathe, heart pounding like the fucking sucker I am.

"You look . . . good," she says, pink tinging her pretty cheeks as she takes in the pearl-snap button-down I usually save for rodeos.

My mouth pulls wide. And I want to tell her she's the best looking thing in this whole damn town, but movement over her shoulder distracts me, and I look up to find the sheriff frowning.

"Bennett," he says coolly. "What a pleasure."

It's all it takes to shut me down as I frown right back at him. "Can't say it's ever a pleasure to see you." I throw him a cold smile. "There a reason you're competing with the staff to welcome me in for dinner?"

I notice Olivia's expression change in my periphery, but my gaze is locked with Sheriff Joe's, and I refuse to be the one who breaks. "I don't know. Is there a good reason for you to be here?"

I snort. "I wasn't aware I needed to prove my intentions to earn a plate of food."

The furrow in his brow deepens. "Unfortunately, son, you've made a habit of stirring up enough trouble for just about everyone in this town, and I'm afraid I don't trust any of your intentions at this point. So why don't we just get to the part where you tell me why you're here. Hell, maybe I can help you."

"I'm not your son," I bristle. For as much as the man always claims he's only ever trying to deescalate a situation, he sure likes to push the buttons he knows will set me off. It's one of the many ways he uses the front of his badge to fuck with me.

"I'm sorry," Olivia says before I can respond. She looks confused, turning around to look at the sheriff standing behind her. "May I ask what this is about? Is there something wrong?"

He doesn't so much as look at her when he replies, "Not yet. But I'm afraid it's inevitable when it comes to this one."

I want to fucking punch him.

I don't know what I expected Olivia to respond with, but the deep scoff that rips through isn't it. "His name, for the record, is Rhett. And unless he actually gives you a reason to bother him, I'd like to politely ask that you sit down and focus on your own dinner."

The sheriff finally looks at her, brows rising in surprise. He definitely didn't anticipate June Danvers's daughter coming to my rescue. "I'm just trying to keep your mother's place of business safe."

"I don't see any reason why it wouldn't be," she says with an icy tone that has me clearing my throat to cover a burst of surprised laughter, "considering I'm the one who asked Rhett to come."

He narrows his eyes, looking back and forth between us. And then something akin to realization strikes his face, and he frowns again. "Olivia," he says, giving her a pointed look. "I want to make sure you understand something. Rhett Bennett isn't interested in settling down or changing his ways, not for any woman. Especially not for such a nice girl like you. Don't let him fool you, sweetheart."

I clench my fists at my sides, seeing red. "Don't patronize her, you fucking prick," I seethe, stepping toward him. What I would *give* to feel his face break from one good, solid hit.

"Rhett," Olivia says softly, pressing a hand to my chest.

It's enough for me to look down at her, my gaze snaring in her eyes. There's a softness to them, an understanding. An unfamiliar emotion sinks into me, spreading out and down my spine.

"It's not worth it," she says simply.

I breathe deeply and take in the point of her nose, the curve of her rosy lips. With every passing second, the anger inside seems to dissipate like a dangerous mist yielding to the sun. And then I nod, stepping back to my original place. For her: I yield.

She turns to face the sheriff again, crossing her arms over her chest and glaring.

An uneasy smile creeps along his mouth as he shakes his head. "Don't say I didn't warn you," he mutters before pulling his wallet from his back pocket. I watch as he shuffles out two twenty-dollar bills and hands them to her. "Thanks for dinner," he says, and then moves around me to walk out the door.

A deeper exhale bleeds out of me when he's gone.

"I'm sorry, Olivia—" I start to say, but she shushes me and takes my hand, pulling me toward the same empty booth she set me up in last time. I feel the attention of everyone in here but keep my focus on her until we reach the table.

"Want something to drink?" she asks as I sit.

I nod, eager to get this train back on its tracks. "Yes please."

She's still wound up when she returns with a soda, setting it on the table in front of me before sitting on the other side of the booth like she's not still on shift. The café isn't exactly full, but there are enough occupied tables that I'm sure she's busy enough. "Is that what it's always like for you?" she asks. "When you come into town?"

I shrug. "I've gotten used to it."

She shakes her head. "That's not okay, Rhett."

I force a smile. "I'm not exactly innocent," I remind her.

"Still, that doesn't mean people can shit on you forever." She's genuinely pissed off, and I have to focus on untangling my straw from its wrapper so I don't shoot over the table and kiss her. "The sheriff, of all people, has no right to treat anyone like that without a good reason. You weren't even doing anything wrong."

"Yeah, well, there's a long history there. And it's not just him hiding behind a position of power." I think of the mayor too, how they both like to tag-team with their bullshit. I sink my straw into my soda and look at her. "It's okay, peaches. Really."

She shakes her head again, that stubborn fire I like so much still raging.

My phone vibrates on the table, skating across the surface in a jagged dance. I see Kasey's name flash across the screen and reach down to silence the call.

"You don't deserve to be treated like that," she says somberly, and it pierces me right in the chest.

But the sound of my phone ringing again distracts me. It's Kasey, *again*, and I frown. I know he's working at the bar tonight . . . I wonder if something's wrong. "Sorry, I need to take this."

She dips her chin. "No worries. I'll be right back."

I watch her disappear into the kitchen as I swipe to answer the call, lifting the phone to my ear. "Kasey?"

There's shouting on the other end of the line. A mix of voices that surge together in a chaotic frenzy that's impossible to understand. "Rhett," Kasey breathes. I've never heard him sound like that—so lost and defeated.

And then I hear it.

Brooks, in the background. Screaming.

My heart stops, eyes squeezing shut with an uncomfortable pressure.

No no no no . . .

"I'll be right there," I say.

I'VE NEVER GIVEN MUCH THOUGHT TO MY OWN mortality, despite knowing I've definitely kissed death a time or two. Between the drinking and fighting and speed of my bike, there's no doubt I've come way too close to meeting whatever comes on the other side of this human existence.

Sometimes I've even scared myself. Once, back when I spent

most Saturday nights selling pills with Colt to knuckleheads at the fairgrounds, we got swindled by our dealer after he decided to take our money and run without giving us any new product. Colt was prepared to accept the loss, but I got so worked up over the injustice that I jumped on my bike to chase the fucker down the highway. But he'd known I was behind him, and he'd gotten fucking close to running me right off the road.

Or there's the time I picked a fight with the meanest cowboy I could find at the rodeo because I needed to burn off some pent-up anger—I don't even remember why I'd been so bent out of shape. But that mean cowboy shattered my nose before I even saw him swing. In the span of seconds, I went from the wild frenzy of rearing my own fist toward him to waking up in a hospital bed with no recollection of what happened. Thank god Kasey had been there to get me some help.

Despite flirting with it over the years, the idea of death and dying isn't something I've feared or obsessed over. We all live, and then we die—it's one of the simplest promises that life can offer us. But I've also been relatively lucky enough that I haven't had to experience the way death cuts into you, the way it breaks and shatters and shreds all traces of light, leaving you starved and empty and numb.

I've never known the true pain it causes for those left behind with a hole shaped like the one they've lost.

Until now.

I can hear the crying inside the house from out on the front steps: the high-pitched sobs of the boys, the deep and desperate moaning of their father. Pushing open the door, I find Kasey on the other side. He's leaning against the wall, his hat clutched in his hand. When he looks at me, he shakes his head, and the panic in my chest grips tighter. Both Wells and Layla sit at the table in the kitchen.

"Where are they?" I ask, watching tears stream down Layla's face as Wells stares hard at his hands.

"Her room," Kasey answers.

I force myself to take the steps that lead me down the hall. Mom is hovering in the doorway of the bedroom Melody's been housed in for weeks, her hand over her heart and her face utterly stricken. On impulse, I reach for her and pull her in close, wrapping my arms tight around her.

She lets out a quiet sob that presses against my sternum. "She's gone, Rhett," she cries, her shoulders shaking. "She just . . . she just *died*."

With Mom tucked against my chest, I can see into the room, where Brooks and the boys are somehow all on the narrow hospital bed. All curled around her.

All of them crying, lost in the devastation.

I force myself to shut down the emotion that rises violently in my throat. "What can I do?" I ask, voice rough.

But Mom doesn't answer me. Instead, she shudders out another sob, and I have to disentangle myself from her. Have to back away from what feels like my heart ripping open.

I turn back and march toward Kasey. "What can I do?" I ask him instead.

His eyes are shining from the light in the kitchen. "Ambulance is on its way. We just have to wait for it." Saddlebrook Falls is too small of a town to have its own hospital—Williamson County Memorial is the closest one to us, and it's a good half hour away. Under normal circumstances, we'd be doing what we can to meet an ambulance halfway for an emergency situation. But both Kasey and I know that won't help Melody.

So, I just nod and try like hell not to put a hole through the wall.

"What happened?" I ask. I mean, *fuck*, she'd looked so much better today.

He scratches a thumb against his brow, a single tear cresting and falling onto his cheek. "She said she was tired and cold after the clouds rolled in, so Brooks got her back to bed for a nap. He went to pick up the boys from school and then horsed around with them out front for a little while before he came back inside to check on her and . . . she was already gone."

A knot forms in my throat, so thick I almost gag.

My pulse thunders in my temples and I need something to focus on, something that will help.

I need something to *do*.

And then it hits me.

I walk back out the front door, my hurried steps carrying me beneath the darkening sky. Pulling my phone out of my pocket, I take a deep breath.

I already know I'm going to hate myself for doing this, but of all of us, I'm the one who deserves it the most.

CHAPTER TWENTY-FOUR

OLIVIA

Rhett isn't at the booth when I come out of the kitchen.

His soda still sits untouched on the table, the only proof he'd been there at all. For a moment I wonder if Sheriff Joe came back for him. Did he take Rhett in the few minutes I was gone? Could Rhett have done something in such a short amount of time that would somehow justify being detained?

My feet are moving in an instant, taking me out the front door of the café. I don't see the sheriff's car in the front row where I know it'd been parked, but I also don't see Rhett's bike, which means . . .

He left on his own.

My shoulders slump. Walking back inside, I think of the phone call he took at the table—I didn't see who was calling, but if Rhett's just suddenly *gone* like this, it might mean there's been some sort of emergency. I check on a few tables as I move back through the dining room, distracted enough that I'm honestly not sure if anyone asked for anything by the time I find myself in the kitchen again. I head straight for my purse where it hangs from a hook so I can grab my phone.

There are no new notifications, and I deflate all over again from the lack of communication. But if Rhett's truly in some sort of emergency situation, he probably wouldn't be able to reach out right away . . . right? It's not like he can text or call while he's on his bike—that would be far too dangerous. I decide to text him a quick *Are you okay?* before tucking my phone inside my apron pocket and forcing myself back to work.

Teresa's holding a food ticket at the expo window, looking at me with a warm smile. "Hey kid, table four's food has been sitting here for a few minutes—want me to take it to them?"

I eye the two plates, one with Mark's chicken pot pie special and the other with a hamburger and fries. "Um, yeah, could you, please?" I ask, giving her my best attempt at a smile, suddenly beyond thankful that she's back to work and here tonight.

The warmth in her eyes changes to something like concern. "You okay?" she asks.

I nod, waving a hand. "Yeah. Just . . ." I have no idea what to say. "Yeah, I'm good."

She stares at me for another beat before grabbing the plates and disappearing through the door. I know she's going to come right back and try to force me to spill, but I still haven't really told anyone about Rhett, and I'm not interested in navigating any half-truths at the moment. Plus, I don't even know for sure that anything's wrong.

So I throw myself into work, determined to distract myself. But over the next three hours, I only grow more and more concerned, compulsively checking my phone whenever I get the chance. By the time the dinner rush is over and Teresa cuts me loose, I'm so tightly wound with anxiety and frustration I can hardly think straight. I have half a mind to head straight for the ranch, to settle the worry in my heart and prove to myself that Rhett's okay. But my car's at home and it's too far to reach on foot. Plus, I don't think I'm comfortable showing up there unannounced—I may have gotten away with it in the name of bravery last week, but this is different.

So I grab my jacket and purse and slip outside, pointing myself in the direction of home. I try calling Rhett as I walk the pathway through the park, eyeing the gazebo with a frown. He doesn't answer, and my stomach clenches uncomfortably as I push myself forward.

I don't hear from him before I finally crawl into bed, and by the time I wake the next morning, there's still no trace of him. It doesn't stop me from looking around my room, the living room —hell, even the kitchen—to see if he might have snuck in to leave some sort of explanation while I slept, a sprig of hope that seems to bloom with the sole purpose of making a giant fool out of me. But there's nothing.

It's like my mind can't justify any of it, because the truth is even if there *was* some emergency he had to take care of, there'd likely been an opportunity by now for him to let me know he's okay. I still don't know what to call whatever this thing between us is, but didn't we *just* agree that, at the very least, we're friends?

I hate to admit it—even to myself—but in the chasm of uncertainty spreading wide within me, Sheriff Joe's words from last night are beginning to take root.

Rhett Bennett isn't interested in settling down or changing his ways, not for any woman.

It's not like I want Rhett to change. I mean, hell, I'm still just getting to know him. But he's let me see parts of him I know no one else does, and that . . . means something to me. It's stirred up an assumption that, despite Rhett's history with women, the way he opens up to me might be different somehow.

Especially not for such a nice girl like you.

Does it make me naive to think I could be actually earning his trust? I know he doesn't owe me anything—not really. It's only been a few weeks of getting to know each other. But dammit if things between us haven't felt inevitable.

My heart beats so fucking fast for you, Olivia, I feel like I'm dying.

I've never felt like Rhett's a liar—at least not with me. Not with the way his words sink into me like sunshine on a cold winter day, warming me from the inside out in a way that feels so right. But I worry that he still might be capable of hurting me, especially with the way I'm beginning to feel about him.

Don't let him fool you, sweetheart.

I swing the door of my fridge closed a little too hard after getting out some orange juice and a June's Café magnet falls to the ground and breaks in two. I eye it warily, wondering if it's a sign. If my heart's about to break just as quickly. Just as plainly.

Rhett might not owe me anything, but I don't like the way this uncertainty makes me feel. As open as he's allowed himself to be, there's still obvious traces of darkness that linger and hold tight to his mind, and I can't let myself get so deep in the trenches of it all that I get hurt in the process.

By the time the sun begins to dip down again to bring in another uncertain evening, I've decided that the next time I see him, I need to lay out some ground rules.

Thankfully, Charlotte comes into the café that evening to visit during my shift. And she's not alone this time: Ivan trails in behind her like a well-trained puppy. She leads him to her usual table, and after dropping off food for Maeve and Gerry—lord knows the gossip ping-ponging between those two—I head over to them.

"If you guys were looking for a romantic date night, I'm not sure my mom's café is the right kind of environment. I'm pretty sure I saw Gerry use his shirt as a napkin over there, and Maeve doesn't seem to understand the concept of covering her mouth when she coughs."

Charlotte rolls her eyes. "Gotta love them."

I smile. "If you insist." I turn to her boyfriend. "Nice to see you, Ivan."

His returning smile is warm and genuine. "Hey, Olivia, good to see you."

"How've you been?"

He shrugs. "Good as can be." I watch him throw a small glance at Charlotte. "I was actually hoping you'd be here. I wanted to apologize for that night at Spurs—Trent was such an asshole, and you didn't deserve it."

I wave it off. "Not a big deal." And I meant it. I'd already forgotten all about it.

"He's sorry too, you know."

"Ivan," Charlotte warns.

I frown at her before I look back at Ivan. "I appreciate it, but you don't have to apologize for him."

Ivan nods. "I agree. He'd actually like the chance to apologize to you himself. And maybe, if you're willing, for a do-over on the whole thing?"

Char lets out a frustrated huff. "Ivan, I said no," she whines.

He looks at her with a mix of guilt and determination. "I know. But it's worth asking!"

"By 'whole thing,'" I interject, "do you mean the double date?"

Ivan's expression turns sheepish. "If you're open to it, yeah. He feels really bad for acting like an idiot, and he knows he messed up." He takes a deep breath. "Look, Trent's not a bad guy. He's one of my best friends, and I promise he doesn't normally act like that. I think he was nervous and pregamed a little too hard . . ."

"Olivia doesn't have time for do-overs," Charlotte states matter-of-factly. "And Trent's not the only interested guy on her roster." She turns to me. "Right, Liv?"

I know she's talking about Rhett. That she wants me to admit I have feelings for him, that something bigger is going on between us. But I'm not going to take the bait.

"I don't know what you're talking about," I say, feigning

confusion. "But there's definitely not a *roster*. Geez, you make me sound way cooler than I am."

Ivan, bless him, laughs at my joke. But Charlotte's face scrunches. "There's not?" she asks.

I shake my head. "Nope."

"What about—"

"Nope," I repeat more firmly.

Her eyes soften, and I'm not sure what conclusions she's coming to, but I'm sure they're close enough: I'm not feeling very secure in anything going on with Rhett. At least not right now, not when everything points to him ghosting me.

"So, you'd be down then?" Ivan asks, hopeful.

Charlotte kicks him under the table.

I laugh. "Can I think about it?"

He shrugs. "Sure."

"Great. Now, what can I get you to drink?"

CHAPTER TWENTY-FIVE

RHETT

$\mathcal{I}$ don't think I've ever seen my family more broken, more crushed than they are right now. With all the shit we've been through during the course of my life, nothing has ripped through us like this—not Dad's drinking, not his accident, and not any of the other stupid bullshit my brothers and I have ever gotten ourselves into.

Brooks is . . . *Shit*. I'm not sure Brooks is going to be able to come back from this. It's like the light inside of his soul has switched off, lost to the darkness of despair that's taken hold of him, and not even the boys are able to find a way through it. I can't imagine what it must feel like to lose so much and still have to navigate raising three children. Thank god for Mom, for Layla and Wells, who all take turns caring for them while Brooks is lost to his devastation.

James doesn't seem to really understand what's happened other than his mommy went to sleep and now lives in heaven. But Liam and Noah better understood how the cancer had wrapped its grotesque arms around her, squeezing her tight with a claim over her life. They saw her fight it, saw her *lose*, and they aren't sure how the hell to process the unfairness of it all. How it's possible they actually lost their mom. They're far too young to be so heartbroken, and with Bennett blood running through their veins, it's anger that they've seemed to turn to.

I come into the main house around lunchtime to find Liam sitting at the kitchen table by himself, glaring at nothing and everything around him. Kasey and Wells are still out with the horses, but I know Layla's around here somewhere, probably busy with James. Brooks retreated to his own cabin yesterday and locked himself inside without a word, and we're all fucking scared of what he might try to do to himself. But we saw Mom march over there this morning, set of spare keys in hand and determination in her gait, and neither of them have appeared again since.

I hope like hell she gets through to him. That he lets *someone* in to help him lay out the next steps of his life.

I grab a loaf of bread and jar of peanut butter from the pantry, bringing them across the kitchen to the open counter. "Hungry, Rooster?" I ask.

Even with my back to him, I feel the way his glare singes. "No."

I nod, pulling a banana from the bunch in the fruit basket. Spreading peanut butter over two pieces of bread, I make quick work of slicing the banana into chunks and adding them to the sandwich, tossing the whole thing on one of the kids' plastic plates with a smiling cartoon puppy and bringing it to the table. I sink into the seat directly across from him and take a big bite.

He eyes the sandwich hungrily—I happen to know it's his favorite, and I'd bet he hasn't had lunch yet. Might be why he's sulking in the kitchen. "I'll give it to you if you tell me why you look like that," I say evenly.

"Like what?" His eyes rise to meet mine.

"Like you want to punch me."

He considers. "Maybe I do."

I nod. "Yeah. I get that. But is it *me*, or is it just your anger talking?"

He frowns. "Both."

I lean back in my chair, spreading my feet out in front of me beneath the table. "Tell you what," I say. "You keep that anger focused on me, okay? When you feel it, I want you to let it out— but not on your brothers, and not with Grandma or Layla. You let it out with me. Deal?"

He looks at me like I've grown a mane and a tail, but I don't blame him. I'm sure the last thing he expected was permission to be an asshole. "I won't get in trouble?" he asks tentatively.

"Fuck no." I shake my head. "Promise."

He looks back at the sandwich, gripping the edge of the table tight in his hands.

And then he shoots out of the chair and hurls himself at me.

As far as I know, Liam's never been in a fight—he's only eleven, and I imagine the bulk of that stupid schoolyard bullshit is still a few years away. But when he pulls his little fist back and swings it at me, I'm surprised with how much power he's able to throw. He lands his punch right in my eye, causing an explosion of pain I wasn't prepared for and a grunt to escape from my throat. But as soon as I open my eyes again to look at him, he's already swinging on me again, this time landing a fucking haymaker to my jaw.

"*Shit*," I mumble, grabbing at my face. I fight the natural instinct to push him away and protect myself, knowing that he needs this. But after a few heartbeats pass, he doesn't make another move.

When I look up at him, he's crying.

"Come here," I murmur, holding my arms open.

He launches into my chest and I wrap my arms tightly around him, letting him cry and cry. I soothe a hand across his back as his shoulders shudder, feeling his tears soak the front of my shirt. "You're going to be okay," I whisper, squeezing my eyes shut. "I promise you, kid. We're all going to be okay. This family *survives*. We always do."

"She didn't!" He slams a fist into my bicep, still clutched tight to my chest.

And dammit if it doesn't almost break me. "I know, Liam. And it's not fair. None of this is fair. It's going to be one of the hardest things you'll ever have to go through, but you *will* get through it. And you'll help your brothers through it too, because you're an amazing kid. But you don't have to do any of it alone, okay?"

He pushes away to look at me, his eyes red-rimmed with the tears still spilling over. He's got his mother's eyes, her sun-streaked hair. But it's Brooks's fire in his heart. "Will my dad get through it?"

My chest squeezes. "Your dad just lost the love of his life. It's going to take him a while . . . but he'll get through it. Your uncles and I will all help him—it's what brothers do."

He nods, wiping his nose on his sleeve. And then he grabs the plate on the table and brings it to the other side where he sits back down and eats.

I stand, rustling my hand through his hair, and head for the door.

We decided to close Wild Coyote for at least the week—none of us have the heart to leave the ranch, especially not to face potential questions from people in town. Melody didn't grow up in Saddlebrook Falls, and I'm not sure if any of them know much about her other than she's Brooks's wife and the mother of his children—that she's a Bennett like the rest of us.

Or *was* . . .

Fuck.

But it's only a matter of time before someone with a connection to the hospital finds out that she's gone. And we sure as shit aren't ready to deal with the way the news of her death will undoubtedly spread through town like wildfire.

Still, closing down the bar is going to hurt financially, and we're already hurting pretty damn bad. I've never cared enough about the business side of things to have a good grasp on the books, but Kasey says money's tighter than he's ever seen it, and I know that's saying something. Now we have a funeral to plan on top of all the medical bills, and we still need to find a lawyer who can help us navigate Huck's potential threat to the ranch—a threat that's more prominent now that Brooks might've lost his legal claim, his *birthright*, to the land.

It feels like a stone's lodged itself in my throat when I think of the call I made two nights ago, after Melody died. When I think of what I have to do tomorrow, the risks I have to take.

But even worse is what I have to do tonight.

GUILT RIPS THROUGH ME WHEN I FINALLY TEXT OLIVIA and ask if I can see her. There are at least half a dozen messages she's sent that have gone unanswered over the last couple of days, and based on that and the calls I've avoided, I know she's worried. And I know I'm the worst kind of asshole for staying quiet.

But the truth is, my need for Olivia has become a sentient, all-consuming beast that I'm not sure will ever be sated. The more I've given into the temptation to push things further with her, the more this need pounds through me and rattles my very bones. Despite everything going on around me, my mind finds solace in thoughts of her. I lie awake at night and think of nothing but her skin, so soft and warm and opposite of everything I am. I think of her eyes, the depths of green and gold that I could get lost in for eternity, an endless pasture of my deepest desires.

I know with my whole stupid heart that I don't deserve her, that just like everything else in my life, this will end in a monumental catastrophe. Especially now, when I have nothing to give her and no room for distractions. But *fuck*—I haven't had it in me to soften the blow. I haven't had the capacity to pull away from her because she's . . . she's so damn sweet and addicting.

But I have to. I care about her more than I thought I even could, which means I need to cut her loose.

I'm sorry for disappearing the other night, I type into my phone as I walk toward my cabin, fingers shaking with the weight of what's coming. *We need to talk. Can I see you tonight?*

Her response comes in mere seconds. *I'm off around seven.*

I'll pick you up then.

My thoughts begin to spiral as I think of Brooks and everything he's experiencing. I think of myself in his shoes, what it would be like to watch Olivia slowly wither away into nothing, whether from something like cancer or from the inevitable chaos of being with someone like me.

I think of what it's going to feel like to lose her—to lose her so I can save her.

I pull my bike into the café's lot right at seven, my mind tumbling when I see her already waiting on the curb. She's wearing a green cotton dress beneath a brown jacket, her strawberry hair spread around her shoulders. And if looks could kill, I'd be a dead man.

I hold the second helmet out for her and she takes it, slipping it over her head and buckling the straps herself before she climbs onto the back of the bike. She doesn't hold me as tightly around the middle, doesn't laugh with the rush of the speed on the highway, and I realize my silence since leaving her the other night has done more damage than I'd anticipated.

Good, I think. This will be easier if she's mad at me. And lord knows I deserve it.

I take her to the water tower, where we'd traded secrets over burgers not too long ago. It's probably too cold to climb up there this late, but it's quiet amongst the trees and far enough away from everything that I know we'll have privacy. I can't bring her to the ranch right now, and I sure as hell don't want to hurt her in her own house.

I park along the fence line and cut the engine. Olivia is quick to jump off the bike, strutting away from me as she works to wrangle her helmet off. I pull mine off and set it on the tank before standing to wait for her.

Once her helmet's off, she whirls back around. "You fucking disappeared," she says.

Oh yeah, she's mad.

"Melody died," I say quietly.

I watch her face change, those hard lines of anger softening into something more like concern. "Oh my god," she says, clutching a hand to her chest. "I . . . I wondered if it might have something to do with her, but I didn't . . . I'm so sorry."

"We knew it was coming," I say. "The doctor all but said it a week ago. But we had no idea it would be so fast." My gaze drops to the ground. "She'd had a really great day too. I think we were all carrying a little hope that things were turning around."

Her eyes close as she lets out a breath. "I'm so sorry, Rhett," she says again.

I move toward her, reaching to press my palm into her cheek. "You have nothing to be sorry for."

"I thought you were ghosting me," she admits. "I thought—I thought everyone was right."

The words are like a shot to the heart.

"I should have known," she adds. "God, I feel like such an idiot—"

"No," I interject. "Don't you dare. You have every right to question things that don't sit right, Olivia. Trusting yourself and your instincts is important in all this. And you were right to question me."

She frowns, and the sight of it guts me. "Did someone hit you?"

"My nephew—Liam. He's . . . no one is taking it well."

She's looking at me like I'm a wounded bird. Like she wants to care for me, and . . . *Dammit.* I need to do it right fucking now. I need to tell her this is over.

"Olivia," I say. But then she's hugging me, her arms wrapped tightly around me as her face presses into my neck.

She hugs me, and it feels like home.

I nearly buckle at the knees as I fumble to get my own arms around her.

"Where are you right now?" she asks, her mouth a hot jolt of lightning against my collar.

"Nowhere good," I concede, squeezing my eyes shut against the anxiety barreling through me. The pain of losing her is already so potent, and it hasn't even started yet.

But it will, because nothing good ever lasts. Whether I take control of it now or it takes control of me later, I *will* lose this.

I feel her still, the loss of her mouth against my skin enough to make me wince. But then she presses a soft kiss to my throat and I can't help but lean into it, lifting my chin to give her more. "What can I do?" she asks, voice gentle and brave. So fucking brave.

I almost cry out in panicked frustration, realizing my hands are shaking as I lift them to pull her in close. I'm supposed to be ending this, telling her all the reasons I'm no good for her—especially with all that I'm about to do—but my hands have a mind of their own. "I need to quiet the noise," I breathe out through clenched teeth. Even as I work to chase away the damning thoughts, I can't catch a breath.

I need you.

"You have me," she insists. I must have said it out loud. It would be embarrassing if I wasn't already coming apart at the seams. Small, delicate hands slide up my jaw and I open my eyes to find her watching, her focus sharp and intent, studying me for the cracks that she can no doubt slip herself through. My beautiful, brave girl, ready to face my demons with me. "I'm right here, Rhett. You already have me. Do you feel this?" She presses my hand to her chest, to her beating heart. "I'm right here, baby."

I take in the warmth of her sure eyes, the confidence in her hands as she holds me together, and finally suck down enough air to fill the lungs in my too-tight chest. I focus on the feel of her body against mine, on the cotton neckline of her dress, and let myself tip over the edge into the chaos.

I want her so bad it hurts.

"Tell me to stop," I force out, trying to give her a chance to stop this now while I still have some semblance of control. I'm not sure what's coming, but if the roaring beast inside of me is any indication, I'm about to lose it.

"No," she says. Simple and clear. Her eyes flash with stubborn anticipation, and if I wasn't currently spiraling, I'd reward her for it.

I stand, hooking my hands around the backs of her thighs as I rise to lift her with me. She gasps in surprise, but her legs wrap around my waist on instinct, and I turn to lay her down the length of my bike. "No pretending this time, peaches," I say, voice raw and breaking with all the ways I'm still failing her. "Right now, I just need you to be mine."

I don't give her a chance to respond before my hands are under her dress, pulling the fabric up tight around her waist. She's wearing a lacy black thong that looks tempting as hell, but I hold strong to a desperate ache to taste her and instead rip the fabric right off of her body.

She moans, but I don't let myself enjoy the sound. This isn't about her or her pleasure, it's about me chasing away the monsters in the shadows of my mind that are threatening to take over. I hate myself for using her like this, for wrapping her so deep in my shit that she's bound to it now. Where there's light, there's Olivia. But where there's pain, she'll be there now too. And it's all my doing.

Dropping to my knees, I let my gaze bounce to her face for one fleeting moment of reprieve, finding her watching me with so much worry marring her beautiful face. Her concern is obvious, even as she shivers from the mix of cold air and the desire slicking her inner thighs.

I'm right here, baby.

I'm so sorry, I think. Hoping she knows it's the truth. That I'm so fucking sorry for ever thinking I could bring her into my life without hurting her.

I rip my gaze away and focus between her legs, letting my torment swallow me whole.

And then I give in.

CHAPTER TWENTY-SIX

OLIVIA

Fear lances through me as Rhett's tongue splits me apart. I cry out from the sensation, writhing on the seat of his bike from the white-hot pleasure of it, but two callused hands rise to pin my hips down, locking me in place. Something's wrong—very wrong. And I think it's more than just Melody . . . but I have absolutely no idea what.

Another torturous lick along my center almost rockets me to the moon, but I force myself to stay grounded, to take in any piece of evidence that might point to Rhett's undoing. Something's happened, something that's cracking him down the middle, and I think it's more than just Melody. He's reckless when his family's in trouble, and if I don't figure it out and show him another way through, I have a terrible feeling I might lose him forever.

As glorious as his mouth on me feels right now, I'm acutely aware of the fact that this isn't about me at all. This isn't one of Rhett's coy and careful lessons. This feels more like a punishment, like he's punishing himself, and it's just more proof he's done something to hurt himself . . .

He moves one hand across my belly so his forearm presses against the bones of my hips, keeping me in place as his mouth lifts from me. With his newly freed hand, he drags the pads of his fingers down the inside of my thigh, eyes locked on where they glide along my skin. He looks back to where his mouth just was, where I'm needy and cold without him. His mouth twists as he seems to suck in through his teeth behind closed lips, and then opens them to spit on me.

The warmth of his saliva lands where his mouth was just deliciously edging me higher, and I watch in fascination as he lifts those devious fingers to swirl himself around me before abruptly plunging two deep inside.

I cry out from the shock of it, my back arching off the leather seat, pushing against the heavy arm that still holds me down. He wastes no time, pistoning his fingers in a brutal assault that forces my eyes closed, overstimulated in the best way, unable to focus on anything but taking what he's giving me. His mouth finds its rightful place where I need him most, and it takes less than a handful of heartbeats before he's hurling me over the edge, nose-diving into ecstasy as I scream his name into the pines around us, mind spinning from the plunge.

Still, he doesn't stop. Pleasure wrecks through me until I'm boneless and hollow and made of only him and this, of the intense need to be what he craves when he's falling apart. When it's clear he's siphoned every ounce of my undoing, I feel the loss of his mouth and fingers as he rises to his feet, eyes roaming over me with a predatorial hunger like I've never seen before.

His hands bracket around my waist, sliding me off the side of the bike and holding my weight until my feet reach the ground. His eyes fasten to mine for a long second that stretches around us, flaring with the war waging in his heart. I know he won't tell me what's going on, that this is his only way of communicating his pain. Still, the resolve to show him that he's not alone is closing in.

He moves to spin me around until my back is to his chest, and shivers scatter down my neck as his lips trace along the shell of my ear. "I've got you," he whispers, a clear sign the Rhett I know and have come to deeply care for is still in there, even as he grips me hard enough to leave bruises.

"I know," I say back. Because I do. No matter what, I know without a single doubt that he's not going to hurt me. He won't let me fall.

One of his hands lifts to apply pressure between my shoulder blades, bending me down over the bike. I hear the rustle of his clothes before his legs press against mine, where I'm still bared to him and the night, and feel him nudge against me. Anticipation rushes through me like a blast of light just as he pushes in.

It's fast and hard and not exactly careful, but I can tell he's holding back.

The groan he lets out is deep and wide open. There's an edge to it, a relief. An exhale. And then he's moving, hands squeezing against my hips as his work against me.

"I can take it, Rhett," I say over my shoulder. His eyes meet mine, steely and focused and still full of so much pain. He looks so tired. "Let me take it."

He grunts in response, eyes flaring. And then he moves faster. Harder. The slap of our skin echoes the beat of my heart, ratcheting higher and higher as he chases the darkness away. It's not long until he's losing his rhythm, becoming more and more frantic. He feels like sin, unmoored and alive with need. It's carnal, wild, and yet I know from the way his thumb rocks back and forth against my back that he's still tethered to me, still holding me through this just like he's always done.

That alone is almost enough to make me come again, but I'm too anchored to his well-being to allow myself to tumble back over the edge. Still, a band of desire pulls taut within me, and despite Rhett's roughness and my worry, I'm climbing higher and higher with him until his thrusts stutter.

"*Christ*," he grunts, pulling out of me, and I feel his release paint my skin as he heaves in heavy breaths. "Fuck," he says, lower this time, his forehead pressing lightly against the back of my dress where it's still wrapped around my chest.

I don't say a word as he moves to pull his pants up around his waist, buckling himself in. "Don't move," he says quietly. He takes off his jacket, then pulls his T-shirt over his head and uses it to wipe away the evidence of what he's just done. What *we've* just done. He gently tugs my skirt back down, smoothing the fabric over my hips as I turn to face him.

His skin is pale in the moonlight, a stark contrast to his dark hair and clothes. I watch as he stuffs one end of the balled-up shirt into his back pocket before tugging his jacket back over his shoulders, his muscles flexing and gliding as he moves. The confidence he wears so easily is nowhere to be found, and his eyes look haunted.

"What did you do?" I rasp, nerves spiking.

The question surprises him. "What are you talking about?"

"You're punishing yourself. You're . . . you're *spiraling*, Rhett. This isn't just about Melody dying. You've done something." I narrow my eyes, scrutinizing the rise of his chest and clench of his jaw. "You've done something to try to save everyone, just tell me what it is."

His eyes harden, and it's all the confirmation I need. "There's a threat to the ranch," he replies coolly, and his words from our phone conversation force their way back in.

Someone might be trying to take the ranch from us.

"Can it happen?" I ask. "Can someone really take it from you?"

He shakes his head as he shrugs, and I've never seen him look so defeated. "It's complicated. The land technically needs to be inherited, and there are stipulations we can no longer meet. My uncle somehow knows that, and he wants it all for himself."

"Wh-what would that mean?"

Rhett's pale eyes grow distant, and I wrap my arms around myself. "Doesn't matter. It's not gonna happen."

"How?" I brave the question.

"We need . . . money. For a good lawyer, for a goddamn funeral . . ." The look he gives me is full of so many emotions I almost can't pick them apart. But it's the apology that scares me most. "There are ways I can get it."

"Rhett," I whisper.

"I will always protect my family, Olivia. No matter the cost."

"But who's protecting *you*?" My eyes burn with tears. "Why don't you ask for help?"

"Who's going to fucking help us?"

"*Me*!" I say louder, chest heaving as my own emotion tears through me. "*I* will help you!"

He frowns. "I would never ask you to do that."

"Why not? You can *trust* me."

"It's not about trusting you, peaches," he bites out. "It's about protecting you."

"I don't need protection!" I shout.

"Yes you do!" he shouts back, and I almost stumble backward from the force of it. "You have no business being in the middle of shit that can hurt you, Olivia. *I* will hurt you, it's only a matter of time."

"You wouldn't hurt me, Rhett."

He scoffs, head tipping to the sky, and it slices into me like a knife. "Of course I would!" When his eyes settle back on me, they're near-pleading. "Haven't I already, Olivia? You were madder than hell when I picked you up tonight."

"Because you just *disappeared*!" I cried out. "One second you were there and everything was . . . good between us. And then you were gone, and I couldn't reach you, and—"

"And you thought everyone was right," he says through clenched teeth. "Isn't that what you said? I ghosted you, and you thought everyone was right."

There's real hurt in his eyes, and I hate myself for it. "I'm so sorry," I whisper. "I should have known—"

But he shakes his head. "No. The thing is, you *were* right. I ghosted you because we can't keep doing this. Not when I can't be who you need me to be." He shifts on his feet, like he hates the words as much as I do, and I want to scream for him to stop saying them. "It was supposed to just be practice for you anyway. I'm not ready for something like this. I'm . . . I'm not the guy for this."

"Practice," I repeat. The word tastes like ash on my tongue. "Practice for what? *Other* people? Is that what you want, Rhett? You want me to date other people?"

His jaw tightens. "I want you to be happy," he says simply. "I want you to be brave. And I want you far away from me."

A tear spills over and glides down my cheek, and I watch him track it, his frown deepening. "I don't believe you. *You* make me happy," I tell him, because it's the truth. "*You* make me brave, Rhett. Why don't you try it? Be brave with me. Let me in so I can help you."

He lets out a frustrated breath. "No. I will *not* pull you into my shit, peaches. I'm sorry, but I won't do it." And I know by the tone of his voice that he means it. He isn't going to budge on this.

My shoulders slump as the reality of his words sink in. The damn irony of it—for all he's done to help me build confidence and belief in myself, Rhett was the one who needed it more. It's . . . *maddening* to think I might have missed an opportunity to prove him wrong about himself.

I want to remind him of all the ways he's shown me the kind of care and attention that's done anything but harm me, want to shove it all in his stupid self-deprecating face. I hate to think of how alone he must feel, the pressure he's put on himself to throw himself in danger for the greater good of others. That he thinks he might deserve it. I want him to see what I do when I look at him: his strength and intelligence and how *tender* he can be, how raw and wide open. His ability to protect is powerful, but not if he loses himself in the process. What kind of a life is that?

But I know I can't win this argument—not now. Rhett Bennett will keep fighting fire with fire, as he's been made to do. To prove he's capable of anything else means playing a long game. He's not going to trust it until I force his hand.

"Take me home," I demand, ripping my gaze from him. I refuse to let myself find his eyes again, to let him see me break.

"Olivia," he breathes. His voice cracks with emotion and I have to dig half-moons into my palms to keep from breaking with him.

But I find the strength to shake my head and move toward the bike. "No, Rhett. *Stop.*"

And I don't have to look at him to know exactly the way it lands, that safe word he's always made sure I know I can grasp hold of.

I pull the helmet over my head and wait for him to do the same. He moves painfully slow, like he knows this is all wrong, but he doesn't say a word as he gets on the bike. It roars to life beneath him before I get on and he slowly points us home.

The engine rumbles through the soles of my sneakers as he opens the throttle down the long empty road, sending shockwaves of heady awareness up the length of my legs and thighs as I keep a careful but distant arm around him. I'm thankful for the helmet as it hides the tears that freely stream down my face, and I wonder if this might be the last ride he gives me.

CHAPTER TWENTY-SEVEN

RHETT

I steer my motorcycle down the worn and beaten drive that leads through Rustler Ranch, white-knuckling the handlebars as I try to avoid fishtailing along the soft gravel. I wore my dark-visored helmet tonight even though it makes it hard to see the ground in front of me—it'll give me the chance to take in the scene when I pull up to the game before anyone spots me.

The old cattle barn appears in the distance, the silhouette of the steep slope of the roof cutting through the warm colors of the dusky sky. The building looks even worser for wear than the last time I was here. The Rustlers built a handful of new cattle barns decades ago, and instead of tearing this old one down, they use it as headquarters for their side-hustle.

My phone buzzes against my ribs from the inside pocket of my jacket, but I ignore it for now as I canvas the half-dozen cars already parked in front of the game barn. There's a white sedan and a gray SUV I don't recognize and an old silver truck and a newer black one that I do, but it's the classic orange coupe that catches my attention. I'd know that fucking car anywhere, unmistakable with the parallel black racing stripes that span from hood to rear.

Mean-Eyed Maverick.

My stomach rolls at the thought of Ellis allowing that hellion back into a game after what happened last time, when his fucking brother was stabbed at the table. For Christ's sake—I'm shocked Colt would allow it after it took over a month before the hospital would even release him back home.

Fucking Rustlers.

Batshit crazy family with no regard for their own mortality. For as much trouble as my family has gotten into over the years, we don't hold a candle to the shit these boys are involved in.

I ease my bike to a stop at the far edge of the narrow dirt lot and push down the kickstand with my boot. Yanking a glove off with my teeth, I reach into my jacket pocket to pull out my phone. When I see Olivia's name across the screen, everything we said to each other last night comes racing back.

Fuck.

A volatile mix of panic and guilt slices through me as I fumble and almost drop my phone. I'm met with the sudden desire to turn this bike around and drive straight to her, leaving this stupid game in the dust where it belongs. The truth is, even though I gave my word to Colt, even though I need this money if we have a real shot at keeping the ranch, walking through those barn doors is the last thing I want to do. I've never cared a whole lot about myself or the trouble I get into, but something's been shifting inside of me, something tired and aching for respite.

I look toward the horizon, to the setting sun and the burst of colors it's leaving behind. My guilt turns sour, like acid. I told Olivia I'd be there for her, a soft space for her to land, and I've fucked it all up. Serves us both right I guess, for ever believing I could handle something as important as her.

Shoving the phone in my pocket, I stand from the bike and pull off my helmet before marching toward the barn, an uncomfortable fire igniting in my veins. It's a familiar call of the wild, a temptation to tear everything around me to the fucking ground.

The pang of knowing I'm letting everyone down—letting *Olivia* down—settles in my stomach, because there's a very real possibility that this goes sideways.

Good, I think.

Maybe she'll finally understand why I'm no good for her.

The thought chafes. Before I know it, I'm turning on my heel and hustling back toward my bike, fishing my phone back out of my goddamn jacket.

She answers on the first ring. "Rhett," she says, her voice warm but tentative, like the first morning of spring. "I'm sorry I called . . . I just—I hate how things went last night, and I was hoping we could try again."

This girl . . . this perfect girl. Still not giving up.

My response is shaky as I admit, "It's not a good time, peaches."

"Oh," she says. The disappointment in her tone is as obvious as my goddamn irritation about what I'm doing. "Are you okay?" There's a trace of fear in the question, and I hate the sound of it.

I lean on the seat of my bike, squeezing my eyes shut. "Yeah, um . . . something came up with a friend of mine," I force out through gritted teeth. I told her I would take care of my family as best as I knew how, but that doesn't mean I'm going to risk sharing details that could implicate her. "But I'm good."

Stop, she'd said last night—and I honestly thought I'd lost her for good, right there on that gravel road. Even though ending things was the whole point, my traitorous heart wanted to walk it all back the second I heard that word leave her lips.

That she's even calling now—it makes me feel like even more of an asshole. I'd meant everything I said, that I can't be what she needs, but I'm not sure I actually have the heart to let her go.

I hear her sigh. "Look, you don't have to tell me what you're doing. Just tell me that you're safe."

"I'm good," I repeat low into the phone as another car I don't recognize makes its way up the drive.

"Come over when you're done," she says in a rush. "I'll leave a key under the mat."

"No, don't leave a key out." The car in front of me parks and two men get out. They both throw uneasy glances my way. "Anyone with bad intentions would look there first. I don't need a key to get in."

"So you'll come?" she asks, and the hope in her voice lights me up.

"It'll be late," I say. "You'll probably be asleep."

"I don't care," she insists. "I just . . . I need to feel you. I need to know you're safe."

"Okay." I nod, looking down at my feet.

It takes her a beat, and when she says a quick "Okay" back, I hear the worry seeping through. "Be safe, please?"

"I will. Promise." I hang up the phone before she can respond and take in a deep, shaky breath. Every ounce of will inside of me is begging to bail on this. To run back home to her.

Home.

"Rhett!" Colt calls from behind me, snapping through the haze of my internal undoing. I turn to find him standing at the entrance to the barn, his face cast in shadow as a dull, yellow light spills out into the dirt around him, illuminating his edges.

I hold a hand up. "Coming," I shout before fiddling with the helmet that rests on the bike's seat, pretending like I'm not having a fucking moment. Tucking my phone away again, I force my way back toward the barn where Colt waits for me. Unlike the last time I saw him at Spurs, he wears a guarded and wary expression that tells me he's not looking forward to this either. "You good?" I ask quietly as soon as I reach him.

He nods his head once, quick and clipped. "Glad you're here. Ellis bit off more than he can chew."

I scoff, annoyed that the eldest Rustler brother would be so reckless. We've all had our fair share of debauchery, but inviting Mean-Eyed Maverick was a fucking dangerous and stupid move. I dip my head toward his car. "Did you know he was going to be here?"

"Nope. I knew there'd be other big players, people we don't know well. But I had no idea *he'd* be here."

"What the hell is Ellis thinking?"

Colt frowns as one of his hands lifts to press against his ribs, as if he can still feel the wound from Maverick's knife where it pressed into him three years ago. "I don't know," he says, his worry evident. "Someone must have him by the balls if he's this desperate for cash."

I don't want to tell Colt it's my own desperation for cash that got me here. A half-million dollar bet puts over a million in the pot, and that kind of money would be life-changing in a way my family really needs right now, even with the unspoken rule between all Rustlers and Bennetts in play: any of us wins the pot, we split it evenly amongst ourselves. It gives us a greater chance at winning when Ellis isn't counting cards. "Yeah, well, if Maverick sniffs out any funny business in those cards tonight, he's going to flay us all wide open."

Colt's eyes snap to mine with a rush of fear that I feel in my own throat. "Thanks for coming."

The words snare and tangle in my stomach. It's never done well to have anyone relying on me, especially with something this serious. But I guess if there's anything to rely on me *for*, it's answering assholes with violence. "Yeah," I mutter. "Like I said on the phone, I can't match the bet." I took what I was able to from the bar's safe, but it's only about eight grand.

Colt looks nervous. "Ellis put aside a few stacks for you, but I'm pretty sure he padded them. Just—be careful betting too high if you don't have a hand. If you have something good, make sure I know so I can bow out and feed you more under the table."

I shake my head—it doesn't take a genius to know fucking around with counterfeit money on a night like tonight is bad news. All of this could go downhill so fast.

Colt throws me a look like he's sorry, and then turns to walk back into the dimly lit barn. I trail behind him, eyes tracing along the empty and forgotten horse stalls that flank either side of us, wondering who might be crouched and hiding within. My mind plays out visions of Maverick's posse jumping out with shiny blades and brass knuckles—their favorite toys to play with—and I scrub a hand down my face.

I force my gaze forward, to a large round table set beneath the single bald light hanging from the rafters, where Ellis sits surrounded by gruff men and . . . "What the fuck is Wylie doing here?" I ask Colt under my breath.

He's already ramrod straight next to me, cursing under his breath.

Wylie, the second youngest Rustler child, is by far the wildest, even wilder than Ellis. At only twenty-three years old, she's already hurled herself so far through her own sordid life experiences that she came out the other side with a permanent scowl on her face and a baby on her hip. Tonight, her blonde hair burns golden beneath the yellow light, spilling around bare shoulders. Her black tank top molds to her body like a second skin, just like the blue jeans she wears.

I'm not surprised that, even in the middle of a biting Texas winter, she's dressed to show herself off. Once, two years ago, I almost made the mistake of letting her into my bed after she'd used her weapons of those curves, a sultry-sweet smile, and captivating banter to unravel the awareness that she was my *very* off-limits best friend's sister. We'd gotten as far as the hallway to the stairwell of the apartment that sits above Wild Coyote before she was already shucking off her shirt and the reality of what we were about to do hit me like a horseshoe to the face. I was able to come to my senses in time to expertly pull her shirt back over her head and gently shove her out the bar's door back downstairs—thank god.

To this day, I'm not sure what her motive was in sleeping with me. But if one thing's for certain about Wylie, she *always* has a motive.

I still don't know if she ever told anyone about it. Doubtful, since her brothers would wring her neck just as hard as they'd wring mine. But it doesn't make me any less nervous to see her, and not because I'm scared of her. The Rustlers are the closest thing the Bennetts have to friends, and I don't want our little almost-mishap to be what throws a wrench in that decades-long alliance.

Ellis watches Wylie like an overprotective hawk as she takes an open seat next to him.

"Oh my . . . Looky here," Maverick says from where he sits between two of his fiercest cronies, eyeing Colt and me like we could be lunch. He wears a ratty denim jacket over a dark shirt, strands of greasy hair falling into his coal-like eyes. A thick, pale scar cuts across one eye from forehead to cheek—it's a wonder he didn't lose the eye itself. "Two of my favorite little rascals."

Colt's back is so full of tension it might snap, but he still finds a way to stiffen further. "Maverick," he says coolly.

The old criminal smiles, crooked and mean. "Good to see you again, young Colt."

Colt's eyes narrow. At nearly thirty, he's hardly the scrawny teenager he once was, but instead of taking Maverick's bait, his eyes move to his sister. "What's she doing here, Ellis?"

Ellis scoffs, clearly annoyed about something as he keeps his eyes trained on her. "Dealing."

Wylie makes a show of rolling her eyes. "So much hostility with you boys, I swear. Good thing I'm here to show our friends some southern hospitality."

"These aren't friends, Wylie Jo," Colt chides through clenched teeth.

"Then why are they on our property, Colt?" Wylie's eyes move to me, and she has the audacity to wink.

Ellis catches the movement and angles a deep frown in my direction.

Jesus.

Maverick chimes in from his seat with a smile. "I heard you're a mommy now, Wylie. My sincerest congratulations."

Colt flinches. That Maverick is keeping up on the Rustler family is . . . not good. I press a hand to his shoulder and hope to god he doesn't do something stupid.

"Don't talk to my sister," Ellis bites out.

"Quit bossin' people around," Wylie mutters.

Ellis whips his head toward her. "Remember the rules, Wylie."

Her face falls for a moment before she regains her mask of indifference. "Yes, boss," she says with a mocking salute before picking up the deck of cards and shuffling.

Ellis pins his focus on us. "Sit down and shut up. We don't have all night for this shit."

OVER THE LAST TWO DECADES, RUSTLER RANCH HAS become a tourist attraction, a destination for families who come from all over the country seeking to experience a wild and western way of life. It was Colt and Ellis's grandfather who'd first decided to split their land in half, designating one side to their own cowboying and cattle and the other to hosting a guest ranch open to the public. It became an opportunity for outsiders to immerse themselves in the beauty of this land while also enjoying accommodations like meal services, daily wagon rides, and horseback riding excursions through the many trails that snake along the rolling hills around them.

As one of the largest cattle ranches in East Texas and its relative proximity to the Gulf Coast, the land is beautiful in pictures and sells itself on the internet without much effort by the family.

Our land in Saddlebrook Falls is big, stretching out in all directions for miles and miles. But the Rustlers own at least double what we have, and the effort to maintain it all is that much greater.

While I'm sure it's gotta be hard to host complete strangers on their property, those guests provide a level of financial stability as the family's cattle business goes through its natural ebbs and flows. But somewhere along the way, the Rustlers found another new way to make things even more lucrative: sniffing out the type of guests who might like to participate in their underground, *unregulated* card games. Through cards—and Ellis's expert sleight of hand—they've made a killing hustling even more money out of folks who are none the wiser.

Still, cheating cards with unwitting tourists is a lot different than at a table with real criminals who will stab first and ask questions later, and though I used to worry Ellis might be dumb enough to try, he's always kept high-stakes games like this honest. With Wylie dealing, it's even more assurance of a straight game—though, with the way she handles the cards, I'd bet she's been practicing some of Ellis's tricks.

On nights like tonight, it's more a game of chance and numbers: the more Bennetts and Rustlers at the table, the higher probability one of us will win to split the profits. Like always, we play two games with restricted bets to knock some of the dust off and get everyone's blood pumping. For a while, everyone's quiet, focused on the cards in hand against the cards on the table. Even Wylie keeps her lips closed as she deals each round. But it doesn't take long for Maverick to reveal he's the same cocky son-of-a-bitch he's always been, eager to slap his dick down on the table and show Ellis's new friends from Cheyenne that he'll win in the first game.

"Straight," he says proudly, laying his cards down. It's not a great hand, but it beats the rest of us who only have pairs and a three-of-a-kind.

I watch the two new cowboys carefully as Maverick greedily pulls his winnings from the table toward himself, trying to figure out how a pair of old boys like them could be strapped with so much cash. They're dressed in basic work clothes, their boots solid but nothing fancy. I can tell from their calloused hands and sun-wrinkled skin they know a hard day's work. They must have an illegal hustle of their own at home . . . or they're making a fucking killing in cowboying, which is hard to do. It amazes me more that Ellis would be willing to risk so much of his family's money to match their bet.

I wonder if his father knows how crooked his son is getting with the family business.

I can't tell for sure if Maverick knows the amount of cash up for grabs tonight. How a mean fucker like him could possibly have that kind of money on hand in the first place. Unlike the Cheyenne cowboys, Maverick hasn't worked an honest day in his life and instead makes his bread clawing and stealing from those around him. He might've won the first game tonight, but Colt takes the second, a flair of retaliatory determination set in his eyes as he watches Maverick fold his hand.

It's enough to set Maverick on defense, watching Wylie's hands carefully as she shuffles the deck for the third and final game—the one that matters most, the real reason we're all here tonight. I shoot Colt a warning look to settle his ass down.

"Ready, boys?" Ellis asks, monitoring Wylie as she deals us all two cards before laying the flop down on the table. There's an uncomfortable tension in the air that I once reveled in, once felt most powerful in, but that now just feels wrong. Looking at my cards, I spot a pair of sevens, and hope sparks. Colt makes the first bet, dropping a stack of cash he pulls from a backpack at his feet on the center of the table with a smug grin. "Ten grand."

All eyes shift to me. I work to keep my expression neutral as I count out a matching bet and set it down next to Colt's.

Both of the Cheyenne cowboys to my left do the same, as does

Maverick's first lieutenant. When it's Maverick's play, he makes a show of examining his cards against the cards on the table before he, too, matches the bet with a knowing smirk that I know is meant to intimidate. The bullish man next to him follows suit, and then Ellis does the same.

When Wylie flips a fourth card down on the table next to the first three, that earlier hope expands. It's an eight—and I have one in my hand.

I've got two pairs. It's a decent hand . . . Not nearly enough to win the game, but there's still one more card left.

Colt tenses next to me, and at first I can't tell if it's good or bad. He takes a long look at his cards. At the cards on the table. And then at Mean-Eyed Maverick, who gives him a hateful smile.

And then he folds, kicking the bag of money at his feet toward me.

It's the permission I need to make a bold move. I set my cards down and reach into the backpack, pulling out enough cash to make anyone at this table without a decent hand squeamish. "Two fifty," I say, stacking two hundred and fifty thousand dollars on top of what's already on the table.

The cowboys next to me give nothing away, but I don't miss the way Maverick's eyes widen in surprise. Which means . . . *fucking hell*. Ellis didn't tell him how big the stakes are tonight.

I look at Ellis and find him watching Maverick with a cold glare. And that's when I realize—he's setting him up. Ellis is forcing Maverick into a corner with no choice but to fold, to make him feel inferior in front of everyone else here.

It takes everything in me to keep a mask of indifference on my own face as the weight of this knowledge sinks in. If Maverick and his men have to fold, this game turns into one between Ellis, me, and the cowboys—both of whom, I note, drop enough cash on the table to match my bet.

Maverick's first sidekick immediately folds, tossing his cards on the table in defeat. Maverick glares at him, and then at me.

And then at Ellis. I'm smart enough to know that look means trouble. Colt must sense it too because he shifts in his seat, and I see the way his hand carefully slides into his pocket.

Turning my gaze back to Maverick, I watch him throw an expectant look to his second man who grumbles before sliding his bank of cash toward his boss, folding his own hand regardless of what he might have had. Maverick counts the money alongside everything else he's brought and what he's already won, and by the skin of his teeth, he has enough to make the bet. "Two fifty," he says, dropping the cash on the table, the malice in his tone cold and biting.

Ellis nods. "Two fifty," he repeats, adding his own cash.

Wylie eyes the money with a palpable hunger, and I don't blame her—there's well over a million dollars on the table. But she needs to keep herself in check in a room full of vipers—these boys will bite.

"Wylie," Ellis chides with a low grunt.

She blinks, looking at her brother before smiling at the rest of us. And then she lays down the river.

It's another fucking eight.

I have a full house.

Adrenaline prickles along my temples and the back of my neck, but I keep my face unreadable. It's a good hand—it still might not be strong enough to win the round, but it's enough to stay in the game. I look around at the others to see how they might be faring: the cowboys give nothing away, but Maverick can't contain his growing temper. I turn my focus to Ellis and find him already looking at me, a glint in his eye that I know all too well.

I watch as he turns to scan the table, his shoulders relaxed and expression easy in a way I've seen from him countless times. Like he already knows he has the whole table beat.

And it dawns on me.

He's actually rigged this game.

CHAPTER TWENTY-EIGHT

OLIVIA

I can hardly see through the dust that's kicking up in front of me as I follow a random blue truck down the worn dirt road toward Wild Coyote. It's a section of town blanketed by heavy darkness, no streetlights or other buildings to indicate a bar would be found back here. You'd have to know where it is to find it, but everyone from Saddlebrook Falls knows where to find it—it's been here for generations.

Gravel crunches beneath my tires, the sound an echo of what my heart is doing in my chest as I wrestle through all the anxiety rocketing through me. Rhett said he'd be late tonight, and I swear I tried to keep it together and just wait for him at home. But I could hear it in his voice—the fear and uncertainty—and I couldn't just sit idly by knowing something bad could be happening to him. He might hate me later for meddling in what he clearly wants to keep me away from, but as long as he's here to hate me, it'll be worth it.

I can't explain the feeling in my gut, the instinct that he's in trouble. I hadn't even meant to call him so soon—not after last night and all the things we hurled at each other. I'd planned to make him wait a few days before starting a conversation again, just like he'd made me wait after disappearing from the diner. But I'd been a fool to think I could hold out—not when I know how alone he is with all that pressure and pain. Not when my stomach is roiling with the worry of all the desperate ways he could be trying to make quick money for his family.

His voice all but confirmed he's already in the thick of something dangerous. Whatever it is, I hadn't expected it to come so soon. I thought I'd have more time to convince him he didn't have to face it alone.

I hated thinking I might be too late.

The truck in front of me makes a slow right turn into a near-empty lot in front of the quiet, unlit bar. There are no lights in the parking lot and no windows in the building that would allow for inside light to creep out. But there's a neon sign on the roof— the words WILD COYOTE beneath the outline of the howling animal—that's also dark.

Something isn't right.

I spot two old men sitting on the front sidewalk. One of them drinks something wrapped in a brown paper sack while the other watches me through my windshield with curiosity. The truck I'd followed parks in the back, but the driver keeps the engine running, probably also confused by the lack of life here. I don't see any other vehicles.

Rolling my window down an inch, I pull up next to the men on the ground, careful not to accidentally run over their feet. "Is the bar open?" I ask them.

The man with the sacked drink in his hand smirks. "Nah, door's locked and we ain't seen anyone around all night. Weird for a Friday." He lifts the drink to make sure I can see it. "But I'm happy to share this with a pretty girl like you."

I shake my head, forcing myself to smile. "No thanks!"

I roll the window back up and turn my car around.

The bar is closed.

I want to scream into my steering wheel.

There's only one place left to go.

ALMOST TWENTY MINUTES LATER—A DRIVE THAT would have been so much faster in the daylight—I pull up the long, winding lane to Bennett Ranch. The weight of what I'm doing presses down uncomfortably against my spine as the white house comes into view, because I know Rhett's *not* in there. But his family is—people who are currently experiencing unimaginable pain—and I'm about to make things worse.

I started second-guessing myself the minute I turned onto their driveway. Rhett said he was with a friend—what are the chances it's for a legitimate reason? I doubt he'd be out on a social call so soon after his sister-in-law's death, but it's totally plausible there's a good reason for whatever Rhett's up to. If that's the case, I'll be walking out of here with my tail tucked.

But simply seeing a friend wouldn't explain the tone of his voice on the phone earlier. I might still have a lot to learn about who Rhett is, but I *know* him. I know him enough to be petrified.

The driveway spreads wide closer to the house and I pull my car far to the left where there's an open spot next to the handful of other vehicles—mostly trucks—already parked here. The ranch is dark and quiet, but the house shows signs of life through half-open shutters sprinkled around the first floor. After pulling my key from the ignition, I sit and stare at it, wondering who might be home. I know Rhett has his own cabin, and I imagine the same is true for his brothers, so it's entirely possible that it's only his parents who stay in the big house at night.

I wish I knew how I could find Kasey's cabin, or Wells's. The last thing I want to do is come clean to Rhett's mother—or his father—but without knowing where else to go, I'm just going to have to chance it.

I pull the latch of the door handle, forcing myself out into the night air, and briefly tip my head up toward the blanket of stars overhead. For a moment, I close my eyes and whisper an apology to the sky. Whatever happens next, I know I'll never regret ensuring Rhett's safety, even if it costs me his trust.

I draw in a deep breath, feeling my lungs expand as I set my sights toward the house's front steps—and I almost jump out of my skin when I see the silhouette of a man standing in front of the door. It's obvious he's looking at me, but I can't tell who it is because his face is obscured by the dark.

"Olivia?" a deep voice calls out. The man steps forward, down the first step, and when the light of the moon washes over his face, I see that it's Kasey. "Is that you?"

"Yeah," I call back, relief rolling through me. "I-I'm sorry to just show up like this."

"Rhett's not here."

"I know. Um . . ." I move closer so we don't have to keep shouting at each other. "That's actually why I came. I think he needs help." Up close, I notice the deep lines set around Kasey's mouth, the downturn of his lips. He looks exhausted, like he's hanging on by a thread, and my heart leaps. "I'm really sorry. I went to Wild Coyote first—I didn't want to just show up like this."

He nods. "Bar's closed for the week." He stares at me for a long minute, like he's not sure how to handle this. "My brother's wife died."

I squeeze my eyes shut for a beat. "I know," I say quietly. "Rhett told me. I'm so sorry."

"You said Rhett needs help?" he asks, brows pulling to a bunch at the top of his nose like he's only just processed the words. "He told us he was going to see you."

The words rake through me. I steel myself with another deep

breath. "I'm just going to cut to the chase," I say. "We got into a . . . a fight last night. It's a long story, but he's mentioned there's a threat to the ranch, and I'm not sure what that means, but last night he alluded to needing money."

Something came up with a friend of mine.

"I called him a few hours ago," I continue, "and he said he was with a friend but . . . something felt off."

Kasey scrutinizes my face. "Off?"

"Yeah." I nod. "Like . . . like he was hiding something. Like he didn't want me to worry. I don't know the ways he might be able to get himself in trouble, but I was hoping you might know where to look."

Kasey scoffs, shaking his head as he pulls his hands up to his hips. He studies the ground for a minute, and I'm not sure if I should keep talking or—

He suddenly straightens, pulling his phone out of his back pocket to look at the time, or maybe the date? "*Fuck!*" he curses loudly, eyes flying back to me. "That fucking idiot."

My stomach plunges. "What—?"

But he's already moving, running for the house. I watch as he disappears inside, the screen door slamming shut before the wooden door thuds closed behind it. I stare at it, stare and wait and hope he's coming back out to explain what just happened.

Thankfully it's only a minute or two before he's flying back outside, struggling to push his arms through the sleeves of a flannel jacket as he fists a shotgun in his hand. Wells trails behind him, a confused expression marring his face, and behind him is a baffled Layla.

"Kasey, what the fuck?" Wells says in a hushed tone, hurrying to keep up with him.

Kasey just looks at me. "Get in the truck, Olivia."

I eye the gun before looking back at him. The dread in his eyes mixed with the demand in his tone sends me tripping over myself. I turn toward three trucks that are parked side by side, not knowing which one he means. But then the taillights flash on the closest two-door after Kasey unlocks it with a fob.

"Olivia?" Layla's voice sounds from across the drive.

I hear Kasey say something low to Wells as I pull myself into the cramped back seat, heart hammering in my chest with a spicy heat of adrenaline coursing through my veins. And then Kasey's sliding into the driver's seat as I watch Wells briefly talk to Layla through the side window before he too is climbing into the truck.

Wells turns around to look at me as Kasey shoots the truck into reverse. "What happened?"

So I tell him what I told Kasey—about Rhett's worry for the ranch, about our fight and the secret plans he refused to share.

When I'm done, Wells turns to Kasey. "Kase?"

Kasey doesn't look at him. With his eyes glued to the road, he mutters, "He's at Rustler Ranch. There's a game tonight—a big one."

Wells leans his head back against the headrest, eyes closed tight. "Fuck."

"What does that mean?" I ask, looking back and forth between them. "What kind of game?"

Kasey's eyes flick to me through the rearview mirror. "Cards," he answers. "The Rustlers are . . . *friends* of ours. Cattle ranchers in Silver Ridge County—out in the hills. They host illegal poker games with dangerous people, and shit has a tendency to go sideways."

"How sideways?" I ask.

But he doesn't say anything.

"How sideways, Kasey?" I demand.

He sighs. "Criminals tend to be an unhappy bunch, especially when they lose their money. And they also like to carry things that can stab or shoot."

Oh god, I think, eyes burning with tears as Wells curses again from the front seat.

And then he turns to his older brother. "Why is he doing this? Why do we need money?"

Kasey frowns. I don't miss the way his eyes flash to me again before he responds. "Long story. Let's just focus on getting this dumbass home safe, and then I'll tell you everything."

It surprises me that Wells doesn't already know whatever it is that threatens the ranch. That the Bennetts keep secrets amongst themselves.

"Should we call the police?" I ask.

Both Kasey and Wells shout out a matching "*No.*"

I blink as I look out the window. The night rushes past us as Kasey guns it down a four-lane highway.

"When we get there," Kasey says, eyeing me through the rearview once more, "you stay in the truck."

"What? No!" I argue.

"Yes." Kasey's tone is sharp. "Stay in the truck where it's safe. If we . . ." He hesitates. "If we need you, we'll come get you. But it's going to be dangerous there, Olivia. And I need to focus on getting my brother out."

He doesn't trust that I won't be a distraction, which I guess is fair considering he doesn't really know me. "I won't be in the way," I assure him.

His jaw ticks. "I'm not worried about you. I'm worried about what we're walking into. If you get hurt—if someone so much as touches you, Olivia—Rhett's going to lose his fucking mind. And we need him to want to leave with us."

"Do you know who's there?" Wells asks.

Kasey shakes his head. "Ellis called me a few weeks ago to try and convince me to come. He mentioned some new boys from Cheyenne and a shitload of cash, but I don't know anything else."

Wells nods, exhaling sharply. And then he opens the glove box and reaches in. A flash of metal glints in the dark as he pulls his hand back out, and I realize he's holding another gun.

Under normal circumstances, I'd probably be burning with fear knowing both of them are armed. I'm not sure why I'm surprised, considering the stories I've heard for years. But right now, all I can think about is Rhett—about getting him out of danger.

"Please don't let him get hurt," I whisper in the dark.

Kasey only looks at me through that goddamn mirror.

CHAPTER TWENTY-NINE

RHETT

$\mathcal{M}$y eyes fly to Wylie who looks just as smug as her older brother, and I suddenly want to retch. Because Maverick is looking at her too, like he's caught on to their matching confidence. Like he knows the tables have turned in the game.

Fuck, I think, turning my gaze to Colt to find a bead of sweat sliding from his temple as he concentrates on the table in front of him. He's *sweating*, even though he's already out of the round.

He knows too, then. Mother*fucker*.

Anger flares hot and bright through my chest at the realization of what the Rustlers have done and the danger Ellis is throwing us in. That they'd kept me in the dark, knowing I likely wouldn't be here if I'd known the truth. A trap for only Maverick and these cowboys from Cheyenne, but one set for me too. Because they know I'll fight for them, despite all their fucking bullshit.

It takes a sharp focus to keep my emotions in check while we still sit around the table. Ellis might be able to get away with pulling wool over the eyes of dumb cowboys or unknowing tourists, but to try to pull it over Maverick is fucking foolish. And

257

we don't know these Cheyenne boys well enough to know we can get away with bullshit like this. He's just upped the ante on the whole thing, from illegal gambling to outright stealing, and when this goes south—because it *will* fucking go south—we're going to have to fight our way out of here.

God, no wonder the pot is so damn high. Ellis never intended to lose.

I look back at him and find him watching me, the corner of his mouth rising. I glare back at the cocky son-of-a-bitch as that molten anger spreads through my body, mixed with a fear I haven't felt in a long time and hoped I'd never have to feel again. "All right, fellas," Ellis says. "Last hand of the night, and all the cards are down. Let's make it count."

Maverick fastens his oily gaze on Ellis, and my pulse kicks up another notch. I look at the cards clutched in my hand, skimming over the full house I've secured. A good hand, all things considered—but I doubt it fucking matters with whatever Ellis has cooking up.

All eyes turn to me, and I realize it's my turn. There's still a small pile of cash in the backpack at my feet for me to raise this bet even higher, and knowing the players from Cheyenne came with half a mill bets means there's still plenty of room to do so. But Maverick looks furious as it is, and I'm worried raising the bet past his limits is going to lead to bloodshed.

I could fold, I think. I could fold and bid this table farewell and get the *fuck* out of here. There's a girl waiting for me, and I want nothing more than to leave Ellis and his bullshit behind so I can race home to her. And if it was just Ellis at this table, I might fucking do it.

But Colt sits next to me, Wylie beside him. And I'm mad as hell they chose to keep me in the dark, but Ellis can't protect them both from the monsters at this table. Not without help. And I'm not particularly fond of the idea of having their deaths on my conscience.

So I wave my hand to stay and hope like fucking hell there's a way out of this without anyone getting hurt.

Next to me, the first cowboy folds. "I'm out," he says nonchalantly, dropping two cards from his hand to the table. He briefly looks at his partner next to him—the first look I've seen them share all day—and then leans back in his chair with an expression that's hard to read.

The man next to him straightens, looking down at his cards. Silence wraps around the entire barn as he considers, and my heart pounds so hard in my chest I don't doubt everyone can hear it. And then he moves, taking a deep breath before saying, "I'm gonna raise another two fifty." His accent is thick, but different than ours. We all watch as he pushes stacks of banded cash toward the middle of the table.

And I decide I can't do this anymore. The amount of money on the table is almost sickening, and I can't bring myself to add to it, to keep playing this game. I'll stick around for the fight that's no doubt about to take shape, to keep my best friend safe, but I'm not participating in Ellis's fucking schemes. He has a death wish as far as I'm concerned.

So I throw my hand on the table in a show of defiance, look right at Ellis, and say, "I fold." His eyes narrow, but I don't care. This isn't a numbers game anymore, and it doesn't matter that I'm not still in play.

Maverick clicks his tongue, the sound sharp enough to whip across the table, and when I look at him, I see it: his terrible temper unfurling. Because Maverick is out of cash. Maverick, who once pushed the blade of his knife through my best friend's ribs, is near spitting with anger at being made to look like a fool in front of the eight other people at this table.

For thieves like him, money is king. Money is *everything*, a direct reflection of status and power in the underworld he prowls in, and I know he would do anything to protect the image he's worked so hard to build over his long devious years. For Ellis to

invite him here and *not* tell him how much cash would be in play .
. . A reckless, foolish mistake. I know Ellis was only seeking
retribution for his little brother, but this was a *mistake*.

In a move so sudden it causes Wylie to scream from her seat,
Maverick launches to his feet, flipping the table over toward Colt
and me. I push Colt out of his chair and fall to the ground to
avoid getting hit by the weight of it as cash and playing cards go
flying around us. The table lands on my legs and a flash of pain
flares in my left knee, but I'm able to kick it off me. When I look
up again, Maverick is pointing a gun at Ellis, who shields Wylie
behind him.

"I'm no fucking fool," Maverick drawls.

"You sure?" Ellis smiles, a corrupt heat in his eyes.

"What the hell is going on?" one of the cowboys says, sitting
up from the floor with a hand pressed against his forehead.

But Maverick ignores him. "You're playing a few different
games tonight, aren't you, boy?"

Ellis simply shrugs.

The second cowboy jumps to his feet beside me, and I'm
surprised to see him point a gun at Maverick. "Put the gun
down!"

The first cowboy also rises, still clutching his palm against his
head. I don't see any blood coming out from beneath it, but I
imagine the table must have hit him hard enough to knock him a
little loose. He holds his free hand out, and beneath the bald light
that hangs above us all, a golden badge shines.

"Oh fuck," Colt mutters on my other side. "Cops."

Faster than lightning, Maverick turns his attention to the men
from Cheyenne and fires his pistol. The cop holding the gun
drops to the ground, clutching the side of his neck. Wylie screams
again.

The sounds must alert others who wait outside, because the
shadows of two more men come creeping into the barn with guns
drawn, and I know in my heart this is all over. Those of us who sat

at the table tonight will either die in this barn or walk out of it in handcuffs. For a heartbeat, Olivia's face flashes in my mind. I'm not going to make it to her tonight like I promised.

It's a sickening feeling, one that almost has me puking right here where I'm crouched—not because I'm going to be arrested or that I'm disappointing my family in one of the worst possible ways when they need me most, but because I'm not going to make it home to *her*.

I look up to watch the inevitable, taking in the new men coming in, no doubt more cops—but my heart lurches when I see their faces.

Another gunshot slices through the air and I startle, turning to find the downed cop has raised an arm to take a shot at Maverick. He misses, hitting one of his cronies instead. The man drops like a bag of feed and doesn't move.

Maverick hollers out a loud curse before firing again, hitting the cop on the floor with another shot before aiming for the other one who still stands.

"Put the gun down!" the cop tries to yell, eyes wide with fear in the face of the barrel Maverick points at him. His own gun, I realize, is still holstered at his hip.

Maverick doesn't so much as flinch before he shoots him. And before the man is even done falling, Maverick turns to point the gun back at Ellis. "Was all this worth it?" he asks in a quiet, menacing tone. "Dead cops and all this money gone when I walk out of here with it—was it worth it, Ellis Rustler?"

Ellis seethes, opening his mouth to say something. But then a loud boom rattles through the barn, heavier than any of the shots fired so far, and Maverick is hurled backward. His back slams into the ground with a thud.

I turn to look at the two men who just joined us in the barn, at the one who holds a smoking shotgun pointed where Maverick had just been standing. His hands are shaking with the force of what he's just done.

Kasey.

And beside him, stands Wells.

They came for me.

Ellis turns to look at his sister with a panicked look. "Run!" he shouts at her before turning to his own brother. "Get out of here!"

Colt turns to look at me, and I nod. He rockets to his feet, turning to grab his sister by the hand before pulling her through the barn's open doorway and out into the night.

Kasey cocks his head toward Ellis. "You motherfucker," he smolders, taking a step toward him, his gun now pointed at the ground between them. "You reckless, dumbass fucking cowboy."

Ellis throws his hands up. "It wasn't supposed to go like this, Kasey."

"Of *course* it wasn't!" Kasey roars. "It's never supposed to end like this, is it? But you're too fucking stupid to see all the ways it can. *Those are fucking cops on the ground!*"

Ellis trembles, his shoulders bunched in fear. And I can't blame him—I've *never* seen Kasey like this. Even with all the shit I've put him through over the years, he's never looked as scared or angry as he is right now.

"Kasey," Wells says low beside him. And I can't comprehend how it's possible, how my brothers knew I'd need them tonight, how they'd known where to find me.

A shuffle sounds from the ground where the other side of the table had been, and we all realize at once that Maverick's second man, who'd seemingly been pretending to be down amidst all the chaos, is very much *not*. He shoots to his feet with a low grunt and races out of the barn.

Kasey glares at Ellis. "This is on *you*, you hear me?"

Ellis nods. "I'll take the fall if it comes to it. For Colt and Wylie. For Rhett. I'll do it."

Kasey stares at him for a long moment before lowering his gun to his side and turning to me. "Get in the fucking truck."

Without another word, he turns and walks out of the barn. My gaze shifts to Wells, to his wide eyes and tight jaw, and realize he's also holding a gun. My baby brother, with a gun in his hand. Rising to my feet, shame curls tight against me as I look at him. "I'm sorry, Wells."

But Wells just shakes his head and gives me his back, following Kasey out into the dark night.

I rise to my feet and throw Ellis a hard glare.

"This wasn't supposed to happen," he says again, voice trembling.

And the weight of all that's happened presses down around us. Ellis might have taken too many risks tonight, but he's not the only one at fault. I should have never been here. I should have never thought this would be the way out.

Still—I look at all the money on the ground.

"I expect sixty percent of this cash to be in my hands within three days."

Ellis frowns. "Sixty?"

I nod. "Twenty for me, twenty for Kasey, and twenty for Wells. Isn't that how this works? We protect each other and split the profits?" He'd be an idiot if he didn't think I'd expect shares for my brothers.

"Fine," he says. "Three days."

"And the rest of it goes to Colt and Wylie. Twenty each, Ellis." I lean down close to his face. "*None* of this goes to you. Nothing but the blame, should it come to that. Got it?"

Anger sparks in his eyes, but he nods.

"Don't fuck with me, Ellis. I'll make sure Colt knows. I don't care if you told them what was happening here tonight—I know you didn't give them a choice. You played with fucking fire and now it's time to feel it burn. If Colt and Wylie don't get their cuts, I'm coming for you."

And then I turn and walk out of the barn.

Kasey's truck sits next to where my bike is parked, and I watch my brothers work together to lift it into the bed.

"I can ride home," I say, looking at Kasey.

But he just shakes his head and looks back at me. "You owe her," he says.

Owe her?

And then the passenger door of the truck is swinging open and Olivia is jumping out. My heart stutters and then stops altogether as she faces me, her eyes so full of emotion that I can hardly breathe. The relief on her face is palpable, and in the light of the moon, I notice the tears that spill off her chin. "Rhett?" she says.

It was *her*. She tipped off my brothers. "Olivia," I say on a rough exhale.

She rushes forward, and I open my arms to catch her body against mine. But when she reaches me, she stops. I watch in fascination as her relief turns into a scowl, her sad eyes narrowing in anger.

And she punches me right in the jaw.

CHAPTER THIRTY

OLIVIA

"*F*uck," Rhett mumbles, stepping back from the force of my hit.

I match his curse with my own as pain sears through my hand. I've never punched anyone in my life, and I didn't expect it to hurt so much.

Rhett's eyes zero in on where I clutch my hand to my chest. "Shit, let me see."

"No!" I yell, turning away.

"Peaches," he pleads.

I turn to get another good look at him. At his stupid eyes and stupid mouth and *stupid* dark waves that cluster at his collar from beneath his stupid hat.

Stupid, stupid man.

Before I know it, I'm hurling myself back at him, reaching to cup my hands around his stupid face. Pressing up to my toes and kissing him. Hard.

Warm arms wrap around my middle and clutch me tight. I sink into them, letting him carry some of the weight that's been crushing me all night. His tongue parts my mouth open as a hand winds its way up my back, tangling into the mess of my hair.

I almost lost him.

I almost *lost* him.

"Enough," Kasey scolds from somewhere behind Rhett. We both turn to find him scowling. "We need to get the hell out of here."

Rhett nods and herds me toward the open door of the truck, letting me climb into the back first before he gets in behind me. There's hardly any space, and our knees are shoved together. When our eyes latch together beneath the dome light, I see a question waiting in his. "How did you know where I'd be?" he asks.

"I didn't." I shake my head. "I just knew something was wrong—I could hear it in your voice."

He faces his brothers in front of us who are both getting settled in their own seats. "So, how then?"

Kasey starts the ignition before biting out, "I told you I knew about the game."

"I didn't know what else to do," I say quietly, drawing Rhett's attention back. "I went looking for your brothers, hoping they'd know where you were."

"You're a damn lucky son of a bitch," Wells mutters from the passenger seat. He doesn't look as angry as Kasey does, but his face is pale, and I have a feeling he might be in shock.

"What happened in there?" I ask, even though I'm terrified of the answer. I heard what I know were gunshots and saw multiple people run out of that old barn.

"Yeah, Rhett," Kasey growls, pulling the truck onto the road that brought us here with a speed that has my stomach flipping. "Tell us what happened. And while you're at it, maybe you could tell us what the *fuck* you were thinking."

Rhett frowns, still looking at me when he answers. "There was a poker game tonight with a *lot* of money, and I thought it was going to be a straight game. I knew it was a risk, but I swear I had no idea what Ellis was planning—"

"Did you know Maverick would be there?" Kasey demands.

"No." Rhett's jaw ticks, finally looking at his older brother. "Colt didn't know either."

Colt. "Who are these people?" I ask. "Ellis and Colt. They're your friends?"

Kasey scoffs.

"They're brothers. Their family has been friends of ours for a long time, since our dads started shit together back in the day. Including illegal card games," Rhett says, and then he sighs. "I was pretty involved in them for a while, but I stopped a few years ago." He glances nervously at me.

"How much?" Wells asks.

Rhett looks at him. "Half-million-dollar bets."

"Holy *shit*," Wells shouts, and I flinch. He whips his head around to look at Rhett. "How much of that cash was legit?"

"Dunno," Rhett answers. "Ellis was good for it. Maverick had a good amount on him but not enough, which is what got him so pissy. And the other two . . ."

"The cops, you mean?" Kasey bites out.

And my stomach plummets.

"There were *cops*?" I demand, eyes fixed on Rhett.

This time it's him who flinches. "Yeah. We didn't know."

I twist in my seat to look through the back window, past where Rhett's bike is strapped in the bed, but I don't see anyone following us.

Cops.

This is so bad.

No one says anything for a while as the pulse of roadway lights beats down around us. An uncomfortable knot forms in my throat, hot and rancid, as the reality of what Rhett's done tonight sinks into me all over again. And those gunshots . . .

I'm not brave enough to ask who they hit.

"No one tells Brooks about any of this," Kasey eventually says. "Or Mom or Dad. This stays here—at least until we know of any repercussions."

He's scared, I realize. And I get it—I am too. Even with Rhett beside me, seemingly unhurt, I'm scared to death of what all this means.

Rhett nods. "I'll stay with Olivia tonight," he tells his brothers.

"Oh no you won't," I declare.

He turns to me, having the audacity to look wounded. "I won't?"

I shake my head. "Absolutely not. Not when I can't trust myself not to throttle you while you sleep." I point a finger at him. "I might be really damn happy that you're still breathing, Rhett, but I am *not* happy with *you*. I'm fucking *pissed*. You don't trust me, and it looks like you don't even trust your family. And now I don't trust *you*."

A new tear slides down my cheek, and I wipe it away in frustration.

"Despite what you might think," I go on, not caring that his brothers can hear every word, "I don't care about the things you've done. I've never cared about your reputation or what anyone *else* thinks—I know you, and I *know* better. But I will not stick around just to be heartbroken by your lack of self-preservation. I can't do it. I asked you to let me in, to let me *help*, and instead you chose to abandon yourself to something like this."

He recoils like I've hit him again. *Good*, I think.

"I need time to process. You just . . . you handed yourself over to danger like it wasn't going to *matter* to anyone, but it clearly mattered to your brothers, Rhett. And it damn sure mattered to me." My heart tumbles as I turn away from him, forcing myself to breathe as the world rushes past through the dark-tinted window.

I spend the next week avoiding Rhett.

Not because I don't want to see him—I'm bursting with the

impulse to text him and see how's doing. But I'd meant what I said about not wanting to set myself up for heartbreak if he was just going to throw himself to the wolves, and I've needed space to really process all that happened the night of the poker game.

Thankfully, things get busy at the café after Mom and Mark leave town on Sunday for a two-night getaway on the coast. Teresa and I take turns opening and closing the restaurant every day, doing our best to jump in and help the kitchen when we can.

Wednesday is Valentine's Day, and Char comes in to hang out while she works, doing her best to needle Rhett-related information out of me after I'd all but told Ivan I'd think about another double date with Trent. I know my tight-lipped responses bother her, but I'm honestly not sure what to say. I can't tell her things are done between us, because I don't think they are. But I also can't tell her the truth of all that's happened over the last couple of weeks because I want to protect the Bennetts'—and Rhett's—privacy.

So instead, I lean into another stream of updates. "I think I'm going to meet my dad," I say, plopping into the booth opposite her and almost knocking over the foiled heart centerpiece that every table is currently dressed with. Pain sears through my hand as I brace my weight on it, and I wince. "Ow."

Her eyes go wide. "Wait, what!" She looks at where I'm rubbing my hands together. "Are you okay?"

I nod, scooching a plate of heart-shaped sugar cookies her way that Luna dropped off from the bakery next door. I asked Mark to look at my hand yesterday after he and Mom got back, claiming I accidentally hit it against a door jam. He's pretty sure there's no broken bones, but it still hurts like hell. "I've been invited to my half-sister's wedding, and I decided it's worth a shot, you know?" Tucking a flyaway strand of hair behind my ears, I sneak a peek out the window where the bright sun warms the town's streets. "I want to at least give it a chance."

"Does your mom know?"

"Yeah. She's going with me." I used the email address listed on the invitation to ask Céline if I could bring Mom as a plus one, and her response had chimed in my inbox within minutes.

Of course! it read. *We're so excited that you've decided to come. Dad will be thrilled!*

Not even an ounce of hesitation . . . at least from what I could tell.

"Oh my *god*, Liv. That's huge. Are you nervous?"

"Terrified," I admit. "But I think it helps that I don't need him to be my dad. I don't *need* this family to be my family—I've got all that I need here in Saddlebrook Falls. So it takes some of the pressure off, I guess? I'll just take the opportunity to meet them and see how it goes."

"It's okay to want more than that," Charlotte says quietly.

I smile. "I know. And maybe I will. But right now, this is more than enough."

Later, I'm making a mental note to plan an afternoon with Mom so we can both find something to wear. The wedding isn't for another three months, but it'll be a nice opportunity to spend an afternoon with her. Maybe we can even go out to the city.

She gives me the night off work, saying it's so I can enjoy the romantic holiday with a date, but I know she just wants to work because Mark's working. It doesn't take long for the lunch rush— all five tables' worth—to disappear, so I close myself out and say goodbye to them both.

I push the front door open to head out of the café and immediately stop short when I spot Rhett. Parked along the curb in front of the building, he straddles the seat of his bike, helmet and gloves still on as he clearly waits for something.

Waiting for me? I think.

He turns to look at me, tilting his head toward the bike beneath him, and though I can't see his eyes behind the visor, I know what he's asking.

Frustration blooms inside me as I firmly shake my head

twice, refusing to let him just *show up* and draw me back in. Tearing my gaze away, I start to march down the sidewalk for the walk back to my house, hoping he gets the hint and backs off. But that hope dissipates when I hear the loud roar of his engine as it bursts to life. I don't have to look back to know he's following me.

A thrill shoots up my spine.

Still, I ignore him. I make it all the way to the corner before the red light at the crosswalk stops me. There's not much traffic on the road, and Rhett must be feeling particularly emboldened because before I know it, he's angling right for me, crossing the path of oncoming traffic to sidle up in front of me and block me from crossing the street.

"Get on," I hear him shout from beneath his helmet.

"No," I say back, squaring my shoulders.

He shakes his head. "Get on the bike, Olivia."

"Why?" The word squeezes out of my throat.

"Because you can't just ignore me forever. Get on the damn bike." His chest heaves. "Please?"

Anticipation snakes through my stomach. I let out a hard exhale, feeling my frustration dissipate through the rush of breath. "Fine," I mumble before reaching for the second helmet and climbing on behind him.

I try not to notice how good it feels to wrap my arms around him, how relieved I am to know he's safe. As upset as I still am, I can't deny the way my heart draws right back into him or the way I want him in my life. That it feels *good* to be vulnerable with someone like this, to give parts of myself I never realized I wanted to give, even if it scares me.

I know it would be a risk to love him, to let myself truly fall.

But I think I would be willing, if he's capable of doing the same.

He brings me down the old back road that leads to the bar, and it's so much different with the sunlight slicing through the trees. Pulling into the empty parking lot, he steers the bike into a spot against the front curb and cuts the engine.

The silence curls around us as we dismount, leaving our helmets tucked together on the seat. I trail behind him along the sidewalk that leads to the front door and watch as he pulls out a key.

"The bar was closed that night," I say. "When I came looking for help. No one was here."

His eyes flash to me as he unlocks it, holding it open to let me in. "We've been closed since Melody died," he says quietly.

"Oh." I nod, shuffling through the door. My arm grazes against his hard chest and my mind narrows to the warmth that spreads from the contact.

Inside, the bar is dark. Without windows or light, it's like walking into a dungeon. Rhett moves around me to flip various switches, and neon lights spark to life all around us. I thought he might be bringing me up to the apartment, but he heads for the bar and pulls out a stool.

"Sit," he orders softly.

So I do. But he doesn't take a seat next to me. Instead, he twists the stool around so I'm facing away from the bar. Toward him.

"Do you want anything to drink?" he asks. "Water? Somethin' stronger?"

I shake my head. "Why are we here, Rhett?"

He takes a good step back before crossing his arms over his chest.

"I have a lot of things I want to say to you, Olivia, and if it's okay with you, I'd like to just say them."

He's nervous. I can tell by the way his brows are pinched and shoulders are raised, a layer of determination only narrowly managing to cover a deeper-rooted fear. Hope sprouts that he might be able to ease the worry in my chest, my own fears that I can't seem to shake. I don't know what he could say that would help me move on from the terror he put me through, but I realize I'm willing to listen.

When I nod, he looks relieved.

"First, I want to tell you how sorry I am for what happened at the water tower the other night. I never should have been so . . . rough," he says with an edge of regret. "Not like that. Not with you. I meant it when I said I don't trust myself not to hurt you. I don't think I can give you what you deserve, that I won't hurt you in the process of *trying*. You deserve to be loved and cared for in a way that feels much bigger than anything I feel like I can offer, and that's why I pulled away from you."

He pauses, and I'm not sure if it's to collect his thoughts or to give me a chance to say something. But I stay quiet, hoping he'll keep going.

He does.

"Melody *died*," he forces through clenched teeth as emotion claws at him. "Melody died, and I watched my brother splinter into a thousand fucking pieces when he lost her. I watched the complete and utter destruction of the strongest man I know, and it scared the living shit out of me because I never want to feel that way. I tried to close myself off from this because I'm so fucking scared I'll have to feel even a fraction of the way he feels right now. That losing you is going to be what breaks *me* apart."

My breaths turn ragged and uneven as he steps toward me. "That's why I didn't call you after I left the diner. Why I was *trying* to end things with you at the tower. Because I'm not sure I believe in forever, or that I'd even deserve it if I did. But you know what I've realized?"

"What?" I whisper.

"That all I was doing was forcing the pain to come early, when there's still plenty of good to be had." His eyes move to my bottom lip, where I've captured it between my teeth, and he reaches to swipe it with his thumb, pulling it free. "You *came* for me. You knew I needed someone, and you came for me. I don't know what the hell you see in me beyond a bad attitude and a black fucking heart, but being seen by you is something I don't want to lose yet.

"I don't want to fight this. This isn't practice anymore, peaches. Nothing about the way I feel for you is pretend. And I'm scared of those feelings, but I've realized I don't have a choice anymore because my heart's already yours. And I don't want to live in a world where you're not mine."

He cups my face with his warm hand. My eyes burn with emotion as I take in the ghost of a sad smile on his lips.

"I'm scared too," I admit. "I'm scared of how you see yourself. Your heart isn't black, Rhett. It's warm and tender and safe. You've shown me what it is to be cared for in ways I wasn't sure existed. You're *important* to me. And that matters . . . *you* matter." I let my gaze wash over his face, taking in all the hard lines of his jaw and the curl of his hair. "Stop believing that this is only going to end. I mean—it might. It's a risk to love." I think of my mother and all that she endured. How she was still able to open her heart again because in the end her love for Mark conquered those doubts. "It's a risk to try. But I *want* to take that risk with you. I want you to believe we can do this."

His thumbs trails softly across my cheek and he nods. "I can't promise I won't make mistakes, but I'm going to be so fucking careful with you, Olivia."

"You're still missing the point." I shake my head. "I don't need you to be careful with me. I need you to be careful with *yourself*. I need you to care about yourself, to believe that you can be loved without the need to sacrifice so much. You don't need to be worthy, Rhett. I see you just the way you are, and it's *more* than enough." Pressure builds in the corners of my eyes as new tears threaten, but I try like hell to look unaffected. "And for the record, I've never minded you being a little rough with me. I thought you knew that."

The corner of his mouth curves, a whisper of his devilish smirk. "I do know."

"So," I continue, "I think maybe you can lighten up and take off the kid gloves."

He considers, his eyes dancing circles along my face. "All right." He stands taller, pulling his hand back. "I'll give it to you straight."

I brace myself for whatever he's about to throw at me and nod.

"At that poker game, four people were killed. One of them was a known criminal we've run into before. Another one a part of his gang. And the other two were cops." I knew about the cops already, but dammit if the words didn't sink fear into me all over again. "We didn't know they were undercover. Ellis thought they were random cowboys from Cheyenne—the fucking idiot. Maverick killed both of the cops after one of them killed his guy. Kasey . . . Kasey shot Maverick to protect the rest of us."

"Oh my god." *Kasey* killed someone?

Rhett's eyes harden. "Yeah. It's fucked. But so far, Ellis says things have been quiet. One of Maverick's guys got out, but if he's smart, he's not going to say anything. I don't doubt more cops are going to go knocking on Ellis's door, but he's been way too loose with his fucking stunts lately, and he's already given his word he'll take the fall."

"Do you think he'll do it?" I ask.

Rhett nods. "His brother and sister were there. He's a prick, but he won't jeopardize them."

"What about the money?"

Rhett's mouth tugs. "Ellis dropped off our cuts yesterday. It's . . . it's a lot of cash. Enough to help."

I frown. "What do you need it for? You said for a funeral . . . but also a lawyer? You said your uncle is threatening the ranch?" Kasey hadn't explained further in the truck, telling Wells they'd talk about it later.

"Yeah. He wants the ranch, and he's not above playing dirty to get it." He blows out a harsh breath. "Apparently, in order for the ranch to transition, its successor needs to be married—some stupid rule in all the fine print. Brooks was always going to be the one who gets the ranch, but . . ."

My chest squeezes. "Melody."

He nods. "My uncle knows my dad's in a wheelchair and not fit to run things anymore, but he's never had much of a fight to the land with Brooks ready to take things over. Unfortunately, Brooks was never in a hurry to officially take things over, and now my uncle thinks he can skirt his way in. We need the money for a good lawyer, someone who can help us shut him down. Maybe even take out that stupid rule that says one of us needs to be married to inherit what's always been ours."

I shake my head. "That's . . . a lot, Rhett."

Something cracks in his expression. "Yeah."

"*Way* too much for you to have ever thought you should handle it alone," I add.

He sighs. "I just didn't want you to get caught up in any of it. And I didn't want my brothers to be disappointed or worried."

I tsk. "How'd that turn out?"

He rolls his eyes.

"Rhett," I say, stepping down from the stool and toward him, reaching my hands out to take his. "Promise me. Never again."

He leans down low, resting his forehead on the top of mine. "Never," he whispers.

"*This* is what it takes," I tell him. "Communication. Good and bad. No kid gloves, no secrets."

He nods. "I promise." He presses a kiss to my temple. Pulls me in close. "I have a lot of making up to do."

I smile. "That sounds fun."

He steels himself, looking down at me with a reverence that makes me feel raw. "I've never begged for anything in my life, Olivia, but I'm *begging* for you. It's scary for me to admit I have so much hope after everything. But I feel it with you—you make me *hope* with my whole fucking chest."

I smile, leaning up into his mouth. "If you ever put yourself in danger like that again, I'm going to make you hurt for it, Rhett. Don't steal my heart just to break it."

He rumbles in agreement with a quiet "Yes ma'am," and a steep longing pierces into me as he finally captures my mouth with his.

CHAPTER THIRTY-ONE

RHETT

*L*ate morning light bends through the trees, sparks of gold slicing through the sky over the pasture. The grass still smells like it does at night, like cold dew and soft earth readying for spring. Despite everything falling apart around me, I still feel hope for the day ahead.

It's a curse I think, after all these damn years, to feel so much damn hope. To want better for my family, to feel something good is always just ahead. Maybe I'm a stupid man to want such things, but after generations of fighting against ourselves and the rest of the world for this land, it's about damn time for a little reprieve. Especially now.

Brooks still hasn't come out of his cabin, but Melody's funeral is today and we'd never let him miss it. Mom's been the only one to see him since he holed himself up in the one place he can be surrounded by his late wife—the home they shared for the entirety of their marriage. She moved in with him only months after their first date, a fast and furious love that, for the longest time, the rest of my brothers and I thought would eventually fizzle and fade. They were so young, Brooks not at all the man he is today, and I remember thinking how wild it was to see him fall so fast for a girl he'd barely known.

But they both must have felt their love for each other deep in their souls, because after all these years and through all our family's struggles, that love never faltered.

Kasey and I head up the dirt path that leads to Brooks's front door, and I can't help but let my gaze trail over all the traces of Melody: the colorful flowers sprouting up through the soil again along the outside of their porch, matching ones that are painted along the beams that run from the porch to the roof so even in winter, the flowers still bloom. There's a worn pair of women's boots tucked against the wall beside the door with bright red roses embroidered into them. Melody was such a vibrant woman who brought endless color into Brooks's life, so much love and warmth that it must have felt like finally knowing what it is to have a *home* in someone.

Olivia feels like that for me.

My want for her smolders like a constant fever. I can't escape it, can't fucking *think* through it, and the truth is that even after our conversation, I'm still terrified.

Terrified of loving something I stand to lose.

Terrified she might *actually* love me back, knowing I'm not half the man she believes me to be.

It still makes me panic to think of all the ways I could let her down. But she's right: having her is worth all the risks. And as long as I have her, I'll do everything I can to be a better man. I've always stood so proud in my own ego, believing everything I do— as disastrous as my actions can be—serves a purpose for my family. But I'm starting to understand I've caused a lot of hurt for them over the years, and I don't want to keep doing that.

Kasey climbs up the front steps before me and raps on the door with firm knuckles. The funeral is in an hour, and everyone else back at the main house is almost ready. Wells and Layla helped get the boys in suits and all of us have talked at length with them about what to expect today so they don't feel nervous or scared about any of it. Sawyer even flew home from school late last night to be here.

Now we just need to make sure Brooks makes it out this door. His sons haven't seen him in days, and I know he's needed space to let the violent waves of grief flow through him, but the boys are starting to worry. They need their father, now more than ever, to help set the tone for what the rest of their lives are going to look like without their mother.

Pain spears through me at the thought.

The door opens and Kasey lets out a surprised breath at what we find on the other side. Brooks stares at us in nothing but a towel wrapped around his waist, his hair dripping water along his shoulders and chest. His neck and cheeks are flushed from the heat of his recent shower.

"Hey," he says, his voice strained and cracking over the word, like he's been yelling. Or sobbing.

"Brooks," Kasey answers, placing a hand on our oldest brother's shoulder. "It's good to see you. Are you okay?"

Of course he's not. But I look to Brooks anyway, a twinge of hope sprouting that he's up. We fully expected to find him prone and disheveled, to have to fight him to do this today. But, other than the dark patches beneath them, his eyes look clear and focused. He shrugs like he's a little kid again, like he's not sure what to say. "I can't find a jacket," he says low.

Kasey squeezes his shoulder. "Don't worry about that—we've got one for you."

I hold up the hanger in my hand so he can see the apparel bag. "We found you a nice suit," I declare. "Kasey and I weren't exactly sure of your size, but there's two in here, just in case."

Brooks looks back and forth between us, eyes glistening. "Thank you," he whispers.

Kasey and I follow him into the house, and while Kasey helps him get dressed, I clear the living room and kitchen of all the empty bottles and dirty dishes, doing what I can to erase the evidence of his pain in case the boys come back here tonight. It's obvious Brooks has been lost in his own mind, using whiskey to drown out what he's feeling, and my heart squeezes at how lonely and scared he must feel. How broken his heart is.

We've given him space long enough, I decide. From now on, we need to be here with him to help him get back to living again, no matter how long it takes.

When Brooks and Kasey come back out from his bedroom, Brooks is dressed in an all-black suit. His dark hair is swept to the side, mostly dry now. Of all my brothers, I look the most like him. We both have the same dark curls, same gray eyes, but where I still carry some of the boyish features of my youth, Brooks is all hard edges. His jaw is sharp, his nose steep, and the weight of his grief makes him look even older than he is.

Still, he looks good. Ready to honor the happy and love-filled life of his wife.

When he looks at me, I recognize the uncertainty in his eyes. So I move to him, wrapping my arms tight around his shoulders, and say, "You look perfect, brother."

THE FUNERAL IS BEAUTIFUL, THOUGH DIFFICULT TO GET through.

We kept it private, holding the quiet ceremony on a section of land that grows wild near a trickling creek where the gravestones of past Bennetts are scattered within the tall grass. Soon the land will be covered with wildflowers, and it feels fitting for Melody to be here when they bloom.

From the moment we step out of the herd of trucks that bring us all here, the boys and Brooks are already crying. But Brooks seems to be aware that they need him as he holds all three tight in his arms as they lean on him and each other. By the end of the short ceremony, most of our faces are wet with tears—including Dad's. I was honestly surprised to see him come down the stairs today on the lift Mom installed years ago, but I'm thankful for his show of support. I know it means something to Brooks.

Sawyer is the only one who doesn't succumb to tears, though I know he's feeling emotion just the same. It's in the way he keeps pressing a hand against Wells's back, a tell he's always had that he's feeling nervous or troubled. He's never been able to express himself as easily as the rest of us.

Olivia stands by my side the whole time, squeezing my hand. When the emotion becomes too much—when it's Olivia's face I see in that casket as the fear of losing *her* rages through me—she pulls me back with her hand on my tear-streaked jaw and her lips quick on my neck.

We watch as the boys take turns dropping pictures they drew for Melody in the ground with her, their eyes wet and noses red. It's going to take them a long time to heal from this, but as I look around at the dozen of us gathered together beneath a hundred-year-old oak tree, I know together we can help them through. For the first time in my life, I realize the weight of our struggles doesn't need to just fall on me. That, as a family, we can bear it together.

When the ceremony is over, Olivia and I head back toward the trucks with Wells, Layla, Sawyer, and Kasey, giving Brooks and his family some space to just be together. Mom pushes Dad's chair through the aisles of other gravestones as they take a moment to visit his parents and grandparents, and all the other Bennetts who came before the ones that are here now.

Later, we take an hour or so to refresh at home before all heading to Wild Coyote for a celebration of life. Though we kept the funeral private, Mom reached out to some folks from town to invite them to the bar for an opportunity to show Brooks and our family support. While I doubt anyone will grieve Melody the way we do—no one ever tried to get to know her like they should have

—I know without a doubt the bar will be packed with the folks who thrive on the pain and suffering of others.

The thought irritates me beyond belief. "I don't even want to go to this," I mutter darkly to Olivia, who's helping me back into my jacket. We spent the last half hour lost in each other above the bar after I opened up to her about how scared I felt during the funeral, how I can't stand the thought of losing her.

Her nails painted my skin in half-moon indentations as I sunk inside of her against the wall, and I want to tattoo them into my skin so they stay forever. It undoes something inside of me, to be marked by her. To be changed by this so completely I know there's no going back.

"We have to," she says softly, smoothing her hands down my lapels.

I know she's right. I'm surprised Brooks is even willing to be here, but I imagine that, for his wife, he'd show up just about anywhere. "Can we make a safe word?"

Her eyes spark. "A safe word for the party?"

I nod, stepping toward her so our chests are pressed together. "Yeah. Like if I need an out from a bad conversation, I can use 'rope' in a sentence and you'll know that I *desperately* need you back up here so I can tie you up again."

"Who the hell do you think I am, Rhett?" she chides, swatting at me.

Mine. The word blares to life in my mind, drowning out any other coherent thought. I reach to press my hand around her throat to remind her of it. "Olivia," I rasp as my thumb slips down her skin, tracing her hard swallow. Her eyes grow dark as her mouth parts open, and I struggle like hell to stop myself from kissing her now. From licking into her mouth with all the need burning inside of me. But I hold it together, forcing a polite smile. "Is that a no?"

She laughs, playfully pushing me away. "If you behave for the whole night, you can tie me up for as long as you want after."

My blood heats at the thought.

I watch as she slips on her earrings in front of the mirror, her brow wrinkled in concentration. She's my wildest dream come true, and I'll spend the rest of my life making sure she knows how fucking gone I am for her. Making sure she understands just how deep this goes for me, how I don't stand a chance against the way I feel for her. "I'm never going anywhere, peaches," I say, the words out before I can catch them. "You have me, for as long as you want."

She turns to look at me, eyes shining. "You have me too, Rhett."

CHAPTER THIRTY-TWO

OLIVIA

The bar is loud with a vibrant hum of conversation as people continue to trickle in through the doors—people I've never seen here before and I can't imagine would be here under normal circumstances. And though I'd like to believe that most of them are here for the right reasons, I know in my heart their presence isn't so much about supporting Brooks as it is being here to witness this moment for the Bennetts.

It grates against me, witnessing them being treated like zoo animals to ogle and whisper about. No wonder Rhett has had such a hard time feeling accepted by anyone other than those who share his last name. I understand how it would be difficult for him to extend trust, and I feel even *more* honored that he's giving me that trust.

It's what has me sneaking kisses when I think no one's looking—nothing indecent, but enough to remind him that I'm here. That he's cared for and respected and *not* for the entertainment of others. Even holding back, each kiss sends a wave of heat through me. Each brush of his hand against mine and the deep rumble of his voice sends a thrill dipping through my stomach. And it's *this*—this fire that burns too hot and bright between us, like even if we had forever to let it burn, it still couldn't possibly be enough.

About an hour into the celebration, my mom and Mark stroll through the doors hand in hand. Despite the nature of the evening, Mom is glowing, and it settles something long-aching inside my chest. To see her happy like this is something I wasn't ever sure would be possible. She smiles when she spots me, tugging Mark our way.

"Hi, honey," she says as she hugs me.

"Hi, Mom. Thanks for coming." I came clean to her about Rhett after he and I talked. She handled it well. Told me I had her full support in all things—especially when it came to the heart. I can tell she's a *teensy* bit worried about me dating a Bennett, but I know Rhett will prove himself with time.

She pulls away, eyes drifting to Rhett beside me. "Wouldn't miss it. I'm so sorry for your loss, Rhett," she says, pulling him in for a hug of equal measure in care and affection, like she's hugged him a million times before.

I'm surprised when he doesn't hesitate to let her. "Thank you, Miss Danvers," he says. "It means a lot to me . . . to my family."

"I was so sorry to hear the news," Mark says next, shaking Rhett's hand before pressing a kiss to my cheek. He looks back at Rhett. "And I'm sorry I didn't know Melody well, but I can only imagine the pain your family must be experiencing. I'm hoping it's okay for me to stop by your ranch in the morning—I've prepared some meals for you all, in case it helps."

Rhett's eyes widen in genuine surprise. "You did?"

Mark's smile is sad and soft. "Of course. No one should be worrying about groceries or cooking at a time like this. It's the least I could do."

Rhett nods, emotion thickening his words. "Thank you, sir. That means more to us than you know."

The door opens again, and this time Mayor Moore walks in. From where he stands nearby, I see Wells notice too. He leans in to say something quietly to Layla beside him before turning to make his way toward the man looking around the bar.

On some distant instinct, I search for Brooks and find him seated at a table with all three of his sons and his parents. They've kept to themselves for the majority of the evening, and I have a feeling Brooks's brothers are running a quiet interference on anyone who may want to approach their table, instead taking condolences on his behalf.

When I face the front of the bar again, Wells is shaking Mayor Moore's hand, though the interaction looks rather stiff.

"We're going to get a drink," Mom says, pulling my attention back to her, "but please let us know if there's anything we can do."

Rhett nods and I smile as they walk away. He turns to me when they're out of earshot. "That was incredibly nice of the chef," he murmurs, amusement dancing in his eyes. "Your mom must be treating him well." He winks.

I roll my eyes. "Quite possibly the last thing I want to think about, but thanks."

His smile widens. But somewhere a voice rises, drawing our focus back toward Wells and the mayor.

There's another man beside Mayor Moore now, an older man who looks strikingly familiar with his pale eyes and dark hair. Rhett curses under his breath before he turns to where Kasey's making drinks behind the bar, letting out a low whistle to get his attention. When he looks up, Rhett dips his head toward the man and Kasey's gaze turns that direction before a deep frown etches into his face.

"What's wrong?" I ask, reaching for Rhett.

"That," he mutters darkly, "is my uncle." He moves toward the men as Kasey rounds the bar, and nerves grip tight. I follow him as he cuts a path toward his youngest brother, his eyes fastened to the man who shares his coloring. "Can I help you?" Rhett asks, not too kindly.

The man's eyes flare as he takes Rhett in with a sweeping glance. "I was hoping to give condolences to my eldest nephew, but Wells here says it's not possible. I'm trying not to be offended," he chuffs. "Is this how you welcome family?"

Rhett laughs. "Family? Considering we haven't seen or heard from you since we were knee-high to a grasshopper, I don't really think you get to play the family card right now, Huck."

Kasey reaches Wells and Rhett, and I realize they're blocking the man's—Huck's—view from the table where Brooks and their parents sit. I wonder if they're hiding Brooks, or if it's Mr. Bennett they're worried about.

Huck's eyes grow cold. "Fine," he says with a distant smile as he briefly looks at Mayor Moore. The mayor simply shrugs, eyes glinting as if he's in on some secret. "You want to keep it to business? I can do that." He pulls a rolled piece of paper from the back pocket of his worn jeans and flattens it against his chest before handing it to Rhett. "Consider this an unofficial notice."

"Kasey?" Wells asks warily.

Huck smiles. "My lawyer is filing that same paperwork now, and I assume you'll receive an *official* notice in the next few days."

"Notice of what?" Wells asks, looking from his uncle to his brother.

Kasey presses his lips together, frustration on full display. "Of our uncle trying to take the ranch from us."

Wells frowns, looking back to Huck. "You can't do that," he says simply.

But Huck's smile only widens. "Indeed I can. Please pay Brooks my respects," he says, turning to head back out through the door.

Rhett is hot on his trail. "You come in here again," he growls, "and I will tear you apart with my bare fucking hands."

"Is that a threat?" the mayor cuts in, looking at Rhett with disdain.

Rhett shoots him an icy glare.

"Enough," Kasey snaps, pointing a finger toward the door. "This is not the time or place. Our family is grieving. You need to go. Now."

We all watch as the men turn to walk out the door, traces of dark twin smiles on their faces.

"Motherfucker," Wells says, looking back toward the door, like he might be able to curse his uncle from where he stands.

"Asshole," Rhett agrees, looking down at the paper.

"He's not going to get it," Kasey says. "The ranch. He's not going to get it." It's almost a relief to hear him sound so sure.

"We have the cash now, right?" Wells asks.

Kasey shoots Rhett a glare.

"What?" Rhett shrugs. "You're the one who gave him a gun and brought him to Rustler Ranch."

"*You're* the fucking reason I had to," Kasey seethes.

"Guys," Wells says, throwing his hands between them. "Not now."

"We've got this," Rhett tells Kasey. He lowers his voice before adding, "We just need a lawyer."

Kasey only frowns, the confidence he held already gone again.

Suddenly the doors to the bar burst open, revealing a tall, slender woman with long dark hair that cascades around her beautiful tanned skin. Her deep brown eyes scan the room, looking at each of us as a smile slowly grows from her plump lips. Golden bracelets around her wrist jangle together as she steps into the bar, her stiletto boots clacking against the worn hardwood floor.

My first thought is that she's a tourist who must have taken a wrong turn into Saddlebrook Falls—based on her manicured nails and stylish clothes, her tastes are far too expensive to have landed here on purpose. But then I see the way her eyes brighten when they land on Kasey, and I turn to find him standing so still it's as if he's paralyzed. His eyes are wide with fear, like he's seeing a ghost.

"Kasey," she says as she saunters toward him.

"Ava?" he asks, shock written on every feature of his face.

And then it hits me. Ava Jones. The sheriff's daughter.

"Looks like a party's already started," Ava says, sweeping her gaze around the room full of people before her eyes glue back to Kasey and she leans in to whisper, "I heard somebody's in need of a wife?"

EPILOGUE

OLIVIA

$\mathcal{W}$e stand beneath a cluster of towering oaks draped in Spanish moss, their gnarled branches spreading wide around us in a romantic, near-ethereal embrace. It's golden hour in South Carolina, and the glow from the setting sun washes over the beautiful bride as she takes careful, confident steps toward the emotional red-haired man waiting for her at the altar.

Unlike most of the people around me though, I'm not watching her. My attention fastens to the older man next to her who leads her down the aisle, soaking in the way his rich honeyed skin contrasts against the dark suit he wears, how his gray-brown hair sweeps to the side in a way that strikes against the formality in everything else around us.

Clive Calhoun.

My father.

It's been two days since we arrived in Charleston for Céline's nuptials to her almost-husband, Nathan. Two days since we were ushered into the sunny sitting room of my father's house and welcomed with nothing but open arms by him and his wife, Colette.

Mom squeezes my hand, and I look to find her expression soft. "She's beautiful," she says quietly.

I nod, shifting my focus to my older half-sister.

A sister. *Three* of them.

My father had written so much about them in his letters to me over the years, and I'd always felt ambushed by it. But to see the way he beams at them, the way I've even caught him looking at me in just the short time we've been here . . .

Well, I suppose maybe I better understand now.

Céline wears a traditional white dress drenched in gossamer and beaded jewels. Her long raven hair curls all the way to her elbows, crowned in a garland of white carnations that her mother designed herself. Colette owns a flower shop in Charleston and designed *all* of the arrangements here today, including the bouquets Amelie and Claire hold as they stand at the altar across from Nathan in matching floor-length mauve dresses.

All three of my sisters are stunning.

"You're *more* beautiful," a low voice says close to my ear, the warmth of his breath sending goosebumps across my bare shoulder. I look up to find Rhett smirking at me, his pale eyes sparking.

"Shush." I swat at him. "This isn't about me."

He kisses my temple. "Don't think I don't have *all* sorts of plans of getting you in a white dress too, peaches."

My eyes fly to his, and it's the steady seriousness in them that nearly does me in. "Rhett Bennett," I whisper.

"What?" He shrugs. "My brother can't have all the fun."

I roll my eyes. We both know damn well Kasey is *hardly* having fun.

I watch his mouth lift higher. He's danger and chaos wrapped in a gorgeous black suit that has my heart skipping like rocks on the creek. He recently had his cowboy hat cleaned and shaped, and now it rests low on the mess of dark waves that I want to wind my fingers through and *pull*. I love seeing him like this, cleaned up and polished. And though it suits him—he looks like a true southern dream—I'm counting down the minutes until I can get him out of all the finery. To pull his tie loose from his throat and press my mouth to his skin. To feel the rough scraping of his calloused fingertips against my thighs.

When I'd braved another email to ask Céline if I could bring a *second* plus-one, she assured me it wasn't an issue at all. *The more the merrier!* she'd written in her response. *I think Dad and Nathan would be happy with some more male energy!*

Once I'd gotten her okay, I asked Rhett. And even though I know it's not a good time and there's *more* than enough going on at the ranch that requires his attention, he didn't skip a beat in wanting to be here with me. To support me through this big and monumental life moment.

I don't know what I expected from any of this—I really didn't have expectations at all, to be honest—but finding Rhett down at the hotel bar last night with a not-so-sober Nathan, both of them laughing and animated in conversation . . . I swear, my heart swelled four times its normal size. He's not just here to stand beside me. He's invested in the outcome, in leaning into this whole new family too. Because he knows how much the opportunity means to me.

Though, he hasn't exactly warmed up to my dad yet. I think Clive has some work to do on that front.

I'd been most nervous about how things would go between Clive, Colette, and my mother, but I never could have imagined the outright emotional reunion she'd had with my father or the warm support given to both of them by his wife. Colette is a force in her sharp confidence and raw beauty, completely unshaken by any of what would undoubtedly shake most women to their core.

"I'm so glad you're finally here," she'd said into my hair when we first hugged. "He's been waiting for this for a really long time." When she pulled away, she gathered my hands in hers. "Of course, it's always been for you to decide *if* and *when*, but he's held on to a lot of hope."

"How can you be so kind about it all?" I ask, unable to stop the question from spilling out. Somewhere along the way, I'd let myself believe it was her that had stopped him from communicating in the beginning, but I'm realizing he might have been fighting more with himself.

She shrugs. "Love is *love*, Olivia. I love my husband, for better or worse, through anything life throws at us. He's not perfect, but I know he's a good man. And he *loves* you. He always has. Your mother too. I can't be mad at him for choosing love over fear or resentment. From what I know, your mother is a good woman. My goodness, she's here with you, and that says plenty."

We'd spent nearly our whole first night here in that living room, taking the time to ask questions and share stories and simply exist together. Rhett had opted to hang back at the hotel to give us all that time. But he'd come to the rehearsal dinner last night when we were introduced to Nathan, Céline, Amelie, and Claire, and he and Nathan hit it off immediately with their shared love of motorcycles.

The ceremony is charming and quick, and soon the wedding party is pulled to the side to take pictures with the newly married couple. I'm surprised when Céline insists I join them for the family shot, unable to hide the tears welling in my eyes after the flash strikes.

"Are you okay?" Céline asks, concern in her eyes.

I nod, springing forward to hug her. "Can I have a copy of it?"

Her arms wrap tight around me. "Of course."

She eventually pulls away with a promise to find me on the dance floor later when Nathan's family swarms for their own sets of pictures. When later comes, I'm delighted to find the Calhoun family goes *hard* with a live band, and we spend hours dancing beneath the bare edison bulbs that line the trees above us, washing away the darkness of night like a smattering of amber stars.

Even Mom pours her heart out in the way she moves, and I

can feel the relief spilling out with it. When Clive asks me to dance, I oblige with a sense of wonder ballooning in my heart. A hope for a better future with a man I've always kept just on the edge of my life. I watch him spin my mother around in a dance after, eyes glued to the way her cheeks flush. And it's not with an air of romance that he moves against her now, but with a sense of love all the same. Maybe Colette was right, that he can still love her through the history they share. Through a child they made together, even when the circumstances were all wrong.

"She seems good," Rhett says, drawing my focus back to him as we sway back and forth. His hat shadows most of his face from the twinkling lights above.

I smile. "She does, doesn't she?"

"So do you. You seem . . . happy," he observes, scanning my face. I've felt his eyes on me all night, his careful consideration, ready to swoop in at the first sign of trouble, but it hasn't been necessary.

"I am." I stretch to my tiptoes and press my mouth to his, meant to be a quick kiss. But he pulls me to him with the firm grip he has on my waist, until our bodies are flush, leaning over me so I'm tipped back and at his mercy. His tongue skates along my lips, and I let him in with a soft sigh.

I *am* happy, I realize. And not in a way that feels fleeting. It's the kind of happiness that spreads out and stays a while, embedding into a string of moments that feels like it could go on in infamy.

It won't of course. It didn't for my parents. It hasn't for Rhett and his family. But despite knowing the truth of how fragile and precious life is, how fleeting these good slices within it might feel, I have no regrets for any of the risks I've taken in the last few months. Not to be here, in Charleston. And certainly not with Rhett.

He pulls away, his eyes unfurling upon me like smoke. "I love you, Olivia." It comes out in a whisper, from his heart straight to mine. It's the first time he's let himself say the words, though I know they've been on his tongue for a while, licking into my skin and my mouth every time he gets me alone.

My heart leaps as my eyes burn. "I love you too, Rhett." I kiss him again. Hard. "So much."

We stay like that, wrapped in each other and the lights and shadows that dance around us, as I wonder how long we can make it all last. But even when the lights eventually dim and the shadows grow, Rhett and I will face it all together.

He'll never again have to face any of it alone.

ACKNOWLEDGMENTS

First and foremost, I want to thank all the readers who have loved on and championed this series so much. Sunshine continues to reach so many new hearts and I feel beyond grateful for the time and effort you all spend sharing these characters with others. It's made me even MORE excited to bring you back to Saddlebrook Falls with Peaches and with the rest of the books still yet to come.

To my team:

Logan: My ride or die. Bestie for the restie. The best damn PA I could have ever hoped for. You've changed my life for the better, and I can no longer imagine my world without you in it. You support me in ways my soul has been craving for a long time, and I'm so happy to genuinely call you a friend. (Also, you brought me Sam, and that's pretty dang sweet.)

Britt: You've pushed my writing so much over the last two years and have helped me to grow into the author I am today. From day one you've been a burst of light over my career, and I'm so happy I get to do this with your support!

Lauren: You never fail to give the best feedback and have the loveliest eye for *exactly* what my stories always need. I swear we have the same taste in the exact type of tender romance that I'm always striving for, and it helps so much that you always seem to understand my motives in the specific ways that make your notes so valuable. Thank you for loving on my writing over the years.

To my family, who makes all of this worth it. I love you.

ABOUT THE AUTHOR

Michaela is a hopeless romantic from the western desert who writes grippingly tender romance novels featuring diverse characters and messy, beautifully relatable storylines.

Stay tuned for exciting announcements at michaelajeantaylor.com

BOOKS BY MICHAELA JEAN TAYLOR

Love In The Rockies

Only You

This Love

End Game

Saddlebrook Falls

Sunshine

Peaches

Sugar

www.ingramcontent.com/pod-product-compliance
Lightning Source LLC
Chambersburg PA
CBHW032346310726
48973CB00007B/1879